Interstellar Islands
Cosmic Ark Book One

Scott Boss

Published by Rogue Phoenix Press
Copyright © 2020

ISBN: 978-1-62420-583-5

Editor: Sherry Derr-Wille

Published in The United States

Dedication
To Mack, the lost dog.

Part I

Prelude

A cold, gray breeze dragged across the barren land once known as Inland Florida. Metal fencing surrounded the backlot of Bride of Christ Pentecostal Church, though no one knew the name, as the sign had been repurposed many years ago. Two ducks were inside the fencing. One, Marvin, lay on its side taking its last breaths and the other, Honey, was dipping its bill into a bowl of water.

Zane watched them from the roof of the church, shaking his head, causing his dark hair to swing in front of his small brown eyes, shielding his view for a few seconds. He was perched like a bird, looking out as far as he could through the unnatural fog. The wind cut through him and he wrapped his coat tighter, letting out a long crackling sigh as desolate tears welled up in his eyes.

Honey looked up when the back door to the church opened with a creak.

"Zane? Will you come down from there?" Marlow called up. She had a blanket over her shoulders, trailing in the dirt as Honey approached, looking for food.

"What's the point?" he called back, not looking away from the ominous gray. "What's the point of any of this? Look at Marvin."

Marlow whipped her head, a long braid of hair swinging with her, and hurried over to the dying duck.

"Why didn't you tell me?" she asked through intermittent coughs. "I coulda…" She trailed off, holding the fragile duck head in her palm. "Oh, Marvin."

Zane laughed a bitter laugh. "What? You gonna resuscitate him, again?"

She looked up towards him. "It's a she. Marvin is a she."

He laughed again, more lighthearted this time. "True." His reply was lost in the wind.

"Would you come down here?" Marlow called.

He sighed again, wiped the tears from his eyes and climbed down.

The chapel was filled with plants, mother-in-law tongue, ferns and dwarf pines, among others. Most of the leaves were browning up and falling off. Marlow stood near the back, holding a steel trapdoor open with one arm and Marvin tucked under the other.

"Come on," she said. "You really shoulda been wearing your mask."

Zane grunted, shrugged and followed, catching the door from her as they descended into the underground bunker.

The bunker had been built by a preacher with a zeal for Armageddon, Pastor Jerry Hill, who warned his congregation time after time that the end was near. Though it hadn't been exactly as described in the Bible, he wasn't far off. It had started with the threat of a nuke by Pakistan, then an actual one launched by the US. Soon, North Korea, Russia and other countries joined in and World War III was well under way. This was forty-five years ago, in 2045. Three quarters of the population was lost during the war and the aftermath, but humans are remarkably resilient. The Earth had a resurgence about twenty years back. People went back to smaller communities, farming and taking care of each other. Power grids were restored for some areas. Nations were re-established, but many years of lawlessness couldn't just be undone. Countries once strong. were now weak and recovering. Others took advantage of that.

The Final War had happened two years ago. Zane, Marlow and their families took shelter at the church bunker during it. "Built for times such as these," Pastor Hill said, but the air was saturated with death. He, and most people with more than a few decades of using their lungs, passed on first, along with children.

It was five degrees the day Marvin the duck died, and it started a string of events Zane and Marlow couldn't have dreamed of.

Chapter One

Marlow set Marvin on a card table, sliding a couple plants with her elbow to make room. Marvin had stopped breathing, and Marlow was bending down to perform duck CPR when Zane grabbed her shoulder.

"Just...don't," he said. "She's dead."

"But maybe I can..."

Zane shook his head.

She sighed and took a step back, still focused on the duck in the dark room. "Then we butcher her and eat her tonight."

Zane threw his hands up. "What's the point? We're down to one fucking duck." His slight Indian accent normally made her laugh when he cursed, but not now.

"We'll go out. We'll—" She tried to continue, but a coughing fit overtook her.

Zane put an arm around her shoulders when she stopped. He wanted to tell her that her cough was getting worse, that it was probably lung cancer or whatever it was that took their families but what good would it do? He was afraid he wasn't far behind, as his own chest felt tight most nights. They hugged for what could've been five solid minutes, both parties recalling memories of their families finding each other as they sought shelter. Finally, they broke away and Marlow looked up at him, wiping tears as she did.

"Let's eat this fucking duck."

Zane wanted to protest but couldn't. *Let her have a last meal,* he figured.

Marlow butchered Marvin, apologizing to her that things had turned out the way they had. They built up their fire pit within the fence and Honey watched as they turned Marvin on a spit. Thankfully, she didn't seem to recognize her and quickly lost interest, scratching in the dirt for long-gone bugs or other edibles.

They sat down inside the church sanctuary, sharing a pew with a plate of duck meat between them. Honey had finally cornered a cockroach and was stomping it into submission as she pecked at it. It was the most entertainment they'd gotten lately.

"Do you think we're the last two people?" asked Zane, staring forward at the window frames taped over with plastic sheeting.

Marlow loosened a chunk of meat from the bone and chewed greedily. "Probably not."

"What if we are?"

"I'm sure there are others. Just not in this wasteland that used to be Florida."

"Do you think they'll ever make Earth *right* again?"

"Maybe, if there's anyone left to do that."

"You just said—"

"I know, Zane. I'm just saying, I'm sure there are people, I just don't know if they *can* make Earth right again."

Zane set a half-finished piece of duck on the plate. "So, why are we even bothering then?"

She looked at him, grease staining her lips and chin. "Because, we have to try, we promised our parents we would."

Zane slapped the pew in front of them. "That was all fine and good when they were alive, but now? No one's here to hold us to that. No one's here at all."

"Then do it for me, Zane. Survive a little longer for me."

He huffed. "Fine." And picked the duck back up.

~ * ~

After Marlow settled in the bunker for the night, Zane took one more trip to the roof of the church. It was his place to think. Eighteen months ago, his dad would do it, looking for a rescue helicopter or some sign of peace. His hope was always in vain. No one ever came for them and eventually, his father didn't have the strength to climb the ladder anymore. He'd died just over a year ago, followed a month later by Marlow's mom, then finally, their last companion, Jason. He was closer to their age, eighteen and vibrant, as much as he could be, given the conditions. Zane could still remember the choking wheeze of his last few breaths. The sound scraped up and down the walls of the bunker, as he lay clutching Marlow's hand while Zane paced behind them. In some ways, he blamed himself for Jason's death, deferring to him to take scouting duty more often and Jason had never complained. He'd just go out, looking for anything useful to keep them alive a little longer and his reward was death. Zane's reward for hiding in the bunker was to watch all his friends and family die out before him. He had half a mind to throw himself from the freezing shingles of the church roof, but he'd promised Marlow he'd stick around. Once she went—and it wouldn't be long—all bets were off.

Zane hugged his coat tighter. The temperature had dropped to the negatives, just a normal July night in Florida. The cold air kept his mind awake. He could almost hear his dad saying, "Once the politicians come out of hiding, they are going to need us to help rebuild. You are young and strong, you can help, have a normal life and maybe a family one day." Zane shook his head at the thought and how wrong it had been. He couldn't blame the guy for having hope but he knew better now.

His teeth were chattering when he headed for the ladder. He caught the first rung and almost slipped when he heard a whooshing sound in the distance. What used to be a norm during the Final War was now odd, to hear sounds of any kind in the distance. Zane craned his neck, trying to catch a glimpse of something, anything else, but the sound was gone. He finished the climb and went back into the bunker, locking the door as he did.

Chapter Two

The next morning, Zane was awoken by Honey quacking about something in the dark. She was impossible to see with her black feathers but he could feel her bill poking him. She wanted outside, to try to scrounge up some breakfast. He was able to get to the bunker door in the dark. With much practice, and matches having to be desperately rationed, they both knew the way like blind people who map their furniture in their heads. He swung the door to get a little light and lifted Honey to the upstairs floor, climbing the steps and opening the back door for her to check out the outdoors. Marlow wasn't anywhere to be seen. She'd probably taken off to collect anything they could burn. It was getting harder to keep water from becoming ice and it made drinking for the three of them difficult, much less cooking and bathing. They'd been surviving on big bags of rice they'd recovered, but that took water to cook. Zane was almost happy to see it gone, until they were starving. Marvin had stopped laying eggs a while back and Honey rarely popped one out anymore. It wasn't until their meal last night that he'd felt truly satisfied for the first time since he could remember. He watched Honey, wondering how long until she became their final meal. Would she beat out Marlow? Zane didn't plan on skinning and eating Honey if Marlow was gone. But if he didn't plan on eating, what did he plan on? He shook away the thought, wrapped his coat tight and went to fill Honey's bowl with some water from the well.

~ * ~

Meanwhile, an old wheelbarrow crunched along the cracked

sidewalk of Third Street. It wasn't Marlow's usual route, with just a few decayed houses stripped bare, but she was sure she could find something to burn, maybe even to eat. They'd become less concerned with the chemicals on the wood they were burning when actual firewood became about impossible to find. She selected a former half-million seller that had made a real estate agent quite a commission back in the day. Now, its second floor had collapsed in on the first and folded up like a Chinese takeout box.

She left the wheelbarrow at the doorstep and tried the handle. It wouldn't budge so she headed around the side in search of another entrance. At the back of the house was a screen door with the screen busted out lying a few feet from a hole that looked like it was once a back door. It had narrowed down to half its normal size, but Marlow was confident she could slip in. She got down on her hands and knees, gave a look around and crawled in the hole. She felt chunks of glass cracking beneath her knees and was glad to be wearing two pairs of pants, only hoping they'd be enough. The roof—or second floor—tucked low. She had to get down into an army crawl and drag her body across the cracked tile below. She was a few feet in, feeling the claustrophobia starting, when she saw a wooden barstool, still intact, just ahead. It would be good to burn, but behind it there were cupboards that hadn't been ripped to shreds. There was a small chance this house still had something edible in it. The support beam splintered and made a V shape in the middle of her path. She tucked around it, putting one arm forward and one to her side, using her toes to push her on. The tile was bitterly cold as her cheek slid across it into the opening. She disturbed a layer of dust and it brought on a sneeze, causing her to smack her head on the beam as she did. Marlow lay, shivering, trying to hold back a coughing fit as a cold sweat came over her. "What is the point?" she could hear Zane's voice from the night before. She knew he was right. How much longer would her lungs hold out? She could make it out of this house with a full meal, but then what? It couldn't heal her. It couldn't bring her mom back, or Jason. It would just be her, Zane and Honey until one of them died and the others followed shortly after.

She closed her eyes, her shivers slowed, her breath focused. Her fists were clenched and her jaw tight when her eyes popped back open, golden-brown orbs floating in yellow pools with splatters of red from burst capillaries. Her toes went to work and she slid around the beam, into the kitchen. There was standing room as she pulled herself up on a chipped, marble countertop and stretched out, giving way to the coughing fit that waited in her chest. The stool stood perfectly in the middle of the kitchen, a tan-stained swivel-top that was a contrast to the Italian marble tile. It was like a flower growing in the middle of a war zone, but Marlow plucked it. She was only five foot two and would need it to reach the upper shelves that hadn't collapsed. She lined it up to the sink, giving the faucet a try just for the hell of it. When no water came, she climbed up the stool and checked the upper cupboards. Cookbooks by some overly tan lady named Paula Deen. Marlow knew you needed ingredients to make recipes and had to look away from the pages to avoid salivating. She slammed the cupboards shut and tried any others that would open with no luck. Finally, she looked in a lower cupboard she'd missed and there it was, a container with one of those sealing tops. As far as Marlow could tell, it was full of some kind of flour. She resisted the urge to open it and give it a smell check. It didn't matter anymore. She was taking it back and they'd figure out some way to bake with it. Maybe Honey would lay and egg to help out.

Marlow had the flour tucked under her arm when she realized the stool would only fit through the hole in pieces. She pushed the container through her entryway and grabbed the stool, raising it to smash against the steel refrigerator when she had a second thought. She set it back down by the sink and retrieved the Paula Deen cookbook. Maybe it had some advice for what to do when you only had old flour, water and a possible duck egg to work with. She slid Paula behind the flour and went to work on the stool. The fridge had some solid dents on it when she was done but it did its job. The legs went first, then the seat and Marlow grimaced as the sharp, metal swivel slit her finger open. She cursed and sucked the blood while she replaced her gloves. She made it through easier the second time and soon was back on the sidewalk of Third Street. She'd gone about a mile from the bunker that morning. It wasn't hard to find her way back, even in the gray skies. Third connected with Church Street and it was a mostly straight shot from there.

At the intersection, she paused for a drink, then tucked the bottle back into her coat. Leaving it out was asking for it to freeze up on her. When she turned onto Church, she saw the usual, dead dirt surrounding the sidewalks, the graying, destroyed buildings and the haze. The cloud of who-knows-what laid across the land, only the haze was darker ahead. She took careful, deliberate steps as she pushed the wheelbarrow and the darkness came into focus.

"Zane? What are you—" She stopped when she saw it was not Zane. It was the first other human she'd seen in at least six months, since Jason had died.

The figure stepped forward, wearing ragged coats on top of one another, an Indiana Jones hat and workman gloves. He had a patchy, yellowing beard down to his collarbone and a crazed look in his eyes. He raised a hand.

Marlow didn't know if it was a greeting or he was asking her to stop. He was directly in her path home, which was still a quarter mile away.

She raised a shaking hand back. "Hello? Who are you?"

He was twenty feet back, but took her greeting as an invitation to close the gap. He labored to reach her. Marlow gripped the wheelbarrow, watching him. He stopped just in front of her and she made sure the steel bucket kept them separate.

"Good to see another person," he said through labored breath. "And such a lovely one at that."

Marlow didn't smile at the compliment. "Are you lost? Do you have a family somewhere?"

"'Fraid not. Family all up and died on me. I saw you come up this way earlier. I was so happy. It's been so lonely lately. Name's Walter." He stuck out a hand that went unmet.

"I'm sorry," she said. "It's been hard on all of us. I do have to get back to my family now."

She went to move the wheelbarrow but he gripped the front edge.

"Family, you say? Do you have room for one more? I won't be a burden. I even have some supplies we could pick up from my camp. Put 'em right there in your wheelbarrow."

"I'm sorry, I'd have to consult with them first." She shook the handles but the tire wouldn't budge.

"Well, let me come with then. I could use the company. Looks like you could, too. I'm sure they'll like me if they get to know me."

She shook her head. "We don't have room. Now, please let go." She gave the wheelbarrow another shake and he finally removed his hands, raising them in the air.

"I'm not trying to fight, Marlow." He smiled a group of yellow and black teeth when he saw her reaction. Then he coughed out a laugh. "Didn't know I knew your name? Can't say today is the first time I've seen ya. If it weren't for your boyfriend perched up there like a damn vulture every night, I woulda been by to visit you already." He raised a bony finger at her. "You got a nice figure under all those clothes. I can just tell. Now why don't we—" He was cut off when Marlow jammed the wheelbarrow forward, slamming into his midsection and knocking him to the ground.

She didn't know how long he'd been watching them, but she knew she had to get back to Zane. She wasn't ready for a fight. It had been a long walk for two bad lungs and a malnourished body. Still, as soon as Walter hit the ground, she planted her feet and was off with the wheelbarrow. She was two steps past him when she felt a sharp pain and her left leg gave way. She went down, spraying her collections from that morning over the sidewalk. The flour hit the ground with a crack and a cloud of dust came up from the jar. Paula Deen's face dragged across cracked pavement. Marlow turned back, wanting to assess her leg, but saw Walter crawling toward her. He had a blood-stained, rusty machete scraping along the cement in his right hand as he went, just a foot away.

"No," she yelled, backing away. Her whole chest and stomach felt wet. She could only use her right leg and wasn't making much progress.

Walter raised the machete over her. "Now, hold on. I'm not trying to hurt you." He looked at the blood pooling around her foot and cringed. "Again. Now just—" He was reaching down as he spoke and caught a handful of flour Marlow had scavenged from the ground. Walter yelled,

10

rubbing at his eyes. Marlow took her chance, scooting out from under him and brought herself upright again, using one of the broken barstool legs as a crutch. Her foot bled a trail behind her and couldn't handle any pressure. It was slow going and soon he was behind her again. She planned her attack, knowing she couldn't outrun him. When he was three feet back, she spun on her good heel, swinging out the barstool leg directly at his head. Walter raised an arm at the last second to deflect her blow. It spun him in a circle as the leg flew off. Marlow tried to balance herself and instinctively used her left leg. When it hit the ground, she screamed out and toppled over.

"Fuck." Marlow was clutching her leg on the ground. "Zane. Help. Zane!" she called to the empty streets. The leprous man stood a few feet away, leering at her.

"You know, I wanted to make this easy on you," he said. "If you woulda just come back to my place with me...there's a nice soft mattress. Hell, I woulda laid out some rose petals for you, but now, we have to do this in the street." He shrugged. "Guess it makes no difference to me. Good way to go, one way or another."

She scooted back against the remains of a lamppost to help herself up again and began unzipping her coat with a smile on her face.

Walter's eyes widened. "Well, all right then." He approached with cautious hands held ready. Marlow tossed out her cracked water bottle, at least happy to see that wetness wasn't blood. When she dropped her coat, she was left with just the barstool seat in her hand. She'd tucked it in her coat after she hit him with the flour, wielding it like some kind of medieval weapon. She kept the sharp swivel hidden from him.

"Oh, come now," said Walter. "You gonna hit me with a seat?" He pulled his machete back out of his coat. "Put it down."

She growled the best she could. "Make me."

He took a quick, hard swing directly at the seat and it stuck into the wood. She pulled him close until she could smell his rancid breath, then used her leverage on the light post and pushed off, twisting the seat and shoving the bottom end into his face. The swivel gashed his cheek. It rode up through his eyebrow and forehead. Marlow finished her push and let go of the seat, staggering forward, staying on her good leg. Walter was on the ground screaming. She couldn't wait. She had nothing left to hit him with, so she hobbled toward the bunker. The cold air bit straight through her wet shirt. She needed her coat, but couldn't go back. Her movement was like a kid playing hopscotch, only using the leg she could. It was slow and awful, but each time she looked back, Walter was still on the ground with his hands on his face. Maybe she'd gotten his eye, maybe his other wasn't good enough. If he couldn't see her...

Then he was up, blood smeared across his face, still dripping as he started after her. He wasn't fast, but she was slower. The twenty-foot lead would not be enough to get her home. She hopped up to the remains of a brick building, looking around for anything and settling for pieces of crumbled bricks. Using the wall for leverage, she heaved a palm-sized brick at his head. Walter ducked and kept on, shielding his face with his forearms. She landed a body blow, then cracked another off his kneecap. The second one seemed to hurt him, but he kept coming and she realized it was too late. Marlow pushed off the wall at the last second, to avoid being pinned to it. Walter countered and took her down with a shoulder to the chest. She hit her back hard on the cold pavement. Her wind left her in a choking wheeze. She tried to raise her arms but couldn't fight his hands off as they pinned her down. He leaned in and drove his right knee into her left bicep.

"Ah. Get the fuck off me," Marlow yelled as she squirmed but made no progress.

"I wanted you to be awake for this," Walter said, again with the sick leer on his face. "Maybe even give a little back. Make the last time count. Know what I mean?"

She mustered the little spit she had and managed to hit his coat.

He looked down and laughed. "Oh, ho-ho, and *that's* why I'm gonna have to put you out first." He leaned forward, his knee grinding her arm into ground.

She let out a groan as he rose back up.

"Oh, sorry about that," he said, then raised a chunk of brick he'd picked up. "But, this is gonna hurt worse. Don't worry, you—"

Marlow heard the sound of one foot stepping down just a few feet from her when she saw a black boot come flying out of the haze and plant itself in the side of Walter's skull. He flew off her into the jutting bricks from the old building and crumpled in a heap. The rock in his hand barely missed her head when he dropped it. She looked up.

"Z-Zane?"

A hand came down that was definitely not Zane's.

"No, but I'm here to help." A tall man leaned over her. He was tan with blond hair and an outfit that made her think of Batman, minus the cape and yellow logo.

Marlow didn't know what to say, she hadn't seen anyone look so *healthy* in a long time. She reached a hand back and he pulled her up, gently, looking her over as she shivered.

"How's the leg?" he asked.

She looked back. "Not good. I can't put any weight on it."

"Bleeding pretty bad. Let me wrap it." He helped her back down on a softer spot of dirt then patted himself, as if looking for a pack of cigarettes. "Shit, I don't really carry…hold on." He went over to Walter, kicking him for good measure, then bent down and tore a strip of his jacket. When he was back to Marlow, she was eyeing him. "I know, I know," he said. "Not the most sanitary thing, but it'll do to stop the bleeding. I'll fix you up better when we get out of here."

"Out of here?" she said as he went to work. "Are you part of a rescue team? Sent by the government? Oh, Zane is going to flip. His dad was right all along."

"Hold on. I am *not* part of a rescue team. I'm really not much different from you. I'm a gatherer."

"I think you're a lot different from me," she said as he hefted her up into his arms.

He laughed. "Guess you're right. Let's go get your coat and we'll head back."

"Back? To the bun—" she stopped herself. Not sure how much she should trust this person after her last encounter.

"Bunker, yes. Don't worry. I'm a friend. A *human*, just like you."

"Oh really? I don't know any *humans* that state their species to me. Makes me think you're an alien or something."

"Huh, I wish. Then I'd have more arms to carry your ass." They'd reached the wheelbarrow and he propped it up with a foot then looked at her. "Hope you don't mind, but I'm not some body builder. I'll wheel you from here if that's okay."

"Okay."

He lowered her down, then grabbed the coat she'd shed earlier and laid it across her.

"Is Zane okay? Do you know?"

"He should be. I can check." He raised a hand to his head, then put it back to the wheelbarrow and started talking as they rolled. "Hey, Ice, how's the boy?"

He nodded for a few seconds, laughed and said, "Get him down, we'll be there soon." The man looked down, reading her confused expression. "Sorry, my partner is at your place. She's trying to talk to your friend but he's up on the roof, holding a duck, yelling curse words at her."

Marlow fought back a smile. "Sounds about right."

Chapter Three

They wheeled back to the bunker and Marlow saw a woman, dark skinned, in a matching outfit to the man, leaning against the church. She had a black braid twisted into a bun on top of her head but no hair elsewhere, just a pair of sleek earmuffs. She was close to six feet, huge compared to Marlow. Her arms were crossed and she used a lazy finger to point up. Zane sat perched in his usual spot, clutching Honey to his chest. He'd somehow pulled up the ladder so the woman couldn't follow him. It sat awkwardly on the angle of the roof, threatening to fall off and leave him stranded.

"Zane," Marlow called up.

"Marlow. What did they do to you?"

She shook her head. "It wasn't them. I found another person while I was gathering wood. He attacked me. This guy saved me."

"He did?"

"Yeah. Could you come down? I think they just want to talk."

Zane looked around. "Okay, but I'm not sure I can set Honey down. She tried to jump last time." The strangers exchanged a glance and the man walked over, raising his arms to the edge of the roof.

"Hand her down. I promise not to drop her."

Zane eyed him for a second, then carefully made his way to the side of the roof, pushing Honey toward the man. She dropped off the edge and Zane gasped.

"Calm. I've got her." The man backed up, cradling the duck to show Zane.

"Okay," said Zane. He reached for the ladder and almost lost his footing. Now Marlow gasped. "I've got it." He slid the ladder over the edge with a clang and the woman helped position it for his climb down. He gave the strangers odd looks, taking Honey from the man and kneeling by Marlow at the wheelbarrow. "What happened?"

"Long story. Wheel me inside and I'll tell ya."

Inside the church, the group huddled in the pews facing each other. Marlow had her leg propped across Zane, while Honey did her normal insect patrol.

"Tell us your names and where you come from," said Zane in an outburst.

Marlow put a hand on his arm to calm him.

The man was leaned back in the pew as he spoke. "Sure thing. I'm Arjen. The J is mostly silent." He raised a thumb to the woman. "This is Isolde, but we call her Ice."

"*You* call me Ice," she interjected. "My mother never meant for me to be called that."

He just smiled. "Then she shoulda called you Sally."

She laughed, revealing bright, white teeth.

"Are you from the government?" asked Zane.

"No," said Arjen. "Like I told Marlow here, we're gatherers. We go around collecting useful things for home. Today, we came across you two and it looked like you needed help."

"Got that right," said Marlow.

"How can we trust you?" said Zane.

"There're not a lot of other options," said Ice.

He looked away, tears forming in his eyes. "My father always said someone would come."

Marlow patted his head. "Let's not get our hopes up." She turned to the strangers. "We really could use a meal. I'd gotten ahold of some flour when that man…"

"We can get you more than a meal," said Arjen.

"What does that mean?" asked Marlow.

"We have a ship," said Ice. "Not far from here. We have a medical bay that can help you get better."

"Better? Like my leg?"

"And your lungs," said Ice. "His too." She pointed at Zane whose eyes widened.

"You can fix our lungs?"

"Our med bay can fix most things. We'll still need to wrap that leg until it heals, but you'll be surprised how fast that is."

Zane eyed them up and down, stopping on Arjen, and leaned in. "Are you from Europe?"

Arjen burst out laughing. "Well, my family was at one point."

"Is that where you're taking us when…" Zane stopped.

Marlow seemed to read his thoughts. "You're just relief workers, right? After we're better…"

"Hell no," said Arjen. "We wouldn't leave you in this dump for another minute. We've got a much better offer for you."

"Offer?" said Marlow. "What does that mean?"

Arjen leaned in, as if telling the group, a secret. "Listen. Like I've told you, we're just out gathering materials. It's our job. Now, if we happened to come across two stowaways and brought them back with us, I'm pretty sure our boss would let it slide. We're all humans after all, remember?" He gave a wink at Marlow that she didn't return.

"But where do you live?" said Marlow. "Is it really Europe? My mom said…"

Arjen raised a hand to quiet her. "This," his arms were spread out, "is not a place to live anymore. I think you know that and I don't just mean this old church. Europe is not a place to live anymore. The Earth…" He looked to Isolde.

"What he's trying to say is," Ice said, "we don't live here. Our home is in space."

~ * ~

Isolde and Arjen stood outside the church, waiting, as Zane and Marlow hurried around the bunker.

"What the hell are they even packing?" said Ice.

"Clothes? Books? I don't know," said Arjen. "Maybe they're trying to decide if they should lock us out."

She looked at him with gritted teeth. "They'd better not, or God

17

help them, I will leave them here."

Arjen just smiled. "No, you won't."

After another minute, Marlow and Zane stepped out. She had an arm around his shoulders, supporting herself while holding Honey in the other arm. Zane carried a stuffed suitcase.

"What's all that?" said Ice.

"Clothes," said Zane.

"Leave 'em," said Ice. "They probably smell."

"Leave them?" said Zane. "But my—" Marlow gripped his side with her fingers until he giggled and dropped the bag. "Hey, no fair."

"I told you we don't need them."

"I've just...never been to space," said Zane. "I want to be prepared."

"It's not space," said Marlow. "They've probably got a cult somewhere in South Africa we're about to join."

Arjen studied her as she climbed into the wheelbarrow with Honey on her chest.

"How do you know our cult accepts ducks?" asked Arjen.

"Because if not, we're not coming."

They followed Ice across the barren landscape, as Arjen pushed the wheelbarrow and Zane strolled along asking questions.

"Asteroids? But how do you survive?"

"Well, it's—" Ice began, but Marlow cut her off.

"Zane, don't waste your breath. It's a tent in the mountains somewhere. They'll probably blindfold us and make us drink juice."

"You know your cults," said Arjen, pulling out a silver pouch and tossing it to her. "Drink up."

Marlow turned the pouch over in her hands. "Seriously? What is this?"

"That's pure nutrients," said Arjen. "Taste is okay. Health benefits are through the roof. Might wanna go slow on it though, since it looks like you haven't had a decent meal in a while."

"We had duck just last night," she said, defiantly.

Zane reached for the pouch and she pulled it back.

"Oh, come on, Mar. I want to try it. I'm hungry."

Isolde handed back another pouch and Zane took it, popping the top and putting it straight to his lips.

"Zane," said Marlow.

"Slow," said Ice.

"Ah, it's awesome," said Zane, through heavy breaths. "Can I drink it all?"

"Save the rest for the plane," said Ice. "Too much at once and you'll probably puke."

Marlow shrugged and took a few sips of hers. A smile broke out on her face. "Well, if you're going to kill us, this is the way to do it."

Arjen laughed. "I've never seen that reaction to a nutrient pouch before."

Ice shrugged. "When you're hungry enough…"

"You were going to tell us about the asteroids?" said Zane.

"Right," said Ice. "What I was saying is, we have technology that supports us. Much like what Earth's atmosphere used to be."

"And what's that?" asked Zane.

"Not poisonous."

They continued walking, the group having to take ends of the wheelbarrow to get Marlow over destroyed buildings and cars. After a small hill of debris, they came to a dip in the ground to see a glassy, black ship about the size of the entire church lot they'd been living in for the past two years.

"There's the *Iris*," said Arjen.

"Holy shit," said Zane. "See Marlow, look."

Marlow's lips quivered and she broke into tears.

Chapter Four

Zane held Marlow's hand as they were strapped into their seats for takeoff. Various crew members gave short, inquisitive glances at them as they found their way to their own seats. Arjen chatted with a few of them but all in all he seemed to be an authority figure to them.

The ship was a wonder to two kids who never even flew in a commercial airplane and barely saw them in the sky. Just the basic hallway they took, after Arjen carried Marlow up the ramp, had them both wide eyed with disbelief. It was meticulously crafted and maintained; unlike anything they'd seen. They were strapped down, awaiting takeoff, in a row of seats with a long window-view. Zane was on the left, then Marlow, Arjen and Ice. Honey was in Marlow's lap still, looking around but not fighting to get away. Zane gave Marlow a squeeze as the final door closed.

"Got a little emotional there?"

"I think we're really getting out. Zane, this is what our parents wanted. This is all they ever wanted."

"I know," he said. "I didn't think it would happen. What do you think?" He paused and lowered his voice. "You still think this is all a play? They can't really be taking us to an asteroid, can they? Where is this ship heading?"

"I don't know," she whispered back. "I didn't think we'd make it this far. I thought…"

Zane nodded. "It's hard to believe. Do you think they can actually make you better? And me?"

"I doubt it, but this ship is pretty impressive. Maybe they have something that can at least give us some relief, buy us some time. That food thing wasn't bad."

"It was awesome. Reminded me of vanilla pudding. Remember when we still had pudding?"

"Yeah. I miss it. And steak…oh, I would kill for a steak."

"Me too. Remember that night? That was the best night, before dad died."

"Yeah. I think I did puke then. We had so much. It was probably the last time we had too much to eat."

Zane nodded, knowingly, recalling the different cuts of steak they tried when they slaughtered their last cow. He had a slight smile that dropped in an instant.

"What if they're using us? For something bad? Like sex slaves or something?"

Marlow laughed as she pet Honey. "Have you seen us recently? And *them*? They're like sculpted gods. What would they want with our scrawny bodies?"

Zane pursed his lips. "I'm just saying, I'm not ready to be somebody's boy toy."

She laughed again. "No, no matter what happens, you'll always be my boy toy."

"That's gross," he said, but didn't drop her hand.

"You know, whatever their plan, it has to be better than where we were."

"I hope so."

"You want me to ask if they have a church you can perch on at night?"

He smiled. "Actually…"

"You two," said Arjen. "Small spaceship. Can hear everything you're saying. Also, it's about takeoff time. You may want to watch this part."

"Or not," said Ice. "I don't want either of you puking."

Zane whispered, "She's like obsessed with puking."

"Heard that," said Ice. "Don't want it floating into my face."

A rumbling began, and they could see the ground below the ship getting further away. Soon they were in the haze. The same haze that enveloped their lives and taken their families. There was a shift as the ship shot upward, picking up speed. Zane was crushing Marlow's hand but she didn't mind. Honey let out a honk at her when she squeezed too tight. They both loosened up as they got accustomed to the speed, smiling like kids on their first roller coaster. Within a minute, all the flying gray thinned out and a black sky of stars took over. Zane and Marlow forgot about their stomachs. They could only see the universe before them. The *future* before them that was so bleak, only a few hours before. The ship carried on, out of the atmosphere with the moon ahead in its sights.

"It's the *moon*," said Zane.

"I know," said Marlow, mouth open. "It's so bright."

"And it's right there." He stuck out his hand.

Arjen and Ice popped their seatbelts and stood up, floating to the ceiling and stopping themselves before they hit their heads.

"You're now free to move about the cabin," said Arjen.

"We can fly?" said Zane, finally taking his eyes off the moon.

"Float," said Arjen. "But you can think of it as flying if you like."

Zane loosened himself and pushed off the seat, joining them at the ceiling, his hair floating around him. There were rungs across the ceiling to grab ahold of like a kid's jungle gym.

"Mar, you have to try this."

"Okay, what about Honey?"

"Float her up to me."

Marlow gave her a gentle release upward and Honey looked at her, confused as to what was happening. When she realized she was off the ground, she started flapping and took off. Zane caught her before she crashed into the ceiling.

"Chill, Honey," said Zane, petting her head but spinning in a circle himself.

The duck tried to focus on Marlow and was struggling.

Marlow released herself and pushed off the seat the best she could with her good leg.

Honey kicked off Zane and tried to flap to her, not realizing her own power, soaring past her down the hall.

"Oh, shit," said Zane. "She's not a flying duck. She has no idea what she's doing."

Ice looked at Arjen and kicked off the wall, down the hall after the loose duck.

"Follow me," said Arjen.

The group flew down the hall, to a T intersection. Honey bounced off the wall and took a right, still flapping sporadically, trying to make herself stop, not knowing how. She was heading for a doorway and Ice was shortly behind. Just as she reached it, the doors slid open and she flew through. A confused man in a blue jumpsuit stood in the entry as Honey flapped by.

"What the hell?" He looked up to Ice flying through as well. "Is that a duck?"

Honey entered a room with low lighting and jacuzzi-type tubs. A tub on the right side was occupied by a naked man. His surprise could not be overstated as the duck fell out of the air and landed right next to him, splashing as she did.

"What is...?" he started, holding his hands out at the flapping duck. "How did you...?"

He stopped when Isolde hit the ground with a roll and approached the tub.

"Sorry, Marlin," Ice said. "She's with them." She threw a thumb over her shoulder as Arjen had Marlow and Zane stopped in the doorway.

"A real, live duck." Marlin said, admiring her while keeping his distance.

"Yep. A pet of theirs."

They watched Honey dip her bill and come up with a few drinks of the warm water.

"Think it's okay if she drinks this stuff?" said Marlin.

"Shouldn't hurt," said Ice.

She bent down and Marlin helped her scoop up Honey, handing her off gently before climbing out himself.

He was fully nude, thin, mid-fifties with no desire for manscaping. Ice didn't seem to care as he took a few steps into an air drycr, lifting his arms as the water blew off his body.

"I'd like to meet 'em," said Marlin, gesturing toward the door.

"I'd get dressed first and remember the rules."

"Yes, yes, I remember." Marlin grabbed a blue jumpsuit and pulled it on. Ice was handing off Honey as he joined them.

Zane was poking an almost see-through wall at the door, marveling at his finger going in and out.

"We're standing again," said Zane.

"Yes," said Arjen. "There's gravity in the bathhouse here. You know, or the water would float too."

Marlin stood, eager, next to Ice, she forced a smile.

"Everyone, this is Marlin, he's from Panel operations."

"Pleasure," he said, sticking out a hand. Zane met it, then Marlow. "I already met your duck."

"Honey," said Marlow.

"Right, hi there, Honey. You two, uh, *three*, enjoy your first ride up?"

"Yes," said Zane. "It was amazing." Marlow nodded with him.

"Well," said Arjen. "It's about time…"

"Yes, well," said Marlin, "I'd best be going. See you around." He stepped through the doorway, floated up to the ceiling and started down the hall.

"Seriously," said Marlow. "We just took off. Why was that guy taking a bath?"

"He's a little *weird* about his baths," said Ice. "Likes to get them in."

"Come on," said Arjen. "The doctors are waiting to see you."

Marlow swallowed hard. "Okay."

Zane patted her on the back. "Don't worry."

"They're the best," said Arjen. "I promise."

They went back out to the hall, floating down until they reached the far intersection. To the left was the bridge, going straight went down to the barracks and to the right was an unlabeled hall. They followed Arjen right, with Honey tightly tucked. Arjen stopped at a dead end and a door slide open as he drifted down to it. The group caught up and tucked in, Arjen stabling them as gravity kicked in. A woman in a white jacket turned, her long black hair pulled behind her. She looked like she could've been Zane's aunt, if he ever had one.

"Hello," she said in an Indian accent. "I'm Doctor Vell. You must be the stowaways." She followed this line with a smile as Zane and Marlow exchanged glances.

Arjen stepped up. "You got it Doc. Zane, Marlow, and Honey the duck."

"Oh, how nice. She'll like it back home too." She waved a finger at honey. "So, shall we get started then?"

"Yes," said Arjen. "Do you want...?"

"Leave the girl...Marlow, with me," said Dr. Vell. "Doctor Crouch will take Zane."

"Next door?" said Arjen.

Dr. Vell nodded. "And take the duck with you please."

"All right," said Arjen, reaching out his arms to Marlow. "I'll take good care of her."

Marlow gave Honey a kiss on the head as she handed her over.

Zane reached out a hand and Marlow took it before they were separated. Dr. Vell watched them go then turned to Marlow.

"Should we start with your foot?"

Marlow nodded and looked down at the dirty fabric that, in her mind, held her foot onto her leg. "It hurts, though."

"I understand. Let me help you onto the exam table."

Once she was up, Dr. Vell propped Marlow's foot and unwrapped it. It was red and swollen from her heel to mid-calf. The gash from the crazy man's machete was deep into her Achilles.

"Who wrapped this? Your friend?"

"Arjen."

"Oh." She clapped her head. "He knows better than to use dirty rags to stop the bleeding."

"I don't think he had much choice."

Dr. Vell looked it over for another few seconds, then lowered it. "You'll be okay. He did well enough. Now, first thing's first. Or, second in this case." She turned to a silver tray with various syringes on it, selecting one and looking her over again. "I'm going to need those clothes off."

"I…" said Marlow, holding her arms to her chest.

Dr. Vell replaced the syringe and turned to her with compassionate eyes.

"Marlow, I don't even need a stethoscope to tell you about your lung issues. Your foot will fall off from infection if you leave it as is and you probably haven't had a regular checkup in how long?" She raised her eyebrows and Marlow looked away.

Marlow began pulling at her overshirt. "Everything?"

Dr. Vell nodded. "Let me know if you need help. With the foot that is."

Marlow stripped down, wiggling off the dirty underwear last. She couldn't remember the last time they did laundry of any kind. It was such a process toward the end. She'd found a pack of new underwear that was a little big when she started wearing it but hit the floor like it belonged to an old, fat lady. Her arms and ankles were crossed when Dr. Vell turned, once again holding the syringe along with an alcohol prep pad. The smell stung Marlow's nose and her head snapped back.

"What is that?"

"Please be calm," said Dr. Vell. "It will all go easier if you're calm." She held up the syringe. "This is hagfish DNA. It's quite amazing really. When joined with…"

"No, that smelly thing."

Dr. Vell looked at the alcohol pad in her other hand and smiled. "It does smell doesn't it? This is to clean the area for the shot."

"Oh."

"As I was saying," she said as she rubbed a spot on Marlow's upper arm, "the hagfish is quite amazing. It has the ability to absorb nutrients through its skin."

"What does that mean? Why are you giving it to me?"

"This will allow you to receive proper nutrients without having to eat."

Marlow's eyebrows sunk into a confused frown. "So, I set a piece of chicken on my arm and it will suck it up?"

Dr. Vell didn't reply.

"I'm sorry, none of this makes sense."

"It will soon enough. Ready?" She held up the shot.

Marlow didn't reply but looked away. She cringed when she felt the cold metal under her skin. Dr. Vell taped down a cotton ball while she tied off her other arm with a rubber band.

"Now we will take some blood, run a panel and see what ails you, besides malnourishment of course. Make a fist please."

Marlow did, feeling the tightness in her arm extend to her chest. Her breathing was picking up as Dr. Vell finished cleaning the skin for her next stick.

"Try a song," said Dr. Vell as she raised the needle. "Singing or humming always helps me."

Marlow couldn't think of any songs. She stared at the ceiling, breathing hard like she was in labor. Soon, she felt a hand stroking her hair.

"You're a good girl. You're going to be healthy and strong again soon. You'll sleep in a nice soft bed with Zane and your duck, looking out at the stars."

The image was enough to distract her from the next poke. It took longer but soon she was done, and another cotton ball was taped to her.

Dr. Vell stepped to a machine on the counter behind her and inserted the blood samples. They disappeared inside it and a whirring sound began.

"We'll give that a few minutes. Now, lay back and we'll begin part two."

"I thought *that* was part two," said Marlow, still sitting up.

Dr. Vell snapped on a glove and squeezed some lube onto her fingers. "Got to check everything."

"What about my lungs?"

"I'm sorry, are you a doctor and I am unaware of this fact?"

"No. I just—"

"Then lay back and I will be as gentle as possible."

Marlow wasn't in a position to argue or run for that matter. She lowered her back to the crunchy paper of the exam table and felt Dr. Vell moving her legs into stirrups. It went against everything inside her but she didn't fight. She raised her arms, linking them over her eyes and began humming a song Jason used to sing her.

Within a few minutes, Dr. Vell was back at the machine on the counter. She hit a few buttons and turned around smiling.

"Ready for a bath?"

~ * ~

In the back of the medical office was another jacuzzi-type tub. The lights were low and resembled a sky full of stars, something Marlow rarely saw glimpses of with all the haze over the years. Dr. Vell helped Marlow limp over to the tub and lowered her in. The feeling was wonderful, making her head spin at the warmth and goodness of it. It took so much effort to come up with hot water in the past few years, she'd forgotten the goodness of a bath. It was rare at any point in her life.

"Feel good?" said Dr. Vell, standing by, watching her expression.

"Incredible."

"Slide over a few feet and there is a spot for your head."

It was hard to even lift her head off the hard edge she was resting it on but she did and spotted the place Dr. Vell mentioned. Her head fit perfectly but now her butt was floating. Dr. Vell tapped the water and pointed down.

"Feel for the bump in the wall, yep there." The seat rose to meet her and now it was perfect. Her arms floated, her head laid back and then a man in a blue suit walked in and ruined everything. Marlow barely noticed him as her eyes had been closing. She quickly covered her body the best she could, banging her heel and causing her to groan in pain. Dr. Vell saw her discomfort and blocked the man's view, taking a glass tube from him and sending him on his way.

"Sorry about that," she said, turning towards Marlow. "That was just Marlin delivering the NutrientPanel I ordered for you."

"NutrientPanel? Like, the drink stuff?"

"Not exactly. You see, with that DNA I gave you, you can absorb nutrients through your skin. It will get more efficient over time, but this should give you a good start." With that, she slid the tube into a small opening behind Marlow. "It takes about a half hour. I'm sure you won't have a problem staying in that long, will you?"

"As long as you keep Marlin out," said Marlow, her eyes already closing.

"I'll lock the door behind me. Just call if you need anything. Otherwise I'll be back in a half hour."

Marlow drifted off.

Chapter Five

Arjen was holding Honey, trying to give a firm talk to the pilot of the ship but failing as he found himself shaking the duck at them to make a point. He sighed and handed Honey to Isolde.

"Listen, that was not the mission. I don't care of it was Stephen Fucking Hawking back from the dead floating out there."

"I'm not just going to leave a person to die," said the pilot.

"He's probably already dead, Davis!"

"He waved at us."

"That could've been anything."

"Sir," said the co-pilot. "I witnessed him through the lenses. He's alive."

Captain Davis put a hand to his ear. "Okay, yes, we'll be right there." He looked up at Arjen. "They've boarded him."

Arjen threw up his hands. "Let's go meet him."

The group began walking to the airlock as Isolde stood, her braid loose and hanging down as Honey nibbled on the end of it.

"We need to find you something to eat." She looked around, pulled out the half-eaten nutrient pouch she'd collected from Zane and sat down on the floor, squeezing a few plops onto her palm and watching the duck eat it up. She giggled. "Oh, that tickles, Honey. You want more?"

Honey was quacking again.

~ * ~

Arjen and the pilots met a crewman at the airlock. On the other side, a man in a spacesuit with the US flag on his shoulder, stood, giving a thumbs up. Arjen looked to the crewman with a clenched jaw and he patted a taser on his hip. Arjen nodded, turned to the man and motioned for him to take off his helmet. Another thumbs up, then he went to work. It was a slow, awful process before he finally revealed his head. Emaciated cheeks covered in black and gray hair that gave way to a head of hair that looked like it was chopped by an axe murder. He had wide eyes and a huge smile. He raised both hands like he'd just won the lottery.

Arjen nodded at the door and the pilots opened it. The crewman waited at Arjen's command as the man stepped through.

"Yes," he said. "You found me. I can't believe it. I saw you passing by." He fell to his knees and took Arjen's hand. "I tried to time it the best I could to catch you on the way out."

"Time what? Where did you come from?" said Arjen.

"Get me out of this suit and I'll tell you. It smells like shit." The man looked around at the rest of the crew and put a hand to the side of his mouth as he whispered. "For good reason."

A few minutes later, after the man had been cleaned up, they sat on the bridge. Arjen, Isolde, the pilots and the crewman.

"So, Sam, you were on the international space station for how long?" asked Arjen.

"Two full years." He was shaking his head, still in disbelief of his own situation, while taking sips from a nutrient pouch. Arjen gave an uneasy look at Isolde and she seemed to read his thoughts, taking Captain Davis aside and whispering something to him.

Arjen continued, "And your crewmates?"

Sam pursed his lips. "Dead. Long ago it feels like."

"When was your last supply drop?"

He looked away. "Around then."

Arjen frowned. "Were *you* the supply run?"

Sam nodded. "Things were bad. You guys from the belt? You're not going back toward Earth. What were you doing down there?"

"Hold on a minute. Me first. You went up to the space station right around the Final War and you've been living there ever since?"

"Yeah. Like I said, things were bad. We knew it might be the last

31

time we'd have the funding to send supplies."

"*We* as in NASA?"

"Well, what was left of them. When I told them I wanted to go with, there was a big debate. We didn't have plans for a return flight, and I felt it deep down there wouldn't be one."

"So, why go?" said Isolde, standing to the side of the seated men, holding Honey still.

"Ma'am?" said Sam.

"If you knew you were going to be left to die up there, why go?"

An insane look spread across his face. "But I didn't die, did I?"

"Point." Ice shrugged. "If we decided to just keep driving…"

"Ah, but you didn't. There's decency left in the universe." He made a flutter with his hands to emphasize his point.

"The question…" said Arjen.

"Yes, yes," said Sam. "I guess I just thought it would be better to be up there and watch the world end rather than be down on Earth living it. And by God, it was a hell of a show."

"You watched the Final War from the station?" said Arjen.

"Well, yeah. Not much else to do but try to conserve resources."

"When did you know?" said Arjen.

"That it was all over?" Sam paused, looking out a window into space. "When the explosions stopped. We watched for almost twenty-four hours straight after that, waiting for another one. It's not something you ever wish for, to see bombs going off on your home planet, but *not* seeing them? It was almost worse because we knew there was no one left to fire them." He put his head in his hands and tears began down his bristly cheeks. "I went up there on purpose, because I feared the worst. The worst came but when it happened…there was nothing to do but wait to die."

Ice looked away, tightening her hug on Honey, feeling tears beginning in her eyes. Arjen looked unphased as Davis walked up and whispered something in his ear. Arjen nodded then turned back to Sam.

"I can't begin to say I'm sorry about your entire planet or your crew mates. I will say, you're safe now. We have the resources to sustain you. When we reach our home, our leadership will decide where to place you."

"Belters," said Sam with a big grin. "You're fucking belters. I knew it. Let's go." He made a blast-off noise with his lips.

Chapter Six

Marlow's bath ended when she heard the door. She was relieved to see Dr. Vell and not the man from earlier. She was holding a blue jumpsuit a lot like the ones Marlow saw on crew members around the ship, only, this one was more her size.

"Thought you could use something clean to wear," said Dr. Vell.

Marlow gave her a lazy smile.

"Bath feel good?"

"Heavenly. Do I have to get out?"

Dr. Vell smiled back. "Yes. We need to get your foot wrapped."

"Okay." She looked around. "Towel?"

Dr. Vell shook her head and pointed at an air dryer like the one Marlin used earlier.

"Just stand in it and raise your arms, it will do the rest."

Marlow followed her instructions, marveling at the speed in which it dried her and soon was walking back into the exam room in her new, baggy, but clean outfit.

Dr. Vell wrapped her foot with a firm but flexible material. Marlow got up to test it out. Dr. Vell was back at her computer monitor as Marlow leaned on the exam table.

"Are you done with me?" Marlow asked.

"For today," she replied, then turned to Marlow. "I'll be following up with you in a few weeks, but in the meantime, I'll be monitoring your NutrientPanel to make sure you're getting what you need. I put some antibiotics and anti-inflammatories in there today so your foot should be okay. Let me know if it flares up on you or gives you pain."

"Okay." Marlow was still in a daze from the bath. "What should I do now?"

"Oh, sorry," said Dr. Vell, lost in the monitor again. "Arjen should be by any second."

Marlow sat, letting her leg rest, hanging off the table. A minute later, the door opened and Zane stood in a matching uniform with a big grin.

"Mar, look at us."

Marlow stepped forward, hugging Zane and pulling back. "You don't smell," she said.

Zane laughed. "You either, for the first time since I can remember. Those baths are amazing."

She looked behind him to see Ice holding Honey, giving a wave.

"What's going on there?" said Marlow.

"I think Honey has found a new best friend."

"She feed her?"

"Yep."

Isolde led them to the bridge where Arjen was awaiting them. The drifting astronaut, Sam, was nowhere to be seen.

They sat around the ovular table while Captain Davis called back, "Approaching entry point."

Arjen smiled. "You're going to want to watch this part."

The ship was back up to speed with a sky full of stars around them. Only, there was one place ahead with no stars, no anything.

"Is that a black hole?" said Zane, staring transfixed on the void ahead.

"Wormhole," said Arjen. "There's still a lot to explain, which we'll get to shortly, but wormholes are how we travel. Otherwise you'd both be of legal drinking age by the time we got to the belt."

"What does that mean?" said Zane.

"Twenty-one?" said Arjen. "Well, maybe that wasn't the case toward the end."

"I'm twenty already," said Zane. "I'll be twenty-one in a few months."

"We'll have to celebrate." Arjen turned. "Marlow?"

"Eighteen. But I've had a drink or two, when we could find them, that is."

"Here we go," said Isolde.

They watched as the stars disappeared for good. Reality smeared across their vision like a wet painting. They were moving, seemingly faster but they couldn't be sure. The pilots released the controls and sat back.

"Uh, shouldn't they be driving?" said Marlow.

"No need," said Arjen. "It's like a river, you just let it flow."

Isolde rolled her eyes. "So new age of you."

"What happens now?" said Zane.

"We sit around on our asses and wait," said Arjen. "Who's up for story time?"

~ * ~

Arjen retrieved a bottle of something dark and four glasses. The pilots left, giving new meaning to the word "autopilot." Arjen assured them they had three weeks of wormhole travel and the pilots would be back in plenty of time to take back over. He poured out shots for each of them, pausing in front of Marlow's glass.

"Don't tell your…" He stopped himself, then shrugged. "Don't tell *my* boss."

Each of them tossed back their drinks. Arjen let out a grunt and set his cup down, watching the faces of the kids. They showed no sign that they weren't just drinking water.

"Well then," said Arjen.

"Just like that," said Isolde.

"What?" said Marlow. "The stuff we found wasn't usually top shelf."

"Fair enough," said Arjen. "So, tell us…"

"Tell you what?" said Marlow.

"Your story. The whole thing. How were you two still alive when we got there?"

"The *whole* thing?" said Zane. "That may take a while."

"Paraphrase," said Arjen. "Or not. We've got three weeks and a ship that pilots itself."

"Okay." Zane looked to Marlow and nodded. "I'll tell my side and she can correct me if she needs to.

"Like I said, I'm twenty, born September, sixty-nine. My family is from India a couple generations ago but I was born in northern Florida. Both of us" (he motioned to Marlow) "grew up during the resurgence." He saw the blank look on Isolde's face. "The resurgence was about twenty years after World War III. The late sixties. The planet wasn't in great shape but it was doing better. People were able to raise kids again without the fear of the hospital getting bombed. My parents gave me a normal life. It's all they wanted after living through the war. They were very strict about my education. We lived in a small community near Tallahassee. Ever heard of it? It's gone now." He paused and lowered his head. "I'm sorry. I'll get to the good part, if you can call it that. Two years ago, in June, I was woken up by my dad in the middle of the night. He was frantic, pulling me out the door of our house. Throwing my shoes at me and whispering for me to put them on. I did as I was told and he dragged me out the back door. It didn't take me long to figure out why we used the back. There were trucks patrolling the streets. US military of some kind. The thing was, during World War III, India had nuked the U.S. After the U.S. nuked them of course. Now, after years of peace, there had been rumors of a new war and it didn't take long for that peace to go out the window. They were rounding up anyone with our skin color to make sure we weren't undercover or something.

"So, Dad and I took off out the back. He told me Mom was already on the way and would meet us where we were headed. I didn't find out until months later that she was the reason we were able to escape."

Isolde's eyes were wide. "She stayed behind to distract them?"

"Yes, but it's not like it sounds. Dad didn't abandon her. She had arthritis in her knees. She could barely walk to the mailbox at that point, much less outrun the military. She sacrificed herself so we could escape."

"Jesus," said Arjen.

"Dad and I ran for about a mile until this brown van pulled up.

One of those big, family vans with the curtains on the windows. A family we knew, the Phans were driving. We rode south, before they closed the side roads. We went as far as the van would carry us, trying to find something rural. Our van broke down in Inland. The neighborhood looked to be mostly abandoned. Some of the houses were in bad shape. Others might have had people in them still. We didn't know, only that there were a few hours of darkness left. We pushed the van to an abandoned post office so we could sleep for a bit."

Marlow tapped the table at Arjen. "That's the building where you…" She slammed a fist into her open palm.

"With the guy?" said Arjen.

"Yep."

"Wow."

"Can I?" said Zane. "So, we were prepared to sleep when we heard a voice outside. It sounded like chanting of some kind. Dad went out to check it out, against all of our advice. He found the guy, Jerry Hill, who said he was out on a prayer walk. I don't think Dad would've told him about us or even trusted him if we didn't see the bombs. They were in the distance; from the direction we'd come. Jerry told Dad he had a shelter and he was praying for God to send him people in need. Most of his congregation had fled the town. When the bombing started, Dad waved for us to come on. We did. Jerry led us to the church. We all spent the night in the shelter. Me, Dad, all five of the Phans, Pastor Jerry and an old couple that were part of his church.

"We waited out the night of bombing. In the morning, there was no power. The radio wasn't giving much outside of, 'it was bad out there and to stay inside.' Dad didn't take long to decide we were staying. Pastor Jerry insisted as well. 'We'll ride out these end of days and wait for the Lord to come back,' he'd said, insisting it would be soon as the tribulation had started. The Phans thought Jerry was crazy, and I guess he was. They wanted out of the bunker. They were going stir crazy with their two youngest, Martha and John. Their oldest, Jason and I became good friends. I knew him from before but had never really dared to talk to him. Now, him and I were out each day, scouring houses for provisions. We didn't tell Jerry where they came from, just in case he was still worried about 'Thou shalt not steal.' A few weeks in, Jason and I were out, near the spot you guys landed your ship. We saw two women heading into one of the old delis. We waited for them to come out. It was my idea, you know, so they wouldn't feel cornered. Well, they did anyway and freaked out and attacked us with bats."

Zane pulled down the collar of his shirt.

"You can see where she got me."

Isolde leaned in and grimaced. "Hell of a hit."

Zane glanced over at Marlow. "Yep, she's got an arm."

Marlow snapped her head at him. "We thought you were cornering us to attack *us*."

Arjen broke into laughter. "*You're* the one that clocked him?"

"We had to protect ourselves out there," said Marlow with a shrug.

"So that's how you two met," said Isolde.

Zane nodded. "Jason got ahold of her bat before she could hit me again. Somehow, he talked them out of attacking us further and to come by the camp. They'd been searching for somewhere safe for long enough that they gave in. We had everyone come out to meet them. Mr. Phan seemed annoyed at the prospect of more mouths to feed, understandably so. Jason took it as his personal mission to make sure everyone was fed. He's the one that started the duck thing. We even had a goat for a bit and a cow. But Jason's dad wasn't so sure about sticking it out. He wanted to go back to their house in Tallahassee. The kids wanted their toys. His wife wanted her kitchen back. I don't think they ever grasped all that wasn't the same anymore, even if it was still there. They spent the majority of the next month talking it out, threatening to leave, then finally, one morning, they packed up their stuff and said their goodbyes. The only thing was, Jason wouldn't go. He thought like the rest of us, that things wouldn't be better back home. They may not be there at all. Also..." Zane glanced at Marlow. "Jason had *other* reasons he wanted to stick around."

Marlow slammed her hands on the table. "I never told him to stay for me. I never..." She was scrunching her face up, trying to fight back the emotions.

Zane put a hand on her shoulder. "I know that. I know you wouldn't do that. It doesn't change the fact that he was—"

"Shut up. Just tell your story."

Arjen and Isolde exchanged glances while Zane continued, almost unphased.

"So, it was hard to watch it happen, but Jason's family left without him. They gave him one more chance to come with and when he declined, they promised they'd come back for him once they were settled again. Of course, that was the last time we ever saw them.

"It was about a year and a half ago, we started losing people. We knew something was wrong with the air. You didn't need to smell it. You could notice in the way the winter came and never left. It got colder each day. The sunshine state was just hazy then. First, it was the older couple. I think that's when the rest of us took notice, like canaries in the coal mines. We did everything we could, wearing respirators and dust masks everywhere. Then, Pastor Hill went. On his last day, he told us he was sad he'd missed seeing the rapture but was happy he was taking the express train instead. He promised he'd put in a good word with the big man for us. After he died, it was down to me, Marlow, Jason, my dad and Marlow's mom. The parents came together to make a plan. I caught them talking about it one night, and it seemed like there was only one goal, to keep the kids alive as long as they could. It was common ground for them and that's what they fought for. My dad was always out on the roof with his mask on, looking for any sign of help or just better days. From time to time, he'd spot something, or think he did, but they never found their way to us. He'd talked about taking a search party to find help, but the haze made it impossible to track anything. Marlow's mom was all about the plants and animals, trying to find things that would sustain us."

"The roof thing…" said Isolde.

"Yeah," said Zane. "That's why I do it. I feel closer to him up there. Anyway, one day, about a year ago, he came down from the roof and he never went back up. He didn't have the strength. He tried spending days recovering but he never got back to his old self. When he died, I knew it wouldn't be long before we all were parentless. Marlow's mom adopted us as her own. She spent her last few weeks on long trips I was

40

afraid she'd never come back from. But each time she'd show up with cans of food, jugs of water, inhalers, anything she could find that would sustain us just that much longer. When she passed, it was just us, the *love triangle*, if you will."

"What?" said Arjen.

"Oh," said Marlow. "That's not…"

"Whatever you want to call it, Mar," said Zane. "You weren't the only one in love with Jason."

"But," said Isolde. "You two…?"

Zane and Marlow looked at each other.

"Ew, no," said Zane. "No offence."

"No, same here," said Marlow. "We're like orphan siblings. Which is why it's not a love triangle."

"Fine," said Zane, "whatever you want to call it. It was just us three. Jason and Marlow did the majority of the runs."

Marlow joined in, "He always gave me the best mask. The one that actually worked. I swear, half the time, he had his up on his head instead of over his mouth. He'd see my look and put it back on." She shook her head and gripped her temples with her thumbs.

Zane continued. "Jason got it next, of course. It was about six months ago. It was hard on us. He was like the backbone after our parents were gone. I might have cried more than Marlow. Anyway, the past six months got really tough. We were down to just a few ducks and we'd pillaged everything within a ten-mile radius. With each journey, we'd hope to find something better than the situation we were in but it was always worse. If we saw people, they'd always be coughing up blood or wheezing out their last breaths. Toward the end, we didn't even see people anymore. Until this morning…"

Zane's story was over. He put an arm around Marlow and they held each other as Arjen and Isolde watched. Honey waddled to the middle of the table, no longer content with being petted by Isolde. She did a slight squat, pooped and waddled off.

"Damn it," said Arjen. "I'll go get something to wipe that up."

Chapter Seven

They all took a bathroom break as Arjen cleaned up the table. When they reconvened, Arjen lined up the glasses again, raising his eyebrows to each of them. Zane and Ice obliged him but Marlow refused. After watching them drink, Marlow slid out her glass.

"On second thought…"

Arjen poured and she tipped it to him as she took a sip.

"I just feel so *alert*. It's weird. Like, too alert."

Isolde smiled. "That's the NutrientPanel. It gives you the good stuff without the bad. The one thing is, you had it later in the day than most people take it. It's like having coffee before bed in that case."

"Huh," said Marlow, taking another drink. "Makes sense, I guess. You're going to explain all that, aren't you?"

"Yes," said Ice. "But let *him* do it." She motioned toward Arjen. "He likes to hear himself talk."

"Excuse me," said Arjen. "I *love* to hear myself talk." He gave himself another shot and began.

"First off, how much do you two know about us Belters?"

Zane chimed in, "We know about that Ramirez guy and the colony he was trying to build."

"*Did* build," corrected Ice.

"Okay, *did* build," said Zane. "We didn't learn much else. My parents just told me he set out to do that while we went to war here. He should've used his tech to save Earth."

"Okay, that's…" started Ice. Arjen held up his hand.

"I've got this. Juan Carlos Ramirez and his partner, Petra Gammen," (he pointed to Ice) "her Great-Grandmother by the way, combined their tech, not hoping to see if colonization was possible but *knowing* it was our only chance as a species if things continued the way they were headed on Earth. Obviously, they were dead on with that prediction. Anyway, they made their first attempt in twenty-thirty. It took them almost four years to get there. You can imagine a lot of people forgot about them. Dr. Ramirez's TechBubble was history-changing stuff, but the Earth was shifting its focus onto other things besides space exploration. He didn't know it but his funding was cut mid-trip. Didn't matter to him and Petra though. They could see the future, or so it seemed. So, Dr. Ramirez was a genius but so was Dr. Gammen. She's the inventor of the GammenVat, which is a food synthesizer. Without it, they would've never made it to the belt and back. She could take basic nutrients and build sustainable meals for them. Sound familiar?"

Marlow nodded. "The NutrientPanel."

"Yep. That came years later but was based off the same tech." Arjen took a drink and held out the cup like a billionaire making a statement aboard his yacht. "That first trip, their entire mission was to try to get a TechBubble to stick."

"Stick?" said Zane.

"What is a TechBubble?" said Marlow.

"You know those almost invisible walls all over the ship? Those are versions of the TechBubble. Probably closer to the original because they don't do much but create some gravity. That being said, the original TechBubbles did quite a bit more. The idea is, if you have water, oxygen and an atmosphere, you can survive almost anywhere. Obviously, there are other needs, but these are your basics. Think about Mars, a little further out from the sun than Earth and yet, it's not hospitable. What about Venus? A little closer but it's hotter than Mercury at times. Why is that?"

"Atmosphere," said Zane. "We know that."

"Yes, and that's what Dr. Ramirez created with his TechBubble. It runs off the sun's energy, so solar powered but nothing close to what was on Earth. His was much more efficient. People thought he was insane for not trying a TechBubble on the moon, or even Mars, before going out to the belt, but he chose the belt for trial and error. There are asteroids as

43

small as six feet out there. He was able to try out a smaller asteroid first. He called it Planet Darwin. A tongue-in-cheek way of saying he hoped the technology 'evolved' so people could live out there.

"His first attempt was a minor failure. The bubble formed but the subject, a monkey they'd brought for such a purpose, died. He tweaked his settings over and over again until he was out of subjects and had to use himself, only Petra wouldn't let him. When he thought she was going to force him to forfeit the mission, she strapped on a suit and went herself. It was a twenty by thirty-foot rock, the size of a big living room. Petra double-checked his settings, looked out at the distant sun and pulled off her helmet. The bubble worked. She could breathe and wasn't freezing to death. They'd created the first man-made atmosphere. It went from there. They experimented some more and headed back, but now his vision for the belt was growing. He didn't just see living on a rock and eating synthesized food. Now he saw a utopia, of sorts, and he knew there was a ton of work ahead of them. The pilot spotted the wormhole, you know, the one we're currently riding, on the way in, and when he spotted the other end of it on their return, Dr. Ramirez told him to take it. This was a risk, as no one had used wormhole travel before. But he knew the manpower it would take to turn the belt into what he envisioned, and they couldn't afford four years each way. They were three weeks in with no end in sight and Dr. Ramirez was cursing himself for trying to take a shortcut, afraid now that this one came out a few miles from the sun. When they exited the wormhole and saw how close they were to Earth, you can imagine their excitement. His reports impressed many people of the scientific community but things had changed globally. As I said, his funding had been cut and he had to search elsewhere to get the support to send another ship out there." Arjen smiled but Ice cut him off.

"This is where he gets big-headed."

"Oh, come on. It's pretty great how my grandparents stepped in."

"Yeah, yeah," said Ice. "Just get it over with."

He made and face and continued, "My grandparents were high up in the political party in the Netherlands at the time. They had a lot of connections. They used those and most of their own money to support the next trip out, only asking for a spot for their son in the future. My dad was only about four at the time Dr. Ramirez returned but my grandparents wanted options for him. The second trip to the belt launched a couple years after the first one returned, which in space travel terms is really fast. Let's just say, he didn't have all the support, but the support he did have went a long way. Every astronaut, retired or otherwise, volunteered. More brilliant minds of science did as well. Soon, they had to create a wait list for the next shuttle. You can imagine at this point, there were plenty of celebrities, businessmen, athletes, and politicians who wanted in. The only thing was, Dr. Ramirez didn't have room for fat. Anyone aboard those ships had a purpose. If they didn't have a skill or knowledge that would benefit the belt, they didn't go.

"The second trip expanded immensely from the first. Knowing what and who they needed changed everything. Soon, they'd established a small community, if you will, but the problem was distance. Asteroids in the belt don't just hang out next to each other. They're thousands of miles apart. You may find a few together but you can't build a colony off of that. On the third trip out, they built a 'Rock-Hauler,' as they called it, to tow the asteroids closer together. It ran off the TechBubble technology and though the sun was distant, the TechBubbles were still able to keep things running.

"Up to that point, they hadn't set up a bubble on anything bigger than a football stadium. The Rock-Hauler had been moving every asteroid it could find closer and now, Dr. Ramirez had his sights on something bigger, Ceres, the lone dwarf planet in the inner solar system. He didn't just want Ceres for its size though. Ceres had materials. Carbon, clay, salt. Things that would make organic chemistry possible. But most of all, Ceres had water and lots of it. We're talking as much as Earth on a rock about as big as the state of Texas. At first it seemed impossible to get a bubble to 'take' on Ceres. Dr. Ramirez had never tried a TechBubble with that kind of output, but it turned out, he'd have help from the planet itself. The thin atmosphere it did have was the building block. It took time, and a lot of readjusting to support the already-present atmosphere, but by the end of the third trip, Ceres was on its way to becoming habitable.

"The triumphant return from the third trip was spoiled. It was

December of twenty-forty-three. The war was looming and everyone knew it. Those who hadn't been to the belt didn't have time or resources for it. Those who had, well, they'd been left there on the last trip. Only Dr. Ramirez and a small crew, for the sake of travel, came with him, and his ship needed repairs before it could embark on another three-week journey. His biggest fear was coming true. There wouldn't be funding or resources to go back. The dream he'd built would be enjoyed by others but he would die on Earth. He didn't take that lightly. He convinced what was left of NASA to work pro bono, even guaranteed some of them a spot aboard the ship. They made the proper repairs to his ship and even got him a launch date. They tried to keep it under wraps, as the U.S. president at the time was very opposed to the belt in general, stating it was un-American.

"The day of the launch came and what was left of Dr. Ramirez's supporters were there, including a thirteen-year-old boy, my dad, Robin Visser. My grandparents dropped him off like he was getting on the school bus. They didn't ask to come. They only asked that Dr. Ramirez made good on his promise and took my dad to 'a place with a future.'"

"Whoa," said Zane. "They just up and sent their kid to space?"

"Those were desperate times," said Isolde. "They didn't see a future for him on Earth. Sounds like your parents would've done the same if they had the option."

Zane took a second. "I guess so."

"So, that's a big chunk of the early history," said Arjen. "That ship was the last one to make it to the belt before World War III."

"*Make it?*" said Marlow. "What does that mean?"

"Well, others tried. I mean, with things going the way they were, it was a slim hope but it was worth a shot. Those ships just didn't make it. They failed in one way or another. Some exploded on launch, some later. Some just flat out ran out of fuel and died. We weren't in the position to send help. We were just developing life some four-hundred-million kilometers from the sun. We didn't have a lot of room for error. We lost some good people back then."

Isolde rolled her eyes and groaned.

"What?" said Arjen.

"You act like you were there. Your dad witnessed all that but you didn't. You weren't born until they were fifteen, twenty years into colonizing. It was all hunky dory at that point."

"I was there in spirit," said Arjen, taking the comment in stride. "So, yes, I wasn't there for that colonization over the first twenty years. But I've been there for the last thirty-five and it's been getting better."

Zane and Marlow could barely form replies. Either this was some elaborate cover story or they really were heading to go live in the asteroid belt.

"So, what's it like now?" said Zane.

"Nineteen-sixties U.S.," said Arjen with a smile. "No, but seriously, it's good. We have a real civilization, houses, trees, animals, jobs, nightclubs."

"You have nightclubs?" said Zane.

"Of course, you'd be excited about that," said Marlow.

"There was only one in Tallahassee and I was never old enough."

"Yes," said Arjen. "There are nightclubs, well, one main one. You'll see when we get there. Not that…I'm not sure I'll be taking you to the nightclub." He gave a nervous look towards Ice and she just shook her head.

"What *will* you be doing with us when we get there?" said Marlow. "Slave labor? Sex workers?"

"Jesus," said Arjen. "Get your mind out of the gutter. You can stay at my place until we figure out the best spot for you. I have space and I'm gone a long time when we do these trips. You'll have the place to yourselves."

"Sounds exciting," said Marlow. "You have food in the fridge?"

"Well…no food, no fridge. We have NutrientPanel, remember?"

"What?" said Zane. "No eating? What about the pouches?"

"Those are more for emergencies. Plus, they're more complicated than just taking your bath each morning."

"Seriously?" said Marlow. "You take a bath instead of eating? You really should've left us on Earth."

"Hey now," said Ice. "We've wiped out hunger, obesity and disease with NutrientPanel. How many times were you two looking for your next meal?"

Marlow nodded. "Okay, okay. It just might take some getting used to." She picked up the empty bottle from the table. "You still drink though."

Arjen smiled. "Gotta have a way to unwind."

"NutrientPanel can't do it?" said Marlow.

"Probably not a good idea considering it's a bath," said Arjen. "In the belt you get a two-drink limit though. On my ship, you get what you get until we hit the end of the bottle. And you don't tell anyone where you got it, ya hear?"

Zane and Marlow nodded.

"Do you…poop?" said Marlow. "If you don't eat…"

Zane broke out in laughter.

"We do still," said Arjen. "But not nearly as much as people did on Earth. Maybe once a week for most people."

Zane composed himself. "How do you know so much about Earth? You've never lived there. You've only seen it when it was bad."

"I studied on it a lot. Obviously, my dad told me some, but we have media from Earth. One of the trips brought us a huge hard drive full of Earth entertainment. Most people on the belt are into one show or another. It's not that we're trying to base everything off of Earth's history. There was a lot of bad that led them to the end but there was a lot of good as well. We're trying to take the good parts into our culture. We're a bit lacking in the entertainment field. Hasn't really been our focus. People need a way to unwind after a long day of preserving our species." He smiled but they just looked at him, taking in the story that was sounding more and more unbelievable and yet true at the same time.

Marlow put her head on Zane's shoulder.

"I really think all your talking did it," said Marlow. "I'm finally getting tired."

Arjen tipped an invisible cap to her. "Glad to be of service. Should I show you to your rooms?"

"Rooms?" said Zane.

"Yes. Where you will sleep."

Ice smacked his shoulder. "They probably want to be together. They've been together for years and now they're up on some strange spaceship, hurtling away from everything they've ever known. Have some sympathy."

"Okay. My fault," said Arjen. "I was trying to be a good host. I hope you can share a full."

"We'll make it work," said Marlow. "Honey too."

"Oh, seriously? You're going to have the duck in there with you?" He looked at their
faces. "Yeah, I guess you are." Arjen stood up. "Shall we?"

Chapter Eight

The room was like a small hotel suite, already better than anything they'd stayed in in years. Arjen showed them the basic controls for the TechBubble. It ran off the ship's power and was adjustable on each level, from temperature and lighting to gravity. Zane was still messing with it after Arjen left. Marlow was walking toward the bathroom and found herself leaving the ground on each step, before gently falling back. Honey sat in the middle of the bed watching them both.

"Would you pick a setting?" said Marlow.

"Sorry," said Zane, his hand frozen at the panel. It was a small touchscreen by the door. "This is just so cool. It doesn't seem like it will go all the way off though."

"Probably 'cause they don't want you floating off in your sleep."

"Yeah," he said, absentmindedly still scrolling through the options but not changing them now. Finally, he turned away as Marlow came out of the bathroom, reveling in how basic it was with just a small toilet and hand sanitizing station. He was smiling at her.

"What?"

Zane walked forward and wrapped her in a hug. "We're going to live, Mar. We really are, and if this place is half as good as they describe, we're going to love it."

Marlow was planted in his shoulder, just her eyes watching the door. "I'm still having trouble coming to terms with it. Why would they just pick us up? Just 'happen upon us while out gathering.' I don't buy that, Zane."

Zane sat on the edge of the bed and Honey crawled into his lap.

"I can't say I'm not skeptical, but you have to ask yourself, what would they want with two emaciated, sickly, starving kids from Earth? We have literally nothing to offer them. I mean, you talked to Arjen and Ice. They may just be nice people. They seem pretty genuine."

"They do," said Marlow. "My mom always warned me about nice people though. They usually have an agenda."

"Yes, like me." Zane rubbed his collarbone and pouted for emphasis.

"Oh, shove it. You were the exception. You and Jason."

"All I'm saying is, enjoy the moment. Think about yesterday. When Marvin died, I could read the writing in the sand. One more duck and we were next."

"I know. I feel good. My lungs especially have felt better than they have in a long time. Maybe they really can heal me with their Nutrient BS. I just have a hard time trusting any of this."

"Funny, right? When they found us, I was the one who didn't trust them. Now you don't."

She shrugged. "Yeah, well, when Arjen found me, he saved me from a lunatic. But who's to say he's not just a better-dressed lunatic?"

Zane got up, raised a finger and said, "Don't worry." He walked to the panel, hit a button and turned back. "We're safe from the lunatics. I've locked the door."

Marlow laughed. "Right. I'm sure that does it and they have no way into one of the rooms on their own ship."

After a few minutes, they were under the covers, staring at the ceiling, side by side with Honey at their feet.

"It's so bright," said Marlow, used to the pitch-black look of the bunker.

"Let me try one more time." Zane walked to the panel again and found a button called 'Blackout' and hit it.

"Oh, that did it," said Marlow. "Can you find your way back?"

"I think so."

"Hey, hey." Marlow was giggling. "That's me."

Zane continued poking at her sides. "Oh, this? It's so bony. I thought a skeleton was in the bed."

She poked back. "Shut up. You're pretty bony yourself."

They were side by side again. Marlow tried closing her eyes, but they wouldn't stay shut.

"Hagfish," she said.

"Right?" said Zane. "That's crazy. Your doctor told you about that too?"

"Yes. You know, *that* might be it. We're science experiments. They want to try out new tech on us and if we die, it's no loss to them."

"That's a long way to travel for two lab rats," said Zane. "You'd think they would've gotten more."

"Maybe they did. Maybe they just don't want us to meet. If the rats start talking, it's all over." She paused for a second before cracking up laughing.

"Are you done with the conspiracies for one night?"

"Probably not, but I won't say the others out loud if that makes you feel better."

"Yes. It does. I would like to sleep in this super-soft bed, in a warm room. So warm I think I need to remove some blankets."

"Oh, please do. I didn't want to say it because it was nice at first but man, it's like seventy degrees in here already. Maybe just the sheet."

"I'll try the panel again. Maybe I can turn it down further."

Honey turned a circle in frustration as they adjusted again.

They finally passed out in the middle of the night, tossing and turning with identical nightmares of their lives on Earth. They awoke to a knock at the door just a few hours later.

"Wuah?" said Zane.

"The door," said Marlow, "who's at the door?"

"It's locked."

"I know."

"Are we...? Where are we?"

Marlow shook her head, trying to clear her thoughts. "A ship? Was that real?"

The knocking came again, followed by a voice. "Marlow? Zane? You guys okay?" It was Arjen.

"I think it was real," said Zane.

"Go hit the lights."

Zane managed his way to the panel, hitting buttons until the lights finally came on at full brightness.

"Ah," said Marlow. When her eyes cleared, she saw a skinny, naked Indian boy's butt facing her as he looked over his shoulder.

"Sorry, I…" He stopped when the door opened. Marlow pulled the sheet up over her own naked body.

"Good morning," said Arjen, stepping in. "Oh, sorry, were you getting dressed?"

"Why did you just come in?" said Zane, covering his manhood while simultaneously turning away, showing his butt once more. "I didn't say come in."

"Sorry." Arjen was turned away. "You unlocked the door. I thought it was an invite. I just came to tell you it's breakfast time. It would be good if you hurried so we can meet Marlin with your special panels." Arjen stepped out the door. "I'll be right outside. Five minutes?"

"Okay, just close the door," said Zane. He did and Zane looked over to Marlow, blushing hard.

"It's no big deal," said Marlow, pulling off the sheets and searching for her jumpsuit.

"I'm not ashamed of being naked," said Zane, finding his own suit and sticking a leg in.

"It's just in front of *him?*"

Marlow looked up and smiled at him. "You got a little crush on the big, tan, blond man? He does look like one of those romance novel dudes."

Zane made a face. "No, he doesn't. Well, okay, maybe one or two of them."

"If we took his shirt off and greased him up, you'd see it, I'm sure."

"Don't say that." Zane was smiling again. "I can use my own imagination, thank you very much."

"Gross," said Marlow. "Just keep him out of your dreams, or we're never sharing a bed again."

They stepped to the door, Marlow holding Honey with a slight limp until they hit the zero-gravity hallway. Arjen was on the ceiling, holding one of the rails.

"Ready? Follow me."

They floated to the bathhouse where they'd first met Marlin. They hadn't seen it at the time, but the room was sectioned off into four personal baths with walls for privacy.

"Wait, where were the dividers yesterday?" said Zane. "That man…"

"Marlin just doesn't care," said Arjen. "And that's not uncommon. A lot of people in the belt are more *open* if you will. It helps when everyone is in good shape, I guess. Kinda hard to be fat when you don't eat." He led them to the back two baths. "These should be open for you. You can control the walls with the panel here." He showed them a touch pad like in the room. The walls went down, then back up.

"Up is good," said Marlow.

"Okay." Arjen looked back. "Normally they load up the basic panel for you up there." He pointed to the front of the room near one of the dryers. "But I'm waiting on a special delivery for you two…ah, there he is." Marlin walked in holding two tubes. Arjen met him and took the tubes as Marlin waved over at them before heading out. Arjen met them back at the bath. "Hop in. The water is warm."

They hesitated.

"Right," said Arjen. "Enough flashing me for one day." He bent down and inserted the first one. "Okay, that one is for Zane." He waved for Marlow to follow him to the next bath and inserted the tube for her. She stared at him.

"Okay…" said Marlow.

"Okay," said Arjen. "Hand over the duck. You don't want poop in your bath."

"Oh, right." Marlow did, but before Arjen could take Honey, Isolde slipped in and snatched her up.

"Oh, I was hoping I'd get some Honey time," said Ice.

"Hey Ice," said Marlow.

"Hey," said Ice. "Sleep well?"

Marlow shrugged. "Not exactly. Still getting used to *all this*."

Ice nodded. "It will take time. You'll probably sleep better tonight after a full day on the ship." She undid the bun on top of her head and held out the end of her long braid to Honey. "You hungry girl?" Honey nibbled at the braid, and Ice squealed in delight. "Looks like she is. I'll find her something to eat and meet you back here if that's okay."

"That would be great," said Marlow, teetering from foot to foot.

Ice grabbed Arjen's shoulder. "Let's give her some privacy."

"Right," said Arjen. "We'll be back."

Marlow watched them go, tucked behind the wall and quickly undressed. She realized her foot was still wrapped and had to sit naked while she undid it, feeling her pulse pick up, waiting for some stranger to come walking around the corner. She couldn't help but flash back to the man in the street. "I wanted you to be awake for this, even give a little back," he'd said and she shivered at the thought. *Was that only yesterday?* When her foot was loose, she jumped in, banging her butt on the seat. She felt the rush a child gets when they think there are monsters under the bed and have to be fully covered so their feet don't get eaten. It took a few minutes before she relaxed and let the water do its thing. She realized the NutrientPanel was no joke. She could feel her body energizing as she soaked. The bath the day before had been the first one in such a long while that even if it were lukewarm, plain bath water, it would've felt life changing. Today was the proof there truly was something happening.

Her eyes closed for a minute, letting the panel work its magic, then they snapped back open. She'd seen Jason on his deathbed, gasping for breath. She shook out the memory and focused on the sounds of the room, which were minimal. There was quiet singing from one of the baths that she recognized as Zane. Despite all the good fortune that had come to her and Zane in the last day, she felt the guilt. If only the gathering trip had been six months earlier. Or a year. The ship, the technology, the belt, the *life* they were heading towards was nothing short of astounding, but it pained her to think of the ones they'd left behind. The ones who fought so hard to survive, so *she* could survive. So she could live one more day while they fucking choked to death. She hoped Zane didn't feel this. Knowing him, he'd probably already come to terms with it. He had a gift for freaking out about things, then letting them go. Like he had to just get it out of his system. She was more of a thinker and she suffered for it.

Marlow as almost relaxed again when she heard a voice. "This one taken?" A man stepped around the corner of the wall and she let out a small shriek. He was in the usual blue jumper she and Zane wore but his hair was short and patchy and the look in his eyes brought back the man from the street, Walter.

"It's taken," she managed, while covering herself the best she could.

The man quickly turned, hanging on the wall for balance. "I'm so sorry. Where are my manners?" He was looking away but didn't leave. "The name's Sam. I'm a refugee like you."

"What are you—" Marlow started but he cut her off.

"I just wanted to say hi. We gotta stick together up here. Know what I mean?"

Marlow didn't know and hoped he wouldn't turn around again. Thankfully, he threw up a hand and stepped away.

"We'll talk again when you're decent." Sam called. "Look for me."

Marlow spent the rest of her bath on edge, keeping to the far side, ready to jump out if she needed to. Finally, there was a buzzing sound and the water stopped moving. She looked around and was thankful to see an air dryer against the back wall that she hadn't noticed before. She was about to pop out when she saw a shadow at the entry again.

"Just me," called Zane, sticking his head around. He was dressed in the blue uniform again.

"Oh, Zane," Marlow said, hand on her heart. "Guard the door while I get dressed."

Zane looked around. "There's not really a—"

"Just, don't let anyone else back. I'll be quick."

"Okay."

Marlow got out, dried off and got dressed. She was shaking out her long, coffee-brown hair as Ice walked in, still holding Honey.

"How was it?" she asked.

"Felt great," said Zane.

"Are there other refugees?" said Marlow. "Like us?"

"What?" said Ice. "No. What do you mean?"

"Did you pick up anyone else from Earth?"

Zane and Ice were giving her strange looks.

"A man came in here, saying he was a refugee just like us."

Ice frowned. "Was his hair all..." She waved a circle around her head and Marlow nodded. "Okay, listen. He's a special case. I'll let Arjen tell you about him, but no, we didn't pick up anyone else on Earth."

"When can we talk to Arjen?" said Marlow.

"He's waiting for us on the bridge." Isolde handed off Honey and typed away at a data pad on her forearm as they walked. When they reached the bridge, Arjen was standing at the window, watching the smearing, endless black in front of them. He turned and gave them a book-cover smile.

"You can see why Dr. Ramirez was so freaked out. It just seems to go on forever with no landmarks. Kind of like those magic eye puzzles. Did you ever see those?"

Marlow and Zane nodded.

"I hate them," said Marlow.

"I could only get them half the time," said Zane.

Arjen approached the table and they all sat.

"Arjen," said Ice. "Marlow encountered Sam this morning."

"Oh, really," said Arjen. "Did he talk crazy to you?"

"A little," said Marlow. "He said he was a refugee, but you said you didn't pick up anyone else."

Arjen nodded. "That's true. We didn't pick up anyone else from Earth. We were on a gathering mission, not search and rescue. We happened upon you two and that was it. You know, outside of that guy I kicked in the head. But on our way out, the captain spotted this guy floating out in space. I honestly thought he'd be dead, but we picked him up anyway. Turned out, he'd been surviving on the international space station for the last two years, according to him. I'm a bit skeptical, but the one thing I do know is he's batshit crazy. I would recommend avoiding him the best you can."

Marlow frowned. "Okay."

"Did he say anything else?"

"Not really. Just kinda freaked me out."

Arjen nodded then smiled. "All right." he clapped his hands once. "We've got a few weeks out here. Ice and I talked. If you're up for it, we wanted to start you two with a little more current history of the belt, then some exercise classes to help you build some muscle back up."

Marlow looked to Zane and back. "I guess so. You think my foot is okay for that?"

Ice examined it. "We'll break you in slowly. You'll see though, with the NutrientPanel, you'll be healed up much quicker than you would've before."

"Yes," said Arjen. "You're getting the super NutrientPanel right now. You can't have that all the time or you'd grow a third arm." He looked around. "That's a joke. I think. I don't know, I haven't tried. Anyway, we could do some light exercise today and amp it up as we go. By the time we get there you'll be ready for some slave labor." He looked around again when no one was laughing. "Also, a joke. Come on you two."

"What are you going to do with us when we get there?" said Marlow.

"Good question. First, I think we'll get you settled in. Then, we'll talk to job placement and see where you'd be the best fit. Everyone has a role within our society."

"What about old people?" said Zane. "You make them build houses still?"

Arjen laughed. "No. Would *you* want your house built by someone who could barely lift the boards? No. We have jobs for them still. We have an extensive library, mostly electronic, but still run by real people with years of knowledge who may lack the physical gifts to continue at more labor-intensive jobs. They run book clubs and study groups as well. Some of them form our government as well." Arjen pointed to Ice. "Her grandma is part of that."

"Hold on," said Zane. "Ice's great-grandma made the NutrientPanel stuff, and her grandma is in the government?"

"Yes," said Ice. "And my sister still works with NutrientPanel and GammenVat tech, trying to improve it even more."

"That's pretty cool," said Zane. "Why don't you do that?"

Ice shrugged. "I wanted my own path. Being tied to a lab your whole life gets old. I still know a lot about it. I could repair most of the machines involved. It was always just assumed I would end up in the lab with my family but it just wasn't for me."

Marlow smiled. "That's cool."

"Oh yeah?" said Ice.

"Yeah, like, making your own path, not following something just because your family did."

"Thanks, but not everyone thinks so. They still think I'll come around one day."

"So, what about Dr. Ramirez and Dr. Gammen?" said Zane. "Are they still around?"

Arjen shook his head. "Nope. Their kids and grandkids are, obviously. So, you can meet more of them if you like. Oscar Ramirez, son of the founder, Juan Carlos, is in our government and oversees the TechBubble team. Mateo Ramirez, his son, is the CSO, Chief Scientific Officer, head of our research and development team. His second in command is the recently promoted, Admani Gammen, sister of Ice. I hope all that's not too confusing."

"It's kinda making sense," said Zane. "What about your dad?"

"Oh, dear old dad," said Arjen. "He's in government too."

Ice laughed. "He practically the president."

"He's not..." said Arjen.

"Since Juan Carlos died and Oscar didn't want that title..."

"He doesn't want that title either."

"So, your dad's pretty much the president?" said Zane.

"He's not—" said Arjen. "He's in government, along with the Ramirez family and the Gammen family. They work together to make sure life continues in the belt."

"So, how many people are there?" asked Marlow. "You said they only took four trips, right?"

"Yes. Once they proved they could survive out there, those ships were crammed with as many people as they could fit. I think the original total was one hundred eight people."

"Total?" said Marlow. "Like, there were one hundred eight people when World War III started?"

Arjen nodded. "We're just over three hundred recently."

"So, that's it?" said Marlow. "For the human race? Three hundred people?"

"In the belt," said Arjen. "There may be people still hiding out on Earth, but the conditions didn't look favorable while we were there."

"That's crazy."

"It's a fine balance out there. We don't have the resources to support a thousand people but we're working toward it. With each generation comes its own challenges."

"What about you two?" said Zane. "You have kids?"

Ice looked to Arjen and back. "No. And if I did, it would not be with him."

"Oh, that hurts," said Arjen.

"Just saying," said Ice. "I couldn't handle that much diplomacy in one household. Besides, my nephew is more than enough."

"I wasn't saying…" said Zane.

"We know," said Arjen. "But no, no kids for either of us. Now, who's up for some exercise?"

"Ugh," said Ice. "I already did my work out for today."

"You can lead the class," said Arjen. "You'll be fine."

Chapter Nine

Isolde grudgingly agreed to and they headed to a small workout studio. She led them in a form of kickboxing that made every muscle stretch to its limits. Zane kept up the best he could while Marlow tried and stumbled with her bad foot. This routine continued for the next two weeks without fail. They'd wake up, take their NutrientPanel-filled bath, go to their belt class lessons with Arjen and workouts with Isolde. They were amazed at the way their bodies changed over the course of those weeks. The protein-rich super-panel, as Arjen described it, had gotten them back from looking like starving children, to lean, muscular young adults in such a short time. Their eyes were clear, their skin had a healthy glow. For the first time she could remember, Marlow realized Zane was not a half-bad-looking guy. If he weren't her gay, adopted brother, she might have had another thought about him. Marlow was excelling in Isolde's class, striking harder and more precisely each time. Once her foot healed, she quickly became too much for Zane when they would spar. He was no slouch of his own, but he enjoyed Arjen's teaching more. Marlow teased that he was studying Arjen's eyes more than his words.

It was one day, sixteen days since they'd left Earth, that Marlow was heading from Isolde's class, splitting off with Zane as he headed back to their room. She was going to meet with other crew members for a game of cards. They held daily games, and with nothing real to gamble for, it was all about wins. Atop the leaderboard was Marlin. Besides concocting the NutrientPanel and taking lots of baths, he was quite the card shark. Marlow had grown to like him despite their initial encounters. He was who he was, and just didn't care if you didn't like him. At the same time, he was kind, like he cared more for your feelings than his own. She was preparing a stupid joke to tell him. If you could get him laughing, you could get him off his game.

"I used to have two kidneys..." she mumbled to herself, trying to remember the punchline, when a man floated out of a hallway in front of her, blocking her path.

"Hey," he said. "Remember me?"

"Um." Marlow stared at him. "Your hair is different, I think."

"That's right. Got me a proper military cut. I'm Sam, the other refugee. If I didn't know better, I'd think they were trying to keep us apart."

Marlow hadn't seen him since their first encounter and was hoping anyone else would be coming down the hall to distract him. She realized she was a few minutes late for cards and they were probably already at the table.

"I don't know about that," she said. "I'm actually late to meet some people..."

Sam doubled down, grabbing the two handrails above to spread out in front of her and block the way.

"Yes, cards. I've heard of that, never get invited. Listen, I just want a minute of your time, then you can go." Without all the hair, he looked less crazy and more menacing.

"Okay. You're the guy from the space station, right?"

"Yep. Now hear me out. I saw them making their trips. You're not the first they took, but you might be the last. Things have been pretty bad for a while."

Marlow gripped the handrails above her. "What do you mean? They've taken other people from Earth?"

He nodded. "Different ship, but same result. Short little trip. In and out. I waited them out, trip after trip. Either they didn't know I was up there, or they didn't care. But I ran out of supplies. I had to risk it. Better to be a prisoner than starve. I jumped, had to time it just right or I'd still be floating out there. Good thing is, I've timed their trips before. They picked me up but they don't trust me. I think they're onto me. I think they know that I know."

"What do you know?" said Marlow, truly interested now. "About the trips?"

"*That,* and that they're doing something with the people. Experiments. Testing. Fucking. Who knows?"

"Who knows? *I* would like to know."

"I'm sure we'll find out soon enough."

"So, Arjen doesn't know that you saw their other trips?"

Sam shook his head. "And don't you tell him. He'll kill me."

"I don't know about that."

"He will." His voice was gruff, and Marlow found herself flinch back from him. "Sorry," said Sam. "I just…I'm trusting you. You're not with them. You're the only one close enough to find out what's really going on."

"Okay. Assuming there is something going on." She looked up and down the halls, less hoping people would be coming now and more, making sure her next comment would go unheard by others. "If I find anything out, how am I supposed to tell you about it?"

Sam let out a quick smile, then brought his voice low, "I bathe at six. It's when they let me out for the tubs. I usually try for the back ones. Where I ran into you the first time. Find out what you can, meet me back there before we land, and we'll come up with a plan. Bring your friend, too. We'll need all the help we can get."

"I'll see what I can do," said Marlow, turning over everything he was saying.

"Hurry, we've only got a few days and then it may be too late." He looked around. "I've gotta get out of here. Supposed to be in therapy. I'll catch up with you. Go to your card games, see if you can get them talking."

Marlow nodded at him as he disappeared down the hall again. "What the hell?" she said to herself and continued to the card game.

~ * ~

"I'm just saying," Marlow said to Zane that night, lying in bed in the dark, "what if he's not totally crazy?"

"But he *is*," said Zane. "Ask any of the people who've met him.

He's *out there*, Mar."

"He *saw* the ships, Zane. Think about it, why would they keep going to Earth?"

"Gathering? Remember? That's the whole point of their ship."

"Oh yeah? What have they gathered?"

"Resources, material for NutrientPanel and soil. You were in the class. You know what their gathering trips are for."

"I'm just…"

"What about this crazy astronaut, huh? How did he *see* them taking people? There's no way he could see that. It's not like they were hanging out the window waving at him."

Marlow was silent but Zane continued.

"And what about the space station? Why was he the only one?"

"Resources, Zane. Everyone else died off."

"So, did he eat them? Did he kill them and eat them so he could live? Because, there's no way his oxygen would've lasted two years without a refill, unless…"

"Seriously? You're saying he got up there and went all Hannibal on them right away? You're sick."

"Times were tough. You know that."

"I also know we didn't eat any of our people."

"Eating your mom is different from eating a stranger who's going to suck up all your oxygen."

"Where are you getting this? This isn't you."

Zane sighed. "Some of the crew have just been talking, but I don't think they're far off."

"Zane, this is your life and my life in the balance here. Help me dig up some dirt. It may save us."

Zane was quiet to the point that Marlow was afraid he'd fallen asleep. He finally replied, "Okay. But I don't think they saved us, got us back to proper health and taught us their history just so they could turn and kill us."

"There are worse things than killing."

"Go to sleep, Mar."

Chapter Ten

The next morning, Arjen showed up before they'd left for their bath. He said the doctors were ready to do one last follow-up appointment now that they've had a few weeks. He led them to Dr. Vell's and dropped off Marlow while taking Zane to his checkup.

"Whoa," said Dr. Vell as Marlow stepped into her office. "The NutrientPanel is treating you well then."

Marlow blushed. "I guess so."

"Look at your hair, so shiny and healthy now, and the foot?"

Marlow lifted her leg and spun her ankle in a circle. "All good. I've been doing kickboxing too. Feels good."

"That's good to hear. Will you jump up on the table for me?"

Marlow tugged at her jumpsuit and Dr. Vell shook her head.

"Nope, you can keep it on this time. I just need to listen to your lungs."

Marlow climbed up. Dr. Vell listened in and smiled.

"Sounding clear. I just need to give you one last shot to make sure it's gone for good and doesn't come back."

"That's good to hear. I really didn't know if I was a lost cause or not."

"No, no. You're a *found* cause." Dr. Vell raised a syringe. "Make a fist...good. All this working out has made your veins easy to find. Okay, look away if you want, it will be over quick."

Marlow saw Dr. Vell pull the needle out and step back, then she was out cold.

~ * ~

Marlow's eyes fluttered. The room was dim. She felt like she weighed a thousand pounds. When she tried to move, her arms wouldn't raise. She blinked, once, twice, on the third she regained enough focus to see she was still on the exam table, though it was laid back like a bed. She could raise her hundred-pound head just enough to see the strap across her body. When she moved her wrist, she could now feel the straps there as well. Her head fell back into the small, built-in pillow and she took a few seconds, breathing hard as she tried her feet. They were strapped as well. She let out a screaming groan.

"Hey."

A man turned with a mask over his face and blue gloves on his hands. He was right next to the table. She screamed again. The man pulled down the mask, revealing a two-day shadow of stubble and penetrating eyes.

"Hello there," he said. He put out a gloved hand as if to shake then pulled it back and laughed. "Probably not, huh?"

"Whu-what is going on? Where's Dr. Val?" Marlow slurred her words.

"Dr. *Vell* should be back any minute. I'm Dr. Crouch."

"What are you doing here?" Marlow squeezed her eyes shut, trying to make her brain focus. Everything felt off.

"I was just checking on you."

"You're not my doctor."

He laughed again, pulling his gloves off and tossing them in a waste bin. "True. I've been seeing to your friend."

"Zane? Is he okay?"

Dr. Crouch put a hand on her strapped arm and she recoiled the best she could.

"Yes," he said. "Your friend is fine. *You're* fine. You just need to relax."

"Why am I…?" she started, but the door opened. Dr. Vell walked in.

"Oh, you're awake, Marlow. How are you feeling?"

Marlow was relieved but still uncomfortable.

"Dr. Vell, this guy has me strapped down, I don't feel right, I—"

Dr. Vell shushed her like a mother to a crying infant. "Slow your breathing, Marlow. You'll feel fine in a few minutes. You had an adverse reaction to the shot I gave you. I've stabilized you, but you're still coming out of it."

Marlow *was* coming out of it and was pulling on the straps.

"Why am I tied down? Did you do surgery on me?"

"No, Marlow. You just needed additional medicine to counteract the other one."

"I want out. Untie me."

"Okay. Just relax and I will remove the straps. It was only for your own safety so you didn't fall off while you were out." Dr. Vell went to work on the straps and it took all of Marlow's strength to sit up. Her head was still spinning, but she held the table for support.

"Is that better?" asked Dr. Vell.

"A little," said Marlow. "I just woke up and didn't feel right. If I had a reaction, does that mean…?"

"No, no, the shot still took. You won't have any of those lung problems again. That's a good thing because I don't want to give you that medication again." She smiled as if it was all no big deal.

"I want to see Zane."

"That's fine. First, let me help you to your bath. You still need your panel for today."

Marlow went to the bath with Dr. Vell as Dr. Crouch left. Afterward she felt clear headed and energized. She met up with Zane in their room, hugging him as soon as the door was closed. Honey waddled beneath them quacking.

"Good to see you too," said Zane. "You okay?"

"Something happened during my checkup. I passed out. I had a reaction or something. I was strapped down to the table like they were doing surgery on me."

"Did they?"

"I don't think so. Will you check my body for scars or stitches or something?"

"Okay. I guess so. I'm sure they would've told you if they did surgery."

She gave him a glare as she undressed.

"Right," said Zane. "We're still on the astronaut conspiracy theory thing."

"It's not..." Marlow stopped herself and sighed, now naked in front of him. "Just check, would you?"

Zane did, even running hands across her back and abdomen. "Nothing I can see. I think all your organs are still there." He said it with a smile but she didn't return it.

"Organs," she said. "Maybe that's it."

"My god, Mar, just listen to yourself. I just checked. There are no scars, much less stitches. Unless they pulled them out of your ass, I think you're good."

She huffed and started getting dressed. "Fine. Thanks for looking. Now, we're going to class and we're gonna ask Arjen about those other trips."

Zane pursed his lips.

"What?" She put her arms akimbo and tilted her head at him.

"Class is cancelled for today."

"Why?"

"Because of our doctor visits. I think Arjen checked on us and said it would be better to hold off until tomorrow."

"Well, let's just go talk to him. I'm not up for kickboxing but we can talk."

"He said there was a staff meeting he'd be in all day. Preparing for our arrival, I think. But tomorrow—"

"Fuck tomorrow. Do you know we only have a couple days? We need to know what we're in for."

Zane made a quick, chirping laugh. "Mar, we're in for a good life. I thought you saw that too. You *did* see that too until you talked to the crazy astronaut."

Her face was scrunched up, she let it loose and it drooped. She fell into his shoulder, and he put his arms around her.

"I can't help it. You know."

"I know," said Zane.

"Mom…"

"Yes, she was very much the same."

They stood in silence as Honey walked across their feet, her webbed feet flopping on their shoes.

"She's hungry," muttered Marlow.

"Yeah."

"Let's go get her some food, but promise me you'll come with to cards tonight."

"To play cards or talk conspiracies?"

"Both."

Chapter Eleven

Marlow spent the day fidgeting. The classes had been her entertainment, the distraction from staring out at the endless void of the wormhole they were in, then wondering if they'd ever come out of it. Now she had the additional question of what would happen when they do come out of it? Zane left the room to float the halls and chat with whoever he could find, probably just to get away from her. Honey stayed with her. There wasn't much for a duck to do in a spaceship either, but what did ducks do but waddle around looking for bugs? She'd started laying eggs again but the NutrientPanel prevented them from needing to cook and eat them. She'd been taking them to Marlin to use in the batches he put together though they weren't really needed. She wasn't sure if he was truly using them or just humoring her. Marlow decided to let her keep one, building her a nest out of fabric from their jumpsuits and bedsheets. She wasn't sure how Arjen would feel about her repurposing, but she and Zane were so used to making do with what they had. He'd have to understand.

Honey sat dutifully on her egg in the corner of the room while Marlow was on the bed, cross-legged, trying to decide if she should tell the poor duck that her egg would never hatch. She didn't have the heart. Honey could sit on it for a few days, then their whole world would change yet again.

"What should we name it?" Marlow asked Honey. "When it hatches. What do you think? Sugar? Sweety?" Honey just sat, watching, her dark green head was shinier than ever before. She really was a beautiful duck and Marlow was sad she was probably the last of her kind.

"No," said Marlow. "Really? Well, I mean, only if it's a boy this time, but okay, we'll name it Marvin. That's very sweet of you."

Honey quacked at her and twisted her head. Marlow was afraid the mention of the name brought back a memory for the duck.

"Sorry. I'm being stupid. Forget I said that. Just watch your egg, okay? It's about time for cards." Marlow hopped off the bed. "I'd take you but you love to poop on that table for some reason. I'll see you later."

Honey followed her to the door, as it closed behind Marlow, she went back to lay on her egg.

~ * ~

The bridge was full of card players and spectators, about ten in all. Arjen, Ice, and Zane were about the only people missing. There were two games setup at the big table. They didn't have chips, so they played games more fitted for tallying wins. Marlow got in a few rounds of Blackjack with one of the crewmen before she had a chance with Marlin. He was between games, so she purposely overdrew to lose, then declined a rematch. Marlin was off to the side of one game, watching and laughing with a drink in his hand. Marlow slid up next to him.

"Evening, Little Earthling," he said, proud of himself for coining the nickname, though he was the only one using it. "No eggs for me today?"

"Naw. I'm letting her keep one. She's happy sitting on it."

"All right, no problem."

"You really use them?"

His head snapped back and he gave her a wide-eyed look. "Well, hell yeah, I use them. Throw 'em right in, shell and all."

"How does that work?"

"It's pretty cool. Come by some time and I'll show ya."

"I will," she said, looking around for Zane again, wanting him to hear whatever Marlin could tell her.

"Oof," said Marlin, watching a crewman stand up and slam his hands on the table. "That Ryder is killing it tonight. I might have to show him who's the top of the leaderboard in here."

Marlow caught his arm. "Do you have a minute first?"

He gave her his kind eyes now. "I've got an hour for you."

She smiled. "Thanks." Then tried to keep her voice casual. "Do they always take you along for the gathering trips?"

He shrugged. "Pretty much. You think you got some gathering in your future?"

"Maybe. How many trips do you think you've done?"

Marlin rubbed his head and took another drink. "Not sure I can count them at this point."

"You guys go to Earth a lot?"

Marlin seemed caught off guard by this one. "Well…once or twice."

"Once? Or twice? Surely you remember."

"I'm not sure what you're getting at but—"

"Did you pick up other people, like me?"

Marlin gave her a weird look. "No. You're the only Earthling I know. Otherwise I wouldn't have used that nickname on you."

"What about Zane?"

"Yes, your friend. He's not much for cards. I haven't had much chance to get to know him but okay, I'll give you that, I know two Earthlings in that case."

"So, what did you do on the other trips to Earth?" She looked at him, defiant, waiting for him to refute her statement.

"*Trip*," he said. "If we're talking besides today. There was one other trip. More gathering. Nothing special."

"Did you pick up any other people?" Marlow was in his face the best she could be with her short stature.

"Whoa, whoa. We're all friends here. What's with the interrogation?"

Marlow took a step back. "Sorry Marlin. I'm just curious, I guess. It's my whole planet, you know?"

He patted her on the shoulder. "I understand. Look, like I said, I don't know other Earthlings. We didn't see anyone last time. It was truly for gathering."

"That was the only other time?"

"*Yes*. Did you see something when you were down there?"

"No, nothing. We wanted something, anything to come along but nothing did. Well, until you guys did."

"Yeah. That's was *lucky* all right. But hey, just know I'm glad we did happen upon you, or Arjen and Ice did. I really think you're going to like the belt." He looked at an open spot at the table. "Hey, there we go. You and me. What do you say?"

"Only if you're prepared to lose."

"Now that's what I like to hear."

~ * ~

Marlow found Zane on her way back from playing cards. He was busy in a conversation with one of the crewmen who left the games earlier. He gave her a wave and turned back to the crewman. Marlow huffed as she floated by. She was in bed, pretending to sleep by the time he got back. Zane climbed in quietly, turning on his side, facing the door. After a few minutes of silence, Marlow spoke.

"There were two trips."

"What?"

"To Earth. They took another trip before this."

"Who told you that?"

"Marlin, but don't tell Arjen. I want to ask him myself in the morning."

"Okay. Don't you think he'll just confirm it?"

"No, I'm thinking he's going to lie."

Chapter Twelve

The morning came and they headed to the bathhouse. Marlow's jaw was set, ready to question Arjen, but the back of her mind told her she was biting the hand that feeds. She'd have to be careful. When she found an empty bath, she turned, waiting for Marlin before she'd undress and climb in. Zane practically undressed on the way to the bath now, but this was part of her routine still. The easy nudity of the belters was still strange to her, despite sleeping naked next to Zane each night. It was different with him. The things they'd been through together was a bond she'd never have with another person, no matter how intimate they got.

She spotted Marlin at the door, holding two tubes like usual, with a big smile on his soft face. He went to Zane first, then approached Marlow but didn't put the tube in right away.

"Listen, Little Earthling," Marlin started, "don't go spreading our conversation all over."

She watched his darting eyes but didn't reply. He went to step past her with the NutrientPanel but she grabbed the tube.

"Why?" she whispered.

"Just, keep my name out of it."

She looked at him and felt pity creeping in. "I will, Marlin. We did nothing but play cards last night." She took her hand off the tube and he finished his job.

"Thanks," he said. "I'll leave you to it then." He gave her a wave and headed out. She watched him go and was more determined than ever to question Arjen.

After their baths, they headed up to the bridge. Arjen was in his usual, casual pose, propped back in a chair.

"You guys getting excited to get out of this black blob?" said Arjen, he looked back at the window.

"Yeah," said Zane. "The *Iris* is a nice ship and all but it's starting to feel like the bunker all over again. Same walls every day. No eating. Duck shit…"

"Hey, the duck is your fault. I wanted you to leave her."

"No," said Isolde, entering the bridge, holding Honey. "How would they leave this sweet baby?"

"Oh, goodness, Ice. You know we don't have ducks out there."

Ice stroked the duck's dark feathers. "That's what makes her so special."

"I'm just saying, eventually…"

"Oh, get on with your lesson, spoilsport."

Arjen turned to the Earthlings. "I really don't have much else to tell you. Some of it, you just have to see."

"I have a question for you," said Marlow and Zane looked away, wringing his hands.

"Oh yes?" said Arjen.

She sat down across from him. "How many trips have you taken to Earth?"

Arjen's brow furrowed. "You mean to build the colony? Four. Remember?"

"No. Since then. How many gathering trips, or whatever you want to call them, have you been on to Earth?"

"Besides this one we just did?" He looked in her eyes, reading the intent behind her question. "One."

Zane let out a deep breath. Marlow tilted her head.

"How many people did you bring back that time?"

Arjen countered her head tilt with one of his own. "None…" He held out the word in a questioning manner, then continued, "I told you, they were gathering trips. We collected tech, broke into an old facility Dr. Ramirez knew about. Thankfully it was mostly untouched. You should've seen the look on our development team's faces. They get off on that kind of stuff."

Ice nodded in agreement while Marlow was taken aback by his

reply. Half her probing questions and counter arguments went out the window when he confirmed Marlin's story and now the other half felt weightless.

Ice was watching her face. "Something wrong, Marlow?"

She put up her hands. "Just hear me out."

"You were talking to *him* again weren't you?" said Arjen.

Marlow pursed her lips. "Yes, but just listen. Sam was up on the space station, right?"

Arjen shrugged. "According to him."

"Where else would he have come from?"

"I'm just saying, two years up there…"

"I know, but let's just say he *was* up there for the past two years because there's no better explanation. He would've seen the ships coming and going, can we agree on that?"

"Yes. So, he saw our trips?"

"He saw more than two."

"Are you trying to say I'm lying? I'm not, Marlow. I have no reason to do that."

"I just know what he told me that there were more than two but the more important detail is when he said, 'different ship, same result.'"

Arjen sat up now, Isolde stopped petting Honey.

"He saw a different ship?" said Arjen. "What did it look like?"

Now, Marlow leaned back, finally getting somewhere. "You'd have to ask him. He says you're trying to keep him away from me."

"Now, listen," said Arjen. "Only for your own safety. The man is clearly crazy."

"Well, now we need to talk to him."

"*We* don't need to do anything," said Arjen. "I'm trying to keep you safe. *I* can talk to him about his crazy claims, but even if he says he saw the Pope flying to the Moon in the Popemobile, it doesn't mean it's true."

"The Pope is dead," said Zane.

"Even more reason we don't have to believe him," said Arjen.

"So, you don't have another ship he could've seen?" said Zane.

Arjen looked to Ice, brow furrowed. "Not one that would've

taken that trip."

Marlow, Zane, and Honey were left on the bridge with strict commands to stay there and not follow.

"Seems like you struck a chord," said Zane. "I guess we'll see if—what are you doing?"

Marlow was at the door, hitting everything she could and getting denied. Arjen hadn't trusted her to stay put and damn him for being right. She slammed her hands on the door and turned back to Zane.

"We've got to know what they're talking about. Help me open this."

Zane stood up but didn't move from the table. "We can't. It's locked."

"Well, think of something. I told Sam I wouldn't tell and now they're going to question him."

"I think we should just wait for Arjen to come back and ask him."

"You really think he's going to tell us?"

"He told us about the two trips. He didn't lie about that like you thought he would."

She waved a hand and paced. "Maybe. Maybe Marlin was in on it."

"So, you think he knows about the other ship?"

"I don't know but the way he was acting..."

"True." Zane plopped back down in a chair. "Still." He motioned at the closed door and it slid open. Captain Davis and the co-pilot came in, adjusting to the gravity and watching Zane, Marlow, and Honey with confused looks.

"There a party we don't know about?" asked Davis.

Marlow waved a dismissive hand. "We were gonna play some cards but forgot who keeps the decks."

Davis smiled. "Ah, that would be Marlin. You know where to find him?"

"Yeah," she said. "Thanks." And headed out the door. Zane was startled from his seat. He got up, grabbed Honey and followed.

Marlow was flying down the halls, as fast as her hands could grab the holds on the ceiling. Zane was behind until she turned back and almost crashed into him.

"Shit," she said, steadying herself next to him. "I don't know which way they went."

"Do they have a prison?" said Zane. "They'd probably keep him there, wouldn't they? How else would we never see this guy?"

"You're right. You know what? I think I even know the door, but we don't have access to it."

"You tried the door?"

She shrugged. "I think I've tried all the doors at this point."

"God. Always got to test your limits, don't you?"

"If we could just…" She looked at the ceiling then snapped her fingers. "Marlin. He probably has access. He delivers the Panel all over this ship."

"Oh, that poor man."

"Why?"

"Because you're about to get him all tied up in this."

"He can handle it, now come on."

Zane held his grip on the handrail and Honey. "I'm not sure I want to."

Marlow looked at him, the anger on her face making him change his mind, then she shifted. "No. Good idea. You take Honey and go to the room. Don't come out until I tell you."

"What? Why? What are you thinking now?"

"Never mind. I'll tell you later."

"Oh, Mar," said Zane. He gave her one last questioning look, turned and headed toward their room.

Chapter Thirteen

Marlow found her way to the nutrient room. A man in a full mask, gloves and apron greeted her at the door through a small, glass window but didn't open it. She mouthed, "Marlin," at him, and he raised a finger signaling to give him a minute. Then, Marlin was at the door, his mask pulled down. He came into the hallway and greeted her with a wave.

"Little Earthling, is today the day?" He motioned back at the room.

She shook her head. "I wish. Actually, I was hoping you could help me."

"Well, sure, what is it?"

"Honey got out. You remember how she is trying to fly in the gravity."

He nodded with a smile. "Most eventful bath I've ever had up here."

"Right, so she got into a door and it locked behind her. I couldn't get it back open. I'm afraid for her. She could be flying into a wall or who knows what."

"That's not good. Which door?"

"I'll have to show you. It's not labelled. Come on." She didn't wait for his agreement, just started down the hall.

"Well, hold on. Just give me a second." He looked down at his mask, gloves and apron as she turned the corner. "Ah." And followed her anyway.

She led Marlin around a couple turns before she reached the locked door. It took him a minute until he caught up and stopped next to her.

"Oh, I don't know about this one. Are you sure she came in here?"

Marlow nodded furiously. "I thought I'd have her cornered but someone must have triggered the door. I wasn't fast enough."

"It's possible they already caught her," said Marlin, looking around nervously.

"No, Zane or someone would've found me by now. She has to be in here."

"Ah, how about I take a quick look and—"

"She'll want me, Marlin. She's probably scared. I don't want her to get hurt."

"Oh, good lord." He looked back down the way they came. It was clear. "Let's be quick then. And this goes with the other thing. Don't tell anyone that I…"

"Yes, you got it."

Marlin raised his arm, brushed back a long glove and hit a button on his data pad, the door slid open and Marlow dropped inside.

~ * ~

Marlow looked around the dim room, it was clear right off the bat that Honey was not inside, unless she'd figured out how to open more doors. Marlin started to mention this fact but she cut him off, trying each door with no avail, then she heard Arjen's voice, low, through the last door. She put her ear to it.

"…you to…exactly…saw…" She could make out a few words before Marlin's hand yanked her back. He was holding her by the shoulders as she tried to shake free.

Marlin spoke in an angry whisper she'd never heard out of him before. "This is not what I agreed to. We looked for the duck. She's not here. We're not spying on people. Now let's go."

She couldn't hide the shocked look on her face. "I have to know what they're saying."

"No, you—" Marlin paused when he heard the mumbling on the other side of the door stop. He gave Marlow a frightened look. "Let's go." It was a sharp whisper now.

As she took her hand off the door, she caught part of the phrase, "Just check it out." She exchanged glances with Marlin. They both looked down the hall and knew, if the door opened, they wouldn't be halfway to the entrance when it did. Marlin raised his arm to an adjacent room and had the door open within a few seconds. Marlow ducked in with him and he hit the close button just as the door next to them opened. They heard footsteps right outside their door, as they took shallow, quiet breaths to avoid making any noise. The footsteps went past again. They heard a slight whirring sound of the door opening and closing. Marlin looked to Marlow, shaking his head. She put a hand on his shoulder, bowing her head in thanks, then stuck her ear to the wall. Marlin threw his hands up in defeat. She could hear the conversation clearer now, which reminded her to not make a sound lest they be found out.

"It was the white one," said Sam. "With the flag on the side. A lot like the one I came up on. The main engine looked like it had been modified though, cabin too. Had to be for all that up and down. That was the part that got me."

"How many times did you see it?" said Ice.

"Three times in the past two years. It was always a highlight. I marked it right on the damn calendar, which was the wall at that point. The last visit was about six months ago. I was planning on jumping out for that one. Making myself known but the timing, fuck the timing. They took longer on the ground than any of the previous trips, yours included. By the time I came around on my orbit again, they were launched well out of range."

"Where were they headed?" asked Ice.

"Toward the moon."

"Like us?"

"I don't know. Maybe. Again, I missed them and they were almost out of sight."

"Just tell me," said Arjen. It sounded like his breath was off. "Was there a symbol on the rudder?"

Sam took a second, then replied. "Yeah, I made a drawing of it the first time, something to do, you know?"

"And?"

"Well, I don't have it with me, probably pretty good for you because I'm a terrible artist, but it kinda looked like a 'Q' with an extra slash in it."

There was a thud then some shuffling.

"Arjen? Arjen?" said Isolde. "You okay?"

"It's her ship. Isn't it, Ice?" said Arjen. "Goddamn it."

Marlow and Marlin waited. The door next to them opened again and closed as Sam was still trying to talk. "Hey, I'm the one who saw it. Who is she? I have a right to…" There was a thud, like a fist against the door. Marlow could feel it down her face as she listened. Isolde and Arjen were headed for the exit, slowly, still discussing Sam's discovery.

"It's just…it can't…" said Arjen. "How can we trust him?"

"Why would he make that…?" Isolde was saying as their voices trailed out of reach. Marlow strained against the door, trying to hear more. Finally, she gave up and looked at Marlin, whispering.

"Who is *she*?"

Marlin shook his head. "You'll have to talk to the big man about that. I could be in enough trouble already. I've got to get back to the nutrient room and you need to go find your duck." He hit the door, peeked into the hall, then stepped out, stopping to look over his shoulder at her. "You know? I'm thinking Honey is fine. Isn't she?"

Marlow gave a sheepish nod.

Marlin huffed. "My mother always told me to look out for the forked tongues of women. Says a lot that she'd say it about her own gender, but I guess she was right." He started toward the exit while Marlow stood in the doorway, looking back to Sam's room. "I'd hurry if you don't wanna be locked in here."

Marlow followed, and Marlin let them out into the hall. He pushed himself up to the handrails and Marlow called out.

"Marlin." He looked back. "I'm sorry I—"

"Save it for when you mean it." He went flying down the hall.

~ * ~

Marlow met up with Zane at their room. She didn't know if Arjen and Ice had already been by the bridge and found it empty or if the pilots told them the story. It didn't matter to her now. She couldn't get the look on Marlin's face out of her head. The look when he said, "Save it for when you mean it." It was a deep cut from one of the few friends she had. The problem was, she couldn't focus on that now. She had to push it out, to figure out who this other person was that was in the ship Sam saw. Who was *she* to them? Was she the one taking the people?

"Mar?" said Zane. "You okay?"

"No." She was in the bathroom, running water into her hands and splashing it on her face. Zane poked his head in.

"Could you save a little water for later? You know it has to run back through that purifier thing every time you do that."

She looked up, water still running, then made a demonstrative motion to shut it off.

"Happy?" she asked.

"No. What's happened to you?"

"We're only a day away from finding out if we're about to be lab rats or sex slaves or something. *That's* what's happening. You think we're really going to stay with Arjen in his perfect little house on his perfect little asteroid eating cake?"

"Well, they don't eat, so…"

"Sam is in prison. Do you get that? Because he knows something. He's probably not getting out again, thanks to me. He'll be lucky if he ever sees daylight again."

"I don't think—"

"You didn't see it. He's in a cell down there. Why? Why are we in this room and he's locked up? Maybe he knows too much about what's coming and we don't know enough. We're still naive enough to think we've reached the promised land that Pastor Hill talked about."

There was a knock at the door and they both froze. Zane was the first to move but Marlow caught him and went herself. She opened it to see Isolde.

"Hello," said Ice. "I see you made it back to your room."

"The pilots came by," said Marlow.

"Good. Sorry about that."

"What happened?"

"He confirmed the other ship."

"And you believe him now?"

Ice looked at her. "Can I come in?"

Marlow motioned for her to step in and closed the door behind her. Honey quacked a greeting to Ice but didn't get off her egg. Ice went over and patted her on the back.

"Good momma you are."

"So…?" said Marlow, staring at the woman crouched down by the makeshift duck nest.

"Yes," said Ice. "We believe him. He described one of our old ships. One we used to use for gathering."

Marlow and Zane's eyes were wide.

"That's what we said," said Ice.

"Are they your people?" said Marlow.

Isolde looked to the ceiling for answers. "We don't know. The crew of that ship disappeared almost three years ago."

~ * ~

They skipped cards that night. With everything that happened, Marlow didn't think Marlin would want to be in the same room with her. Zane did head off to find crew to chat with, again, probably to get away from her. Marlow turned over Isolde's words, wondering where the ship landed the times it touched down on Earth. Sam would know, but she couldn't get to him, and she worried that her nosiness condemned him. She had to find Arjen, to plead for Sam's life and to find out the significance of that ship.

She headed for the door, giving a wave to Honey, who didn't leave her egg to see her off. Honey may already have been sensing the lack of movement beneath her and was hunkering down. Marlow searched hall after hall. She found Zane sitting around with the pilots and a crewman, telling bad jokes. Then she made it to the nutrient room and turned back, not wanting to run into Marlin if he was still inside. The doctor's rooms were empty. Finally, she found Ice in the workout studio, sweating, propped against a floor mat she'd turned into a backrest. Her eyes were closed.

"Uh, Ice?"

"Yes?" She didn't open her eyes.

"Sorry. I was just looking for Arjen."

"Haven't seen him. Haven't tried."

"Okay. Are you meditating?"

"Trying to."

"Right, sorry. See ya."

Marlow left the workout room. Given her luck, she guessed Arjen was holed up in his bunk. She made one last ditch effort, turning into the bridge and found the card games were over but there was a lone man left, with a bottle of something dark in his hand, staring out into the black.

"Arjen?" she said.

"Yeah." He was in the pilot's seat, watching the nothingness.

"Can we talk?"

He patted the seat next to him. "Be my co-pilot if you wish."

She joined him and he held out the bottle. Marlow took a drink and handed it back.

She got right to the point. "Are you going to kill Sam?"

He coughed out a laugh. "No. Why would you...? We're peaceful folk you know."

"I just thought..."

"He's given us some pretty profound intel. Ice told you?"

She nodded.

"I set him up with a bunk." He turned to face her and she could see the redness of his eyes. "I had to do it. We didn't know we could trust him yet. You know, he's still a bit *out there*."

"But you could trust us?"

"You two." He waved a hand. "You're harmless."

"I'm not—"

"You're tough. I get it, but you're harmless. Different things." He turned back to space and took another drink, shaking his head.

"Who's on that ship?"

He pursed his lips. "I don't know anymore. Ghosts."

"You believe in ghosts?"

"No. But I see them in my dreams."

"What does that mean?"

"Every night since they disappeared, I think of them. Sometimes I dream of them, the last conversations we had before they took off. I never thought…"

They sat in silence, watching the blackness of the wormhole together. Marlow felt like she was forming a picture, just like the magic eye puzzle he'd mentioned before. She blinked it away.

"I'm sorry for not trusting you," said Marlow.

"Hah, I wouldn't trust me either. Look where it led them."

"It's not…I'm sure you couldn't have done anything."

He nodded, elbows resting on his knees, bottle held by just his thumb and index finger. "Nope. But if we ever see that ship again, I'm taking it down and making them tell me what happened."

Chapter Fourteen

Marlow met Sam at the bath in the morning. She walked in with her back to him.

"Oh, I don't care if you don't," he said.

Marlow sat down at the edge of the bath and kept her eyes on his.

"Good," he said. "I'm glad you found me."

"You're free now, aren't you?" said Marlow.

"I've got my own room if that's what you mean. Are any of us free?"

"Are you back on that? I thought we cleared that up with Arjen."

"Just a joke. I think he's okay with me now. Now, if only *I* could be okay with me."

"More cryptic shit?"

"Haha." He clapped his hands and water splashed in his eyes. He rubbed at them for a second. "You know, all that being alone can do something to you. It's a good thing you had your friend, or you'd be woo-woo like me. Or dead."

"Maybe." She looked over her shoulder. "Guess we'll have a whole colony of people now."

"I guess so." He rubbed his short hair. "Hey, I think a thanks is in order."

"For what?"

"Getting them down there to talk to me. They've done nothing but try to get me therapy the whole time I've been up here. God knows I need it, but I do still have something good to say."

"I was afraid I'd gotten you killed. I did exactly what you told me not to do."

"Aw, well, it was a good time to disregard an order. And hey, two years on the station didn't kill me. Don't think that tan piece-of-shit can do me in that easy."

"Not fond of Arjen still, huh?"

"I'll be happy when I can go my own way."

"So, how did you do it? Live on the space station that long."

Sam visibly shivered at the question and keep his eyes on the swirling water.

"I'd rather not get into that right now. Maybe someday over dinner." He cracked up laughing. "But these bastards don't eat. I wonder if that's how they say, 'when hell freezes over.' We'll discuss it over dinner, honey."

Marlow forced a smile. "Well, I should get going."

"If you wanna wait, I should be out in a few. The water only takes a few to recirculate or whatever the hell they've got it doing."

"I would, but I'm still getting a special panel. Marlin meets me here at seven."

"Right." Sam saluted her. "On your way then, Marlow. See you on the other side."

"Sure."

She came back at seven with Zane, watching the door when Marlin showed up. He gave his usual wave and went through his usual motion of starting with Zane, then meeting Marlow at the back, right tub. She gave him a shy look as he inserted the panel in silence. His back was to her at the wall exit when he finally spoke.

"Sounds like they got some good info out of the looney astronaut then."

She nodded, though he couldn't see her do it.

Marlin continued, "Next time you want to play secret agent, let me in on the plan beforehand."

"I will," she choked out.

He raised a hand and stepped out.

~ * ~

Later that day, they were in their last class with Isolde. She had them striking hard, harder than they ever imagined they'd be able to. Ice had to brace the training pads as Marlow had her off balance.

"Good, good," said Ice. "Most people just try to keep their strength up while they're on one of these trips. You've gotten so much stronger."

"It helps that we were almost dead when you found us," said Marlow.

"I don't know. This one," Ice pointed at Zane, "could shimmy up a roof faster than most people I know."

Zane laughed. "Lots of practice."

"Speaking of," said Marlow. "You got a good church for him to climb up when we get there?"

Ice shook her head. "Actually, no. There's really not any organized religion in the belt."

"Really?" said Zane. "What about people's culture?"

"Dr. Ramirez was pretty adamant about that when he founded the belt. Saying that religion played a big role in the Earth's downfall. You know, 'my old book is truer than your old book.' Plus, as we've told you, he wanted everything to be science based, to serve a purpose. He always said, 'If God was on Earth then he didn't come with us to the belt. We are truly alone out there.'"

The door opened to the workout studio and Arjen stepped in.

"I knew I'd find you here. I just wanted to let you know, we should be hitting the opening around midnight. Most of the crew has seen it but if you wanted to join the pilots on the bridge, you're more than welcome to."

"Sounds great," said Zane.

"We'll be there," said Marlow.

Chapter Fifteen

They waited until eleven-forty-five and couldn't wait anymore. Sam was in the hall as they turned toward the bridge.

"You going for the viewing too?" he asked.

"Yeah," said Marlow. "Hey, Zane, this is Sam the astronaut, by the way."

"Hey," said Zane.

"Sam the astronaut," said Sam, twisting his head. "Better than 'that crazy guy.'"

They continued on to the bridge to find the pilots looked sleepy as they stared into the black, waiting for a sign. Marlow, Zane, and Sam stood behind them.

"Might be dull for a bit," said Davis. "You can have a seat at the table while you wait."

They took his advice and were glad they did when one AM approached. Zane was resting his head in his arms on the table. Marlow was next to him but keeping an eye on the windows. Finally, Captain Davis waved them up.

"Think we got something here."

Marlow bumped Zane as Sam was already on his feet. They stood watching the small window of stars ahead. It was like a tiny TV, growing with each passing minute. Soon, the swirl of the wormhole was barely visible on the edges of their view, then it was gone. The sky was full of stars but more intriguing was the cluster of rocks ahead.

"Holy God," said Sam. "They weren't lying."

Before them lay a scattering of asteroids, some large as football stadiums, some as small as two-story houses back on Earth. There were many in a closer group with only a mile between them. They all had the glow of the TechBubble. It was more profound than the ones on the ship, like God took a bubble wand and waved it over the galaxy. The clear domes around each asteroid hugged the sides of the rock, creating life-giving atmosphere just as Arjen described. It was a wonder to watch and they grew closer.

"Hold on," said Davis. The ship started turning and the asteroids shifted from their vision. There was a slight break before more came into view, again, in clusters but these were bigger, all of them stadium-sized and up. One looked like a giant forest. There were trees jutting all over the surface, taller than any Marlow and Zane had ever seen. Another was like an industrial complex, with large buildings scattered over it. Captain Davis lined them up with the biggest yet, far outsizing the rest. It was planet-sized and they were headed right for it, glowing a white light at them. Marlow looked over to Zane.

"Is that…?"

"Ceres," said Davis. "Home base. We'll be there in a half hour."

At any other time in life, telling Zane and Marlow something was happening in a half hour would be cause for them to find something else to do in the meantime, but that day they found themselves staring at the dwarf planet. They could see an endless ocean as it grew in their viewpoint, then mountains rose up at the shore, large gray rocks that went on for miles. This was their view for most of the trip and they didn't look away. The other asteroid zipped past them as they approached Ceres. When they were ten minutes out, Arjen and Ice joined them on the bridge.

"Like what you see?" said Arjen.

They all said they did but Zane had more questions.

"Are we going to land in the mountains?"

"Close," said Arjen. "Our shipyard is just on the other side."

"I can't wait," said Zane.

"Then follow me," said Arjen. "We've gotta get your strapped in for landing."

They headed down the hall, stopping to grab Honey and their few possessions. Soon, they were back to the seats they'd been in for takeoff three weeks before when their lives had just been turned upside-down.

Now they were completely flipped as they strapped in. Marlow stuck out a hand and Zane took it. They entered the atmosphere of Ceres and watched the mountains approach, then pass under them as they gave way to plains of swaying grassland. There were more ships in sight and a clear landing place for theirs.

As the *Iris* touched down, Zane and Marlow felt their guts sink, then all was calm again. Arjen and Ice were already moving, and they could hear the door ramp lowering to the ground. Sam took off, desperate to touch the ground, as he hadn't been on land for years, then Arjen was behind them.

"You guys coming or..."

Marlow's trance broke. She'd been watching men and women in the shipyard, other people, healthy people on a new land.

"Ready?" said Zane.

She nodded, butterflies crashing around her stomach. She tucked Honey under her arm as Zane gripped her hand. They walked together with Arjen and Isolde flanking them, down the ramp until they touched the soil of Ceres.

"Welcome to the belt," came a voice.

Part II

Chapter One

Marlow stood on the fine, white gravel just one step off the *Iris*. She was taking it all in, the feel, the smell, the people breezing past her to do their jobs aboard the ship. It was like a slow-motion scene in a movie she'd never seen. The air on the *Iris* was cleaner than anything she'd ever taken in, but this was different. It was crisp but not too cold, expanding her lungs like a newborn just getting the first taste of life outside the womb. Marlow looked around and saw other ships towering nearby, then a man standing in front of them, an older version of the tanned, romance-novel-cover model they'd been travelling with.

"I'm Robin," he said. "And you are?" He held out a hand.

She took it. "Marlow. I'm from Earth."

He laughed and showed a beautiful smile full of white teeth. His hair was mostly-blond but forming a widow's peak as it retreated from his forehead.

"Arjen mentioned something about 'extra cargo.' I see what he means now. And a duck?"

Marlow nodded. "Honey."

Robin gave a short bow to Honey then stuck his hand to Zane.

"Robin."

"Zane."

"Good to meet you, Zane and Marlow."

"They're quite the pair," said Arjen.

Ice nodded in agreement.

Robin looked them over again then turned to Arjen. "The

homestead then?"

"I thought so," said Arjen. "We could make a little room for them until we get them placed."

"Sounds fair," said Robin. "The man over there laying in the dirt, is that the astronaut?"

"Sam," said Arjen. "Yes, that's him."

Sam was swooping his arms like a child making a snow angel.

"I'll get him settled if you want to take them."

"What about the rest of the cargo?"

"We can let Marlin sort it out with the Haulers. They'll get it processed just fine."

"Okay, but the *ship*...when can we—"

Robin held up a hand. "You just got back from a six-week trip. Take a minute to rest, and we'll talk tomorrow. Oh, and stop in on your mother in the morning. She'd like to see you as well."

Arjen looked to the sky tentatively. "All right." He turned to Marlow and Zane and let out a sigh. "One more ride for the night. It will be much shorter, I promise."

They followed Arjen and Isolde once more, walking through the shipyard, passing a green behemoth with giant drills on the back of it.

"Rock-Hauler," said Arjen, sticking out a hand toward it but not stopping.

Zane and Marlow gave it a glance, but the universe before them was what had their attention. Everywhere they looked it was as if they could just walk right off into space. Without a sky full of clouds or even haze, they could just see the expanse before them. The TechBubble provided light, collecting and spreading the sun, but it didn't block their view.

"Kind of unnerving," Zane said to Marlow.

She nodded, trying to keep her stomach in check.

There was a group of smaller ships on the other side of the Rock-Hauler. They were red and flat-nosed with a thick, glass front, revealing a row of seats two-by-two. Arjen clicked at his data-pad and the one nearest to them opened up, the glass hinged out like a Pez dispenser. There was room for six but it would be tight.

"Want to sit in the front?" asked Arjen. "It drives itself. You just get to watch."

Zane agreed and jumped in the front row. He patted the seat next to him. Marlow sighed, then joined him.

Arjen and Isolde sat behind them and the glass door closed. The little ship Arjen called a Rock-Hopper led them straight up. With their view, Marlow had to close her eyes and grip the seat when she saw the mountaintops retreating below them. Arjen tapped her shoulder.

"Relax," he said, tapping on his data-pad. "See? I couldn't open the door if I wanted to." Ice grabbed his arm and pulled it back.

"Stop it. That's not helping."

Soon, they were out of the atmosphere of Ceres. The dwarf-planet growing smaller as they turned towards a cluster of asteroids in the distance.

"How far is it?" said Zane.

"About fifteen-hundred miles or so," said Arjen. "This thing gets moving, though. We should be there in about ten minutes."

As the cluster grew closer, the rocks grew further apart. Marlow opened her eyes again and saw the ship was focused on one in particular, an asteroid the size of a Walmart parking lot. Everywhere around them was the endless black of space. She felt like she was hanging on a cliff edge just waiting for a breeze to push her over. Her stomach rolled again and she leaned her head back, groaning. She stared at the glass ceiling rather than the floor. It wasn't much help. Features of the "homestead" came into view. There were three house-like buildings with giant clusters of trees near them, like a mini forest had sprouted up just outside their doors.

"Look at those trees," said Zane. "Wow, I've never seen them so big." He was leaned up against the glass and Marlow pulled him back into his seat.

"Zane!"

"It's all right," said Arjen. "He's not going to fall out." He went to tap the glass and Isolde caught his arm, shaking her head at him. Arjen sat back down.

Marlow gripped her seat, allowing herself to look out, as Honey seemed to have no interest in the view.

"It's like a little island," said Marlow. "All of them." She was looking around to the other asteroids flying out of sight.

"This is where you live?" said Zane.

"Yep," said Arjen. "Me, my dad, my brother and his wife. Well, and you two now."

"Can we climb the trees?" said Zane.

The cab broke into laughter.

"Yes," said Arjen. "I don't see why not."

Ice leaned forward and patted him on the shoulder. "I climb the ones at my rock. You try out those ones, then you can climb mine someday if you want."

Zane smiled. "Sounds fun." They were getting closer, more details were emerging, and Zane was on the glass again. "What kind of trees are they anyway?"

Ice scrunched her face. "Well, they're a version of the banyan tree."

"I thought so," said Zane. "My grandparents were from India and those trees were all over the mythology books they'd read me. It was called something else though. Kalpar-something. I can't remember. I wish I still had those books."

"We'll have to take you by the library sometime," said Ice. "We may have a version of them in our database."

"I'd love that."

The Rock-Hopper closed in on Arjen's homestead. It looked like it was going to crash right into the side. Marlow closed her eyes again and groaned as it slowed itself. A row of lights projected on the TechBubble surrounding the asteroid. The ship cruised right into the bubble, lining up with the lights and slowed like it was caught in Jell-O. It then slid through and perched on a patch of grass, swaying from the engines settling. They landed on their first asteroid. It was hilly, leading to the houses in a small valley, with the towering clusters of the banyan trees watching over. There was bright-green grass across most of the surface, and the houses were made of beautiful, dark wood.

It was different from Ceres, but the same features of the other asteroids were consistent here: they were all laid out with one populated, upright side (relatively), with the other side barren. As if they chose the best part to live on and didn't waste the resources creating atmosphere for the other. The TechBubble surrounded the top side like a dome while only clinging to the bottom like plastic wrap. They were truly a bunch of rocky islands, floating in space.

The group exited the Rock-Hopper and Marlow bent down to rub her hand through the grass.

"It feels so nice," she said, looking back at the edge of the rock where the thin line of the TechBubble separated them from the vastness of space and instant death. "Can we walk through these? Like on the ship?"

Arjen shook his head and tapped the bubble to emphasize his point. "That would be a bad setup. I'm sure with enough force…but the Rock-Hoppers send a signal, with the lights you saw, to dock with each location. Otherwise, you're not getting through."

Marlow set down Honey. "You're safe, girl." The duck quacked away, happily waddling through the grass.

Arjen waved them on, and they followed him down the hill toward the housing. Honey saw her owners go and fell in behind them. The air was still as they went. They admired the calm around them with reverence. The settings hammered home the distance they'd come. It was silent, outside of the footfalls. The universe gawked at them on their parking-lot-sized rock. The Earth was out of sight. The few souls in the belt represented most of the human race. Marlow felt a panic attack coming on, though she'd never had one before. The deadly planet they'd come from was home, it would always be home no matter how great life in the belt may turn out to be.

Marlow swallowed hard as she walked, eyeing the globe of the sun in the distance. It was much smaller here. Isolde put a hand on her shoulder.

"It's a lot to take in. You'll get used to it, though. I think…I was born out here so it's easy for me to say, isn't it?" She smiled.

"Yeah," said Marlow, looking at the ground, keeping her focus on her footfalls.

They reached the houses. There were three almost identical, square cherrywood buildings, two in the front and one on its own behind. The roofs were slanted, like houses on Earth, but they weren't shingled or tiled, just more of the smooth wood.

The final path to the houses was made up of flat, smooth stones splitting to each entry with an atrium of stone between. There was a wooden table and chairs in the common area. A man with short brown hair and an athletic build sat, as if he'd been waiting for them all night.

"Little Brother," he called. "You brought friends home? In the middle of the night?"

Marlow and Zane looked around. It didn't look like the middle of the night. There was the blackness of space but the TechBubble released a soft glow, gathering the sun's light and spreading it around.

"Wes," said Arjen, shaking his brother's hand as he stood. Arjen was pulled into a hug. When they released, he stepped to Ice, kissing her on the cheek, then turned to the Earthlings.

"Hello. Wesley Visser." He stuck out his hand. "I'm the lowly, humble older brother of this guy who found you."

"Oh, come off it," said Arjen. "Wes is one of the top woodworkers in the belt. His designs are all over, from the houses to that table."

"No, don't tell them that," said Wesley. "They're going to nitpick the house now."

"We were living in a bunker," said Marlow. "The house looks nice."

Wesley's face pulled back. "Right, sorry. You'll probably like it then. So, I don't know about you, but I've got a long day ahead of me. It was nice to meet you. When I'm home, I'll be next door if you need to get away from Arjen." He smirked at his own joke, turned and headed into his house.

"Shall we?" said Arjen.

"First let me say my goodbyes," said Ice. "I've gotta get home. My bed is calling."

She hugged Zane and Marlow, then waited for Marlow to hand over Honey. She gave the longest goodbye to the duck, telling her to come visit and that she'd be by to see her. Then she handed her back to Marlow and headed for the Rock-Hopper.

Arjen led them into the house. The lights flicked on on their own revealing a living room on the left with a white vinyl couch and chair facing a blank wall. On the right was a door that Arjen opened. He looked around at his bedroom and waved a hand to trigger the light.

"I hope this works for you. The bed is soft, big enough for the two of you. Bigger than that one on the ship for sure."

Marlow and Zane scanned the room. There was a window facing the front walkway and a gorgeous, oak dresser with a scattering of different colored rocks and minerals on the adjacent wall. Zane was admiring a shimmering black specimen that looked like a model of a cliff face.

"Is this stuff you've found?" said Zane.

"Yep," said Arjen. "Just don't tell anyone you saw my petty collection. I always save a good one from my trips for myself."

Marlow joined Zane, eyeing a reddish-black rock that had smooth bubble-like shapes across the surface. Her eyes were glazing at yet another new thing to take in.

"Well," said Arjen. "I don't know about you guys but these middle-of-the-night returns always wipe me out. The Earthlings nodded in agreement. "The bathroom is right through that door." He pointed to the left of the room. "There's a built-in fan in the wall that kicks in from time to time to move the air for you. Don't worry about it if you hear it. I'll be out here if you need me."

"You're going to sleep on the couch?" said Zane. "We can't—"

Arjen held up his hands. "No, no, no worries. The couch is actually pretty comfy. Not the first time I'll spend a night on it. Tomorrow, I'll pull some strings and get another bed out here."

"Okay..." said Zane.

Marlow pulled the bag out of his hands. It was the last of their possessions. No clothes, no food, just a few faded pictures of their bunker family, taken on a Polaroid camera they found in an old house, a little box of their parent's jewelry, claimed when they passed on, and Honey's makeshift nest. Marlow set the nest in the corner of the room and Honey went straight for it, looking around for the egg, as she just now realized it'd gone missing.

It took a few minutes to calm the duck down as they took turns in the bathroom. She searched each corner of the room and Zane even lifted her on the bed for a look about. Finally, she settled in the nest, defeated. She would produce a new egg in the morning.

The house had a better feel to it for them than the ship had. There was something to be said about solid ground. They slept hard, diving in and out of feverish dreams, waking just long enough to recall their whereabouts in the universe, before falling headlong into another grand adventure.

Chapter Two

"But I have to go," said Arjen. "It's my team out there." He'd gotten up early to meet with the belt counsel.

Kaia Gammen, mother of Isolde, shook her dark braids at him. "You're too involved, Arjen. Your actions would be tainted."

"*Tainted?*" he replied. "Come on. I want the best for them, for *all* of them. Not just her."

"Arjen," said Robin, looking across the broad, oak table at his son. "You have *other* responsibilities here. You've only just returned. Let Lisa's team go. It's just for a look. We don't even know this Sam character is telling the truth. They'll probably see nothing."

"First off, I'm not a babysitter. Second, we know he *is* telling the truth because he knew the markings of the ship. *The Mac*, there is no way—"

"He could've figured that out elsewhere," said Oscar Ramirez, son of Juan Carlos, the founder. "It's not hidden information."

Arjen threw up his hands and paced the room. Pictures of the founders looked down at him as he did.

"We accept," said Isolde, quiet until now, giving Arjen his chance to make his point. "We want to be the first to hear if they see anything."

"You will be kept in the loop," said Oscar.

"Thank you," said Ice. "When are you sending them? It needs to be—"

"They've already left."

Isolde's face froze.

Robin joined in. "We needed a quick turnaround on this. After talking to that man, I felt there was more to learn about than just the ship."

Ice looked back for Arjen just as he slammed the door behind him, shaking the founders on the walls. Ice gave one last stare, singling out her mother, then followed. She caught him down the steps of the government building, looking side to side as if waiting for a taxi-cab to show. There were no streets on Ceres or taxis for that matter.

"What do they think?" said Arjen without looking back.

They'd been working together close to ten years and he knew her solely by the way she walked. Her light steps barely scuffed the rock road below. "That we wouldn't be the best to intercept that ship? Supposedly it's why we were chosen for the last mission and now we're just second rate."

Ice knew better than to put a hand on his shoulder. He wasn't looking for comfort.

"They do know we're the best," she said, standing a few feet back, just off the last step. "But they didn't plan on this. *We* didn't plan on it either. If not for Captain Davis…"

"I know, I know, rub it in. I was hard-headed and almost missed out on it all. Remind me to thank Davis when I see him." He flipped a hand in the air in a dismissive gesture.

Isolde looked to the soft glow of Ceres' atmosphere. "I'm thinking he's on that trip."

"No way," said Arjen. "They'd give him a turnaround flight just like that?"

"I messaged him this morning about doing a modification walkthrough of the *Iris* and I haven't heard back. He always messages back. Unless…"

"He knows how pissed you'll be…well, *I'll* be, to find out he's going and we're not."

Ice was at his side, giving up only a few inches to him that she made up with her hair. "I'm pissed too. I know it hits a little closer to home for you, but those were my teammates too."

Arjen let out one more grunt. "Well, shit. There's nothing we can do about it now except wait." He looked down the road toward a row of buildings. "Want to help me carry a mattress?"

~ * ~

Marlow awoke ravenously hungry. Her stomach had been getting better day after day with no food going down her throat, but it still called out to her. The first few days on the *Iris* had been the worst. Feeling the wracking growls but being satisfied at the same time was a strange combination. She wasn't sure of the current time but knew it had been more than a day since her last 'Panel. She slipped out of the bed and into the bathroom, half expecting Marlin to show up with a tube for her as he had for the past three weeks. The tub was full of water. She tested it with a hand, finding it luke-warm to the touch and hit a few buttons on the control panel. The bubbles began and she saw two tubes of NutrientPanel in a holding rack on the side of the tub. There were etched letters on each of them, spelling out "Zane" and "Marlow." She slid hers out and inserted it the way she'd seen Marlin do it. The tub displayed a simple command to enter a code Arjen had given her to begin the bath. She hit the button. By the time she undressed and climbed in, it was already warm. As weird as these baths were, they'd become her morning happy place, her moment of Zen.

Zane got up when he heard the bath, waiting for his turn on the edge of the tub. Honey checked on them both, then went back to sit on her freshly hatched egg.

"Are we sex slaves yet?" said Zane with a smirk.

She splashed water on him. "Shut up." He brushed it off, giggling and she continued. "Everyone knows sex slave training begins after lunch."

Zane laughed again. "Guess we're off the hook then."

When Zane was done with his bath and dressed, he went to the window to see Marlow practicing her kickboxing routine under the banyan tree closest to Arjen's house. She was on point, just as Ice showed her. Her baggy blue jumpsuit always made her look a bit silly but the look on her face did not. Zane joined her, standing under the tree, marveling at the hundred horizontal branches shooting in every direction and the canopy of green above. He couldn't begin to decide which branch to start climbing so he chose the closest one to him, jumping up, latching on and swinging himself up to a standing position.

"This tree is awesome," he said, hopping to the next branch up and catching one above his head for balance.

"It is," Marlow agreed, continuing her kicks and punches.

They heard the hum of the Rock-Hopper as it pushed through the TechBubble, into its landing spot. There was a trailer attached to the back this time.

"Hey," called Arjen, as the glass door opened. "Who wants to help carry a mattress?"

Chapter Three

After they unloaded the trailer, the living room was setup with a mattress leaning against the blank wall. Marlow carried the bag of grain Arjen brought for Honey, and she happily pecked away at a pile of it.

"So, you *do* grow real food here," said Marlow, examining the bag before setting it on the dresser.

"For the panel," said Arjen. "We grow and produce a lot of panel ingredients on Ceres, since that's where all the water is. You're lucky I have connections."

"Yes, we know you hate Honey," said Marlow.

"I don't *hate*, I just have no affection for animals. We don't really have them out here as pets. They serve no purpose."

"I think Ice would beg to differ," said Zane.

Arjen shrugged and changed the subject. "I'm sure you two are sick of your jumpsuits by now, am I right?"

They both agreed.

"Let's take you in and get you fitted for something more your size."

~ * ~

The Rock-Hopper cruised the endless vacuum of space. Other asteroids sailed by as they tuned in on a rock the size of a city block. Half of it resembled a city, with buildings set around a crossing of dusty streets. The other half was farmland, rows of brown branches with creamy puffs on top. They crossed the TechBubble and found a landing spot just between the fields and buildings next to a row of other hoppers.

Marlow climbed out and looked toward the field. "Is that cotton?"

"Yep," said Arjen. "Straight from the source." He pointed to one of the buildings on the block. "They process it there." Then pointed to another building. "But we're headed there. Carol will get you sized and show you a few designs."

They walked together into the building made of a lighter oak with broad windows above the door. The first room featured a rectangular table with scraps of fabric strewn about it. Deep blues and light greens, dark purples and vibrant yellows. An older woman stepped out of a doorway at the back. Her gray hair was tied back to hang down to the middle of her back. She wore a multi-colored skirt and solid violet shirt.

"Well, looky here, Arjen, you brought me some fresh meat." She cackled at her own joke, and Marlow thought of a witch she'd read about in a storybook growing up.

"Carol, this is Marlow and Zane. They need something to wear."

"Don't look naked to me," she said, "but may as well be in those nasty rags." She pointed at the Earthlings' jumpsuits. "They use an old pattern to make those. I'd never condone those leaving my shop."

"Right," said Arjen. "Can you help them out?"

Carol looked them over one more time. "Give me an hour. No, make it two."

"Okay. I'll be back in a couple hours." Arjen walked out, and they were left on the witch's island of cotton and clothing factories.

Chapter Four

Sam ducked around the corner of the government building as he saw a tan white man, a Hispanic older man and a black woman with braids, walking out together. They were discussing something he desperately wanted to hear but couldn't give up his position. *Playing the 'crazy astronaut' card may only work once if I were to get caught, and maybe not even once,* he thought.

Robin, Oscar, and Kaia finished their conversation and parted ways. Sam used a Rock-Hopper, right along the side of the building, for cover as Robin passed. He'd heard mutterings around the apartments he was staying in, rumors that confirmed his suspicions. He just wanted some visual evidence, then…he wasn't sure what, but it would be a start. When the coast was clear he walked as casually as possible, dropping the secret agent moves and heading to the back door of the government building. His hand was on the handle when he heard the hum of a Rock-Hopper's engines. It was just above him and he had to retreat back to the 'Hopper he'd just been behind. The other 'Hopper landed, not far across the grass surrounding the building. Sam watched the door open. He counted six heads before he had to get out of sight completely. All he could do was listen to their footfalls and murmuring. There seemed to be an argument about something. He couldn't make out the words and his guts turned when he thought about taking another peek. He heard a growl, then yelling and knew it was now or never. He stuck out his head, with no regard for anyone looking his way. The back door to the building was open. He saw the back of a woman in a black suit, much like Arjen and Isolde's form-fitting outfits. She had reddish-blonde hair pulled into a bun and pale hands that directed the other people into the doorway. One by one they disappeared. They were shorter than her. Though she didn't look much more than five-six. Sam was gripping the edge of the 'Hopper when he saw the last two being led, no, *pushed* past the woman by a man with short black hair and similar dress.

Sam hit the ground with a soft thud. The last two people to be sent through the door were children, maybe four years old. The man forced their last steps into the building, and the woman closed the door behind them. Sam pulled himself from the grass, once again trying a casual walk but found himself running. Maybe they were just their parents. Maybe they had an argument on the ride over, but something didn't feel right. He was rounding the corner when he heard a voice.

"Sam. Sam, where are you headed?" It was Robin Visser, wearing his blue 'authority' suit.

Sam turned. It was too late to pull the door and follow the group he'd seen. Robin would be on him in a few seconds and his trust would be completely gone. He put on his crazy face and turned to Robin.

"Wow. Did you see it? Robin, did you see it?" He was a few steps away from the door with his back to it now. Robin slowed and approached cautiously.

"See what, Sam?"

"Up in the sky, look." Sam pointed towards a bright object. "It's Jupiter. I've never seen it so close."

Robin sighed, and Sam saw the tension release from his shoulders.

"You're right. Now, let's get you to Dr. Godsey, you wouldn't want to miss therapy."

Sam smiled and followed him, resisting the urge to look back at the door.

~ * ~

Zane stepped out of a makeshift dressing room, starting with a black, pin-striped leg until he heard woops from Marlow and Carol, then he slid his other leg to meet the first, standing up straight now.

"What do you think?" he asked.

"Suave," said Marlow with a smile.

"I've outdone myself," said Carol. "And on such short notice, too."

Zane did a turn in front of a mirror, looking like a nineteen-fifties gangster.

"When are you going to wear something like that?" said Marlow.

"Whenever I want," said Zane. "Are you jealous already? Your suit looked pretty good, too."

"I know, I'm just saying, when's the party? I thought they were going to find jobs for us."

Carol put an arm on her shoulder. "There's plenty of time to work, and you will, believe me but having one good dress-up outfit is still important."

Marlow tucked the other outfits Carol designed under her arm, her "daily threads" as Carol called them, then she picked up her suit. It was luxurious, nicer than anything she'd ever worn before and felt intimidating when she looked at herself in it. She'd changed out to a regular black shirt and tan pants. They were incredibly soft, "a modal blend," Carol had said. She could get used to it but the shoes she really loved. They were light and had a smooth stride. She felt like she could run faster and jump higher in them.

Arjen picked them up shortly after Carol gave them final washing instructions. They flew off and on the ride home, Arjen explained they would be starting their job placement schooling the following day. He was even bringing them a private tutor.

Once again, he dropped them and was off on another errand. It wasn't until the evening that Wesley showed up. They were sitting at the outdoor table, watching Honey run the yard as he walked in. Zane had finally changed to his "daily threads."

"I'm home," Wesley said. "Wait, you're not my family." He waved a dismissive hand. "Ah, who cares? As long as dinner's on the table." He watched them and they stared back, unsure how to reply. "No dinner? Jesus. What's a man gotta do? I put in a solid twelve-hour day for *this?*"

Finally, Zane replied. "You all talk about meals but you don't eat.

Have you ever eaten?"

Wesley looked to the stars. "No, not really." He joined them at the table. "Do you miss eating?"

"A little," said Zane.

"Well, I'm sure you'll get used to it." He wrapped his lips around his teeth. "Until your teef fall out from un-use."

"Does that happen?" said Marlow. "You still have yours."

Wes shrugged. "Who knows? I'm sure the scientists have better things to worry about, plus, I can still catch a mean frisbee." He made a chomping motion, as if snagged a frisbee out of the air.

"So, you're the funny brother then?" said Marlow.

"To some people. Obviously not to you guys."

"Those are dad jokes," said Zane. "My dad made them all the time. Oh, and Pastor Hill was the worst." Marlow nodded in agreement.

"Ugh, the one he'd always tell when we were going on a supply run, 'Better leave now so you beat the traffic.'"

Zane laughed. "Yes, and my dad's favorite when we'd go was, 'Take the shovel, it's a groundbreaking invention.'"

Wesley laughed with them. "See, those are good. They sound like nice fellas, I'm sorry I didn't get the chance to meet them."

"Yeah," said Marlow. "We wish they could be here."

"Sorry," said Wes. "Didn't mean to bring you down. Totally the opposite of what I was trying."

"It's okay," said Marlow. "It's just been us for a while. We're happy to be alive out here."

Wes nodded. "Well, my wife will be home soon. I'd better get dinner on the table." He stared at them and got one smirk from Zane. "There we go. I'll break you eventually." He stood up and headed for his front door. "We watch shows. That's why we all joke about food. People were constantly eating on Earth." They gave him blank looks. "Ah, really? Arjen didn't show you the media player? Figures. We're limited, but one of the nerds brought all the TV shows and movies they could fit on a hard drive back in the day. Most houses have a place to watch. You guys are lucky you're with us, not crammed in those apartments on Ceres."

"Isn't that where we'll end up once we're placed?" asked Marlow.

"Oh…" Wesley scratched his head. "I don't know, probably not."

"Probably?" said Zane.

"It's not up to me. Just talking. Anyway, I was serious about my wife being home soon. I'm going to head inside for a bit but why don't you come over later for a movie since my fuddy-duddy brother won't show you anything. If Tiffany isn't set on anything, I'll let you choose."

"Thank you," said Marlow. "Sounds nice."

"I haven't seen a movie since we found that portable DVD player," said Zane. "We got to see most of *Ocean's Eleven* before it died."

"Ugh," said Marlow. "You dreamed of Brad Pitt for the next month."

"No, the other guy, with the silver hair."

Wesley jumped in, "George Clooney?"

"I think so," said Zane. "I didn't have the case and we didn't make it to the credits."

"Can't blame ya," said Wes. "He's a looker, all right. You ever seen the sequel?"

Zane shook his head.

"Well, hell," said Wes. "I'll see if I can convince the wife. She's a fan of George too. Might not be too hard." He waved goodbye and went into his house.

The Earthlings were inside when Tiffany returned. They were setting Honey up in the room with her nest, though Arjen told them she was free to roam, they didn't feel safe leaving her outside by herself. The prospect of a movie had them both excited. It had been a long time since they could do anything leisurely outside of reading by candlelight in a cold bunker. They waited as long as they could, both pacing the house while Honey watched.

"I mean, he just said later," said Zane. "It's later."

"And she's been home for a half hour at least," Marlow agreed. "Surely they're not…"

"Before we…?" Zane said. "No, he would've set a time then, or come to get us."

"You're probably right."

They went out the door and down the stone walk. Behind Wesley and Tiffany's house, sat Robin Visser's. He hadn't made an appearance since their introduction on Ceres. They approached the door and waited, Marlow with her hand up, ready to knock when they heard raised voices, "...just not a good idea...you know what will happen..." It was Tiffany, then Wesley's voice came in. "We don't know. We think. But the doctors—"

She cut him off, "The doctors agree with me."

Wesley sighed loud enough for them to hear the end of it. "So, you really want to wait another year? We're not getting any younger, you know."

Tiffany was furious. "Yes. I know. I'm an old barren, hag."

Zane looked to Marlow with wide eyes. Both of them knew they should turn and walk right back to Arjen's house but neither were able to move a foot.

"You're not," said Wesley. "I just want you to be healthy when it happens."

Tiffany sounded calmer now, "It might not even be a year. The *process* is already started, who knows how fast they'll figure it out."

Wesley grunted. "It might still work on..." He stopped when he heard a sneeze.

Marlow gave a shocked look at Zane as he tried to apologize, looking cross-eyed at the nose that had just betrayed him. She decided running would be a bad look, so she gave three quick raps on the door. It opened almost immediately.

"Hey," said Marlow. "You just said later..."

"Right," said Wesley, still flustered, looking back at his wife.

"We can come back later if..."

She joined him at the door. "No, now is fine." She ran hands over her temples and back through her strawberry blonde hair, then stuck one out. "I'm Tiffany."

"Hi, I'm Marlow and this is Zane. We're from Earth."

Tiffany let out an unexpected laugh. "That's cute. Good way to introduce yourself up here. Not many of them left."

Marlow noticed now how beautiful she was. She was approaching her forties gracefully. Her features didn't stand out in any special way; they all just complimented each other to form a narrow face with high cheekbones. Her green eyes looked hurt, yet compassionate. She wore tan shorts, much the same color as Marlow's pants, but the legs she showed must have been part of what hooked Wesley in the first place. They were long for someone not considerably tall, though most people were taller than Marlow. There were sporadic scratches along her arms and a few on her neck, as if she owned a feisty cat.

Marlow had to look away to avoid staring. Wesley invited them in and they found themselves in a replica of the house they'd been staying in. The couch was black instead of white but looked to be the same material. The door to the bedroom was open with a black outfit laid on the bed in a heap.

"Make yourselves at home," said Tiffany and they found their way to the couch.

"I'll be right out," said Wesley, stepping into the bathroom.

Tiffany joined them from a loveseat in the living room.

"So, mean old Arjen won't let you use the media player at his house?"

"We didn't know he had one," said Zane. "We're going to ask him now."

"Oh, he's probably got it hidden. I'll show you where it is if he won't."

"Thanks," said Marlow.

"Anything," said Tiffany. "If you ever need anything, I'm right next door. When I'm not at work that is."

"Where do you work?" said Zane. "Wesley does woodworking, right?"

"He does. When his heart's in it, he's the best out here. Give him a boring project and he'll give you a boring result. It's just how he works." She shifted in the seat. "I work with kids. Teaching, counseling them to find the best placement for them in the belt."

"Sounds great," said Marlow.

"It could be...*can* be. It can be challenging sometimes. Sometimes kids just want to do their own thing. They don't want to fit into a mold, but out here, everyone serves a purpose."

Marlow nodded. "I hope we can, too. We don't want to—"

"You will," Tiffany cut her off, smiling big.

"Everyone ready?" said Wesley, joining Tiffany on the couch. "Once this Clooney train gets rolling, it ain't stopping." He tapped on his data-pad and a light projected on the wall. Zane looked back to see a lens up near the ceiling by the bedroom. The screen scrolled through as Wesley typed away and filtered down to *Ocean's 11, 12, 13* and *8* as well as one that said "Original" by it. Wes selected *12* and the screen darkened.

When the movie ended, they said their goodbyes and walked the twenty feet home. Arjen had slid the couch to the back wall and was laying out the mattress when they got in. He had to keep picking up Honey and putting her back on the floor as she would wait a few seconds, then hop back onto the mattress.

"Evening," said Arjen. "A little help with the duck?"

Marlow picked her up. "You don't have to sleep out here. You can have your bedroom back."

"It's fine as long as Honey stays with you." He looked them over. "Out late, huh?"

"Hard to tell," said Zane. "We went from gray every day, to sunny every day."

"Yeah, we keep faced at the sun, the dome needs it for energy. That's why we keep the rooms dark so you can get a break." He pushed himself off the mattress and stood up. "You get to meet Tiffany?"

"Yes," said Marlow. "She's very nice."

"Glad you like her. She'll be your teacher tomorrow."

"Really? She didn't say anything about it."

Arjen scratched his neck. "Yeah, she might not know yet, but she'll be happy with the assignment, I can assure you."

"Aren't we taking her away from her class?"

"Not really. They're having a little break at the moment, so the timing worked out great. Most kids are in classes from age one to ten to learn and find where they'll best serve the belt, then eleven to fifteen to train for that job. You guys are getting the crash course, but don't worry, Tiffany is great."

"Kinda young isn't it?" said Zane. "They start school at one?"

"Well, it's more or less a daycare at that age, but there are still things to be learned. The parents have the option, one year of leave. So, mom or dad can take the full year, or they can split it however they like. After that year, they are needed back at their job and the child begins their learning. Anyway, you both have skills of your own. Tiffany's job is to find and place those skills the best she can, then you'll begin training."

"How long will that take?" said Zane.

"Just depends. We'll see. You should rest, we can talk more in the morning."

Chapter Five

Zane and Marlow woke to arguing outside, by the time they were dressed and at the door, it had ended. They caught the back of Robin Visser walking to a Rock-Hopper, Tiffany storming back to her house with her hands in the air and Arjen standing just outside the door watching.

"All right then," he said to Zane and Marlow. "Why don't you get your baths and we'll be ready."

"Uh, okay," said Zane.

An hour later, Tiffany was at the table between the houses, visible flustered and muttering to herself. Arjen approached her with the Earthlings in tow.

"You ready for them, Tif?"

"Right, sure, okay," she said, not looking up.

"Okay. You need anything from me before I go?"

Now she did meet his eyes. "Talk to your father. Would you?"

"You know where that will get me."

"Just try."

Arjen nodded. "I will." Then turned to Marlow and Zane. "All right then. I'll see you later." He headed to a Rock-Hopper and Tiffany invited them to sit at the table.

"I'm sorry," she said. "I'm a bit out of sorts at this late assignment. You see, I teach the younger class. Usually kids are years into work by the time they reach your age." She looked at the few items she had on the table, wood blocks, paint brushes and a puzzle and sighed. "We'll start with some basics and see how it goes from there."

~ * ~

Tiffany spent the next week teaching and testing them the best she knew how. They did math equations, science experiments, art projects, even some physical activities. Marlow felt patronized doing kid's school activities. She could tell Tiffany was humoring them on most occasions but Zane seemed to enjoy it, all of it. Maybe he was just happy to be busy. Marlow tried to keep a good attitude, not wanting to bring the guy down when all along she questioned what jobs were going to come out of this kind of learning.

Tiffany seemed to just be making it through each day until Wesley came home and school ended. Then, it was as if all was well. They went over for movies most nights and sometimes Arjen even joined them. Wesley had grown fond of Honey and started making them bring her to movies as well. They'd become a weird little family, and it was reminiscent of the good times they had in the bunker back when their parents and Jason were still around.

Finally, on the seventh day of school, Arjen had mercy on Marlow.

"Can you spare Marlow this morning?" he asked Tiffany.

She looked up and nodded while Zane sat, eager for another lesson she'd have to scrape from the bottom of her barrel of teaching knowledge.

Marlow didn't bother to ask where they were going. She jumped up from the table and followed him. Zane waved goodbye then turned back to Tiffany.

As the Rock-Hopper pulled out of the 'Bubble, Arjen looked over at her.

"Thanks. Dr. Vell contacted me. They do constant monitoring of NutrientPanel. They do it to all of us, no worries. When they notice your body pulling more of some vitamins, they'll adjust to make sure you get all of what you need. Every now and then, when you keep pulling more each time, they'll bring you in and run a blood panel to make sure there aren't any underlying conditions. It's totally happened to me before. It was all good and I went home. Probably the same for you, Dr. Vell is just being extra cautious because of your past."

"What about Zane? He's fine?"

"Far as I know, or they would've asked me to bring him too."

"How do they know? How do they know it's not him, or *you*? We all share the same bath."

"That number you type in. That's your code. That alerts the panel and sends the report when you're done."

"That's crazy."

She watched an asteroid below them. Giant trees jutted far above the surface. It was the forest island they'd seen when they first entered the belt. Marlow had dreamt of it a few nights into their new life. She hadn't forgotten it since. "So, I finally get to skip school and you're bringing me to the doctor? You really are trying to recreate Earth out here."

Arjen laughed. "I'll take you out somewhere fun afterwards. Isn't that how it works? We don't have ice cream but…"

"The forest," said Marlow in a snap. "I want to see the big trees."

Arjen looked back towards the fading forest. "Okay, but I warn you, they only grow them so they can cut them down."

~ * ~

The medical complex was all on one big asteroid. There was a group of single-story buildings with Rock-Hoppers lined in front. Their 'Hopper pulled in next to them. There was a row of trees towering behind the buildings. Six clusters of banyans, compared to the two they had at the Homestead. Marlow thought about letting Arjen off the hook and having him just let her wander behind the medical buildings after her appointment but thought better of it. If this was her one day off of school, she was making the most of it.

They walked in through wide double-doors. There was a woman at a lone desk with halls on either side of her heading deeper into the facility. The floors were smooth, polished stone. The woman acknowledged Arjen, then went back to the screen in front of her.

"Excuse me," said Arjen. "I've got Marlow here. Dr. Vell wanted to check on her 'Panel absorption rate."

The woman looked confused for a second, then said, "Okay. She's ready for you." She stepped out from the desk and led them down to an exam room. Dr. Vell entered with her familiar, pleasant, but forced smile. It broadened when she saw Marlow.

"Well, hello Marlow. How have you been? Getting accustomed to life in the belt?"

"Getting there."

"I already gave her the warning," said Arjen. "Checking her blood for 'Panel absorption."

Dr. Vell nodded a frown at him. "Yes. That will be all then." She turned to Marlow. "I'll just need some blood then. You pick the arm."

Marlow rolled back her sleeve and soon they were headed off to the belt forest.

Chapter Six

"Can I trust you, Zane?" asked Tiffany, only a few minutes after Arjen and Marlow had left.

He looked up. "Yes…"

"I'm really winging it here. I'm sure you understand that. I need to check on my other students but I just haven't been able to with this schedule."

"Okay. Do you need…?"

"I've just gotta go real quick, then I'll be back. Shouldn't take a couple hours. But I'm supposed to be teaching you and my boss would be very unhappy if I were to just leave you unattended."

Zane didn't want to mention he was twenty years old and been practically alone on an entire planet before this. Despite enjoying parts of the schooling, he was ready to get off their rock.

"So, take me with you."

She looked around, the two of them were alone at the homestead but still she whispered, "You can't tell anyone. Understand?"

Zane nodded slowly. "Of course. I've got nothing to say."

"Not even to Marlow."

"Okay, sure."

Tiffany looked around one last time then jumped up from the table. "Let's go."

She had to call a Rock-Hopper as Arjen took the last one when he left. The 'Hoppers were more-or-less shared between the islands. They waited a few minutes by the landing spot before one approached, passengerless, and landed. Tiffany hit her data-pad and they took off.

~ * ~

The belt forest was all Marlow wanted it to be. The sweet smell of oak, maple, and cherry trees mingling together. It wasn't as huge as she'd expected. The trees were incredibly tall, and there was no end in sight when she stepped up to the entry but it was only about five acres of forest. Surely not enough to support all the belt's needs. She didn't care as she looked back at Arjen, still catching up to her.

"Can I just…?"

"Hold on," he said, looking over to a group of workers, shaving the bark off a couple of fifty-foot timbers. He approached them and after a minute, Marlow saw him walking back with Wesley.

"Hey, Mar," he said. "Arjen says you want to see the forest?"

She gave him and excited nod.

"Well, don't let this stiff show you around."

He took off the hard hat he'd been wearing and plopped it on Arjen's blonde locks, then removed his gloves and tucked them in his utility belt.

"Keep an eye on 'em for me, would ya?"

Arjen frowned at him. "Don't be long."

Wesley gave a short bow then waved for Marlow to follow him. They headed deep into the trees until it was dark as dusk. Marlow couldn't get over the smells. The woody, bark smell, the sweet sap from the maples, she'd chosen well.

"They're so tall," she said, looking up and feeling like there was no end. Some must have been two hundred feet high.

"GMO," said Wesley. He patted one. "This one is based on a cherry tree. So, we mixed in redwood DNA for height, bamboo DNA for growth rate and there ya go. There's more to it than that. I'm sure the eggheads would hate the simplistic explanation, but it's how we do it for all of them. The cherry is my favorite to work with."

Marlow petted the tree alongside him like it was a prize-winning thoroughbred. "Gorgeous."

They continued walking.

"How's class?" said Wes. "Skipping today? Tif finally piss you off?"

Marlow laughed. "No. I had to see the doctor so she could check my blood. Apparently, I'm pulling too much something from the 'Panel. I don't know."

"Huh, well, good to check that out, I guess."

"Yeah." She held her thought for a minute, then asked anyway. "This job placement stuff...it's weird. I feel like I have no clue where she's going to recommend me. Like, Zane is doing fine. I feel like he's headed toward something woodworking related. You'll have to talk to him about it, but I feel lost, like she's not even trying with me."

Wesley looked troubled and took a few seconds while Marlow backtracked.

"Don't...I'm sorry, that's your wife. I wasn't trying to..."

"No. I understand. It's a weird position for you. Sometimes it takes a little longer from one person to the next, and you gotta remember, she's used to teaching kids. I mean, toddlers. You're a bit beyond that. Just give her time. You'll find the right place here."

"What if I don't, though? What if there is no place for me here?"

"Mar, there is definitely a place for you here. Trust me."

Marlow took a second to digest his words. "Okay, thanks."

They'd reached the end of the trees, the TechBubble glowing not far beyond them. The edge of the island gave way to infinite space.

"Should we?" said Wes, turning back the way they came.

They began the walk back and she looked up at him. "I really didn't come out here to cry about my schooling."

"I know. Lots of people want to visit the forest. Most of them don't get the personal tour. Good thing you got an in with your neighbor, huh?"

Marlow smiled.

They were about to the opening when he spoke again, "Marlow, if you ever need time to *think* or just take a walk, let me know. You can come out here anytime. Don't hesitate. I find these trees are the only thing that gets that vast universe out of my head."

"You feel it too?"

"A lot of us do. Look, we're alive out here, but even if we weren't physically born on Earth, our bodies still belong there, if you know what I mean."

"I think so."

"It took us a long time to evolve to live on Earth. We're only a few generations out here and it seems like our instincts still miss a planet a lot of us have never been on."

"Do you think we'll ever go back?"

"I don't know, you tell me. How is it back on the motherland?"

"Not good."

Arjen approached them. "You get your fill?"

"For now," said Marlow. "I'd like to come back sometime."

Wesley nodded before Arjen could reply. "Just tell me when."

~ * ~

Zane sat in the 'Hopper while Tiffany ran in to the government building. He'd told her he would stay, but what was ten minutes of wandering? There was a small housing community just up the road with people coming in and out of the buildings. He missed the human interaction on the *Iris*. It wasn't much but it was more than the same island of three people.

He jumped out of the 'Hopper and jogged up the rock road. It was smoothed down for foot traffic but would be awful for cars. *It was a good thing they didn't have cars in the belt*, he thought.

When he approached the courtyard, he realized the buildings were good old-fashioned apartments. The people coming in and out must be second shifters that worked the twelve hours Wesley and Tiffany didn't. Nobody was making themselves available for greetings, though he waved at a few of them. He wasn't having any luck. He spotted a man standing at a second-floor window. He was staring in a way that Zane didn't like. Maybe he should've stayed in the 'Hopper. Regardless, his time was spent. He needed to head back and try socializing another day. He gave one last look at the window and it was empty.

Heading down the road, he couldn't help but look back. Someone came out the front of the apartments. He looked away, surely it was just another person leaving for work. When he looked back, a man was jogging in his direction. He picked up his pace, not wanting to run but power walking at least. The 'Hopper was a hundred yards away now. If he went to a dead sprint it would look strange but the man was catching up and he was pretty certain it was the one from the window.

Zane ran. He was faster than the man once he got going but about twenty yards out, he had the thought that once he got to the Rock-Hopper, what would he do then? If he went to the government building, he'd get in trouble with Tiffany. He heard his name.

"Zane, it's me, slow down. I just want to talk. I need you to give a message to Marlow."

The voice. He'd barely spoken to the guy on the ship, but he knew it had to be the crazy astronaut. He slowed and turned around, letting the man catch up.

Sam was out of breath when he reached Zane.

"Man, you got some wheels, buddy. Didn't mean to scare you. I saw you from the window. First familiar face I've seen since we've landed."

"Hey," said Zane. "Sorry, I'm really supposed to be waiting for my teacher."

"I'll be quick. I need you to pass a message on to Marlow. It goes with what we talked about on the ship."

Zane sighed. "Oh, not more of that."

Sam put a hand on his arm. "Yes, because it's life or death out here."

Zane rolled his eyes. He'd been living the best part of his life since they'd been in the belt. He was even being prepped for a job, no, a *career*. His father would be so proud.

"You don't have to believe me," Sam went on. "Just tell Marlow, it's the kids. They're doing whatever it is to the kids."

"Whatever it is?" Zane repeated. "And what is that?"

"We don't know. It's what Marlow and I were trying to find out on the ship." He rubbed his chin. "I'm hoping you two are safe, being that you're old enough."

"Safe from what?"

Sam flung his arms in the air. "That's what we don't know." He pointed a finger down at Zane's nose. "I need you to help find out. I've been monitoring that door as much as I can but I haven't seen them moving again. I think the kids are still down there. The door is locked though."

Zane looked back. "Down in *that* building?"

Sam nodded, then both their faces froze as a figure came down the steps of the government building. "That's her," said Sam. "She's back for them."

"No," said Zane. "That's just my teacher. Look, I've gotta get back."

"That's your teacher?"

He gripped Zane's shoulder, squeezing too hard. "She knows what's going on down there. You've gotta find out."

Zane pulled away, giving him a crazy look. "I'm sorry, I can't help you."

Sam seemed to ignore his reply. "Get her to talk. Find out what she knows." Zane was jogging off as Sam yelled after him, "Tell Marlow to find me."

Zane met Tiffany at the 'Hopper. She gave a concerned look to Sam as he turned back towards the apartments.

"Everything okay? Who was that?"

Zane watched him go, shaking his head. "Just some crazy guy."

~ * ~

In bed that night, Zane spoke in a low whisper.

"I saw your friend today."

"What friend?"

"The crazy spaceman."

Marlow turned. "You saw Sam? Wait, where? How?"

He looked at the closed door then to Marlow in the dark. "You can't tell, not Arjen, not anyone, okay?"

"Okay, fine. Did he come here or did you leave?"

"We left. Tiffany wanted to check on her other students and I got to come with. I didn't do anything nearly as cool as you, but we were at some government building. When she went in, I took a walk and ran into Sam. He wanted me to give some crazy message to you. Something about what you two were trying to figure out on the ship and he thinks it's the kids. 'The kids are down there,' he says and that you and me may be safe because we're older."

"Goodness," said Marlow. "He thinks they're using the kids? Then why us?"

"No, no, this is not why I told you this. We're not getting back on conspiracies. I only told you because I thought you'd find it funny now. Now that we have a nice place to live and Tiffany is teaching us, trying to find the right jobs for us. We're not sex slaves. We're not experiments. I think that's pretty obvious. Can you at least agree to that?"

"Oh, fine, Zane. I guess, but why would he say that about the kids?"

"Do I really have to answer that? Because. He's. Crazy. Mar."

"You didn't talk to him as much as me."

"Probably for the best. Now, please forget I said anything, and definitely forget about Tiffany taking me out. I promised her I wouldn't tell."

Marlow didn't reply, she was staring at the ceiling, her head in a war between conspiracy and comfort.

Chapter Seven

Another week went by with minimal conspiracy talk. They continued with classes while Marlow worked out a deal for them to get some "off rock" time. It was always chaperoned, sometimes with Arjen, sometimes with Isolde. Generally, they were split up. Marlow settled on her walks in the forest with Wesley, when she could, while, after a little exploring, Zane finally convinced Ice to take him to Club Earth.

They were two weeks into life on the belt when Ice landed in a Rock-Hopper, dressed to a T in a violet gown. It was the first dressy dress they'd seen. Tiffany wore flowing skirts from time to time, but they didn't have the effect that Ice's did that day.

"Whoa," said Zane, stepping out the front door of Arjen's house in his pin-striped suit. "That is wild."

"I love it," said Marlow, in her daily threads, leaning on the door frame. "You guys are really going to a club?"

"*The* club," said Ice. "It's the only one. I can't believe we even have one out here but after thirty to forty years of stable settlement, leadership finally gave in. Part of it is the nostalgia factor. Its themes are based on decades of Earth life. Today is a nineties day, as in, a hundred years ago. None of us were alive but we have the archives of media from back then. We'll see what they come up with. You ready?"

Zane stuck out his arm and Ice took it.

"Too cute," said Tiffany. "Let me get a picture of you two." She raised her data-pad and they posed like a couple on the way to the prom.

"Okay, see you later," said Zane and they were off.

Tiffany and Marlow watched them go.

"You didn't want to go?" said Tiffany.

"Ugh, no," said Marlow. "I'm not fond of big groups, dancing, singing…you know, that kind of stuff. But Zane? He thrives on it. I'm glad he can have it again."

"That's sweet. How you care for each other. I think you've got a leg up on most married couples out here."

"You think so? I don't know. I don't think I'm wife material. My gay husband might be as far as I go."

"Oh, come now." It was all Tiffany said.

Marlow expected the cliché "I'm sure you'll make a great wife someday." Or, "Give it time." At least. No, this only further solidified Tiffany's hatred for her. Zane was on the fast track to becoming a woodworker apprentice while Marlow wasn't even cut out to be a stay-at-home-mom according to her teacher. Though, she knew that wasn't an option on the belt. "Everyone serves a purpose, everyone serves the belt," she'd heard Robin Visser say at one of his few visits to his own home rock. But what purpose could she serve? She was going to the forest for her outing, not to take in the trees this time but to find Wesley and implore him to talk some sense into his wife.

Arjen arrived a few minutes later, and she took off jogging toward the 'Hopper.

"Where you headed?" called Tiffany.

"Out," said Marlow, feeling the biting tone of a teenager rip off her tongue. She wanted to follow it with, "none of your business," but thought better of it.

They rode mostly in silence. Arjen broke it only to tell her he'd have to drop her today and be back in a few hours. He'd asked if she'd be okay for a few hours and she assured him she would. They hadn't been gifted with data-pads to have practically grafted to their arms like everyone else but Wesley had given her an old electronic reader, loaded with his favorite books. She was currently making her way through *The Talisman* by Stephen King. She was particularly enthralled with the part where Jack and Wolf end up in the school for troubled children. She couldn't help but compare Tiffany to the evil Sunlight Gardner, though there was no real parallel. She'd sit and read for two hours, if she had to, at the far end of the forest.

Arjen dropped her and she didn't stick around to watch him go. A few of the workers stopped to say "hi" to her as she approached, looking for Wes. He appeared from the lone office building across the open portion of the rock. He pointed toward the trees, then tried to perform a walking motion with his fingers across his palm, but from the distance it was hard to tell.

Marlow yelled, "I'm going for a walk."

Wes gave a thumbs up, then put up five fingers, and she gave a thumbs up in return before heading to the trees.

There was a giant cherry tree at the very end of the forest that Marlow had marked as her favorite. Being a bookend meant it got the most sun and likely was one of the taller trees. There was a neighboring giant oak, but she picked cherry because it was Wesley's favorite. She was a few pages into her chapter, hoping Jack and Wolf would find a way out of the school, when she heard his footsteps.

"Getting into *The Talisman?*" Wesley leaned a hand on the tree, instinctively stroking the wood.

Marlow marked her page and looked up. "Yeah. Getting rough. I love it, though."

"Good. Want to walk?"

"Yeah."

She joined him for a slow stroll. His pace dragged, unlike other times where it was a purposeful jaunt. She'd always been able to see him checking out trees and making mental notes about some detail. Today it wasn't that way. Today he seemed to be searching for the right words, just the same as her. *How do you tell someone you think their wife is a witch?*

"Hey," said Wes. "Come look at this spot. I don't think I've shown you it before."

She followed and they tucked around a fat maple. It had found a way to grow right up to the edge of the TechBubble, and when they sat at its base, their feet could rest against the 'Bubble.

"Pretty cool, huh?" said Wes, putting his two boots against the 'Bubble and leaning back. Marlow did the same, having to stretch her legs further and feeling her stomach jump as she saw the edge of the rock.

She grabbed his arm.

"Sorry, it just caught me…" She'd meant to let go, but his hand rested on top of hers.

"You're safe."

They sat for a minute, Marlow feeling the pulse of contact running through her body. It wasn't like Zane or even Arjen. It was different and the meter between her hatred for Tiffany and herself right now was jumping around in her brain. She knew it wasn't right, but nothing in her life had been right or fair, for that matter. Jason and her mom had been ripped away by the damn Earth, along with anyone else she ever cared about. It had always been about surviving, and the small months of mild happiness with Jason hadn't been enough. Trying to find a place to hold each other while wearing respirators wasn't exactly romantic. She'd take her moments with Wesley, however wrong they felt and however short they might be. Once she was placed, it would all end. She'd likely be in an apartment working a job she was no good at, thanks to Tiffany, and then she might never get walks in the forest.

Her thoughts were a mile a minute, staring out to the universe as his hand was now caressing hers. She knew he wouldn't go further. He had a gorgeous wife back home. Marlow was a short, refugee from Earth. He was probably just—

Wesley kissed her cheek, right at the corner of her mouth. She looked up at him in shock.

"W-Wes…?"

His hand sprang off of hers like it was on fire. "Shit, sorry, sorry."

He was trying to stand up as if she were also on fire but he was having trouble in the cramped space between the tree and the 'Bubble. He settled for scooting a few feet away. His hands were up. "I don't know what the fuck I was doing."

Marlow's head was tilted as she watched his actions of the last few seconds. "It's okay. Don't be sorry. I won't…"

He let out a sigh and slumped to the ground. "It's just been testy at home lately. I probably don't need to tell you that. You've seen. She won't even sit by me most nights, afraid if I get too close, I'll…" He stopped himself, watching Marlow as he did.

"You'll what?" said Marlow. "You're not violent. At least, I don't think you are."

"No." His head was hanging. "She's afraid I'll get her pregnant."

~ * ~

Marlow was unable to get back into her book. She just sat at the usual landing place, leaned against a Rock-Hopper, waiting for Arjen. She held the e-reader up for appearances and to avoid following Wesley with her eyes. Never in her life had Marlow wanted to pry more into a sentence than the one he ended with. She couldn't understand how Tiffany couldn't want to have a child with him. She knew the belt needed the population. He had all of Arjen's good looks *and* a sense of humor but with a stronger dose of honesty. It was the thing that pushed him over the edge for her. Arjen, she could resist. Wesley, she had to fight back the fluttering feeling each time he entered a room. It was fucking pathetic and she knew it, but it didn't stop her from taking those trips to the forest. Now she wasn't sure what would happen. Who knows, maybe they'd find her and Zane a different place to live soon and that would be that.

She hadn't pried though. He gave a strong impression that he'd said enough, *done* enough at that point of the day, and was shutting it down. He'd waited for her to get up from the ground but didn't offer a hand to help. It was a first. They'd walked in silence. Every sentence began in her head like, "If I don't say anything, can I still come visit you?" or "Don't worry about it, we can still be friends." But none of it felt true. The sinking feeling was, their friendship was over.

Arjen landed not far from her seat, and she shut the cover to the e-reader with no need to move her bookmark. When she reached the 'Hopper, Arjen jumped out.

"I just need to chat with Wes for a minute. Can you wait here?"

She nodded, feeling her guts sink. *Had Wes told Arjen what happened? No way.* She found her seat in the second row and watched. They were about thirty yards away. All she could do was read facial expressions. Arjen was excited about something, slapping Wesley on the shoulder, forcing a handshake on him, while Wes stood nodding and pursing his lips. He forced a smile at his brother. Marlow could tell it was forced even from her vantage point. They shook hands one more time and Arjen turned and walked back.

Chapter Eight

Isolde and Zane landed in the first legitimate parking lot Zane had seen in the belt. It was black, like asphalt, with yellow lines painted for the Rock-Hoppers to land in. The front of Club Earth had a pretty basic entrance with the name in big block letters.

"This is it?" said Zane.

"It's more interesting inside," said Ice. "Just stay close to me."

"What does that mean?"

They walked in through the sliding doors and were immediately blasted with MC Hammer's "Can't Touch This."

"Oh my god," said Zane.

"You know this one?"

"No, but I like it."

The main room was surrounded by tables with a few people lounging. The dance floor, a multi-colored checkerboard, was a different story. Swarms of strange outfits, piloted by sweaty heads, spun, lunged, and shook their knees. They were belt outfits but mixed and matched to look like they didn't care. Lights flashed on all sides. A giant screen on the back wall played the music video to accompany the song. The crowd was trying their best, or worst, to mimic the dance moves. Some people on the side just stood pointing at the baggy pants the dancers in the video wore. Zane looked to Ice and she flipped a hand toward the floor, signifying to jump in. He smiled, grabbed her arm and dragged her with him.

They danced for the better part of an hour to various nineties hits from Nirvana and Metallica, to Alanis Morissette and Mariah Carey, all the way to Dr. Dre, Snoop Dogg, and TLC.

When Ice finally convinced him to get a drink at the bar, Zane stood next to her sweating through his suit, but happier than ever.

"I thought the two-drink limit was a joke," he yelled over the music.

"No, but you're still not getting served here." She turned to the bartender. "Vodka on the rocks and water for my friend."

"Oh, come on," said Zane.

She didn't budge, and they found a table to set down their drinks.

"Silly question," said Zane. "Do you turn down *every* guy that approaches you?"

Isolde gave a hearty laugh. "Most of them."

"Why? There are only three hundred people. Can you really be so picky?"

She took a drink and looked out at the dance floor. "I had a boyfriend for a while. He wanted to be more serious than I did, so I broke things off before this last trip. It was a good point to give him time to forget about me."

"Poor guy."

She shrugged. "He's better off."

"What about Arjen?"

She took a few seconds. "Ah, he's still heartbroken from the last one. It works for us gatherers. Not the best profession for long-term relationships."

"So, you and Arjen never…"

She frowned at him. "What's with all the relationship questions there? You meet someone special I need to know about?"

Zane took a turn looking at the dance floor. "No. *Never*. Every crush I've ever had has been on a straight dude."

"Oh, honey." Ice put her hand on his arm. "I'm going to tell you something about the belt."

"Okay."

"Not everyone out here is into monogamy. And you being…inexperienced…I don't want you to get your heart broken. You could probably find a guy out there today, like the one whose number I have in my pocket." She paused to smile at him.

134

"What? Really? Who?" Zane was scanning the floor.

"If I tell you, you have to understand the rules first."

"Okay, okay, just hurry before he leaves."

"He's not going anywhere." She darted her eyes out, then back to Zane. He tried to follow her but couldn't tell where she looked. Ice continued, "There are no STDs out here. The 'Panel prevents the spread of disease. But you can get your heart broken. You can get used by someone just looking for a hookup. Do you understand that?"

"Yes, fine. I've never even dated. By the time I was ready to be open with my family, the world went to Hell again."

"Okay. Take a look over by the right of the screen. See the guy watching the video."

"I...yes. The tall one? Oh, he's not bad. I should have a closer look. He really gave you his number for *me?*"

"Yes, I could see his intentions from a mile away. I intercepted it. It's not like you have a data-pad to call him on anyway."

"Let's go." He stood up and she pulled him back down.

"Me first. I'm going to lay some ground rules. Give me two minutes."

"Oh, you're killing me."

Ice stood up, spun her braid into an intimidating bun on top of her head and held up two fingers. "Two minutes." And walked down to the dance floor.

~ * ~

The Earthlings had a lot to recap that night. Marlow alerted Zane that there might not be a movie at Wesley's house that night and told him she'd explain later. They convinced Arjen to put on *E.T.* for them and spent the time half watching and half talking.

"He was tall *and* funny," said Zane. "I need a data-pad so I can call him. It will be weird to call him from Ice's or Arjen's."

"We should have them by the time we have jobs," Marlow said. "That's what Tiffany made it sound like."

"You still think she's out to get you?"

"If she wasn't before…" Marlow looked to the door, as if she was expecting a guest, but only Honey was in the house with them, laying on her egg.

"What is it? What happened?"

"Wes…he, *we* had an incident today." She shook her head. "Ah, I don't know."

"You're killing me, Mar. Just say it."

Even though they were alone, she whispered, "He kinda kissed me."

Zane's eyes went wide. "Kissed you? I…but…Tiffany. Does he *like* you?"

"Well, I don't…"

Zane kept on, "I mean, he must, but what about *her*?"

"Zane, no, it's not about…I think he was just having an off day."

"Did you like it? Was it *nice*?"

"Zane!"

"Sorry," he said as he watched E.T. light up his finger. "So, what happened after? Did you like, make out?"

"No. It was one little kiss, if that. He knew it wasn't right and we walked back to the camp."

"That's all? Just swept it under the rug?"

"Well, no. I'm sure it's going to be weird for a while. At least for me, but he did say one thing I found especially strange. He said his trouble with Tiffany lately—and *you've* seen them—is that she's afraid he'll get her pregnant."

Zane's eyes narrowed. "Isn't that how it works?"

"I thought so, especially out here."

"Maybe she just doesn't want kids."

"Could be. He just seemed extra sad about that."

Zane nodded, his eyes fixed on the movie, mulling over the situation. It was a few minutes before he spoke again.

"So, you two were just out in the forest kissing?"

Marlow gave him a death glare.

Zane put his hands up. "Just saying, romantic." He braced for the smack on the arm as she delivered it.

~ * ~

Arjen came back later to an alien saying goodbye to his human friends and two Earthlings asleep on the couch. He was tipsy from the bottle he'd opened with his dad, brother and sister-in-law since it turned out he was the main one drinking it. He would've been offended, but by the third drink, he just didn't care. He spent a minute smiling down at the kids on his couch. Just kids to him but so important. Arjen draped a blanket over them and went to sleep in his own bed for the first time in two months. He was out within minutes.

Chapter Nine

A week later, Sam came out of his apartment and moved with a purpose. It had been five minutes since he witnessed the government building clear out. It was the first chance he'd had since he saw the man and woman leading the children into the back door. He was power-walking down the road where he'd chased Zane. The parking area was empty and quiet. It was off-putting for a place usually bustling with officials. He couldn't let it bother him. This was his second, and likely, last chance. If he was found today, he didn't think the crazy astronaut act would work again, though he did have a story in his back pocket for such an occasion.

There was no Rock-Hopper to hide behind this time. He had to continue on, straight to the back door. It was locked, but he'd expected that and had a screwdriver handy that he'd borrowed from a guy down his hall. There was no deadbolt, just the handle-lock. Sam jammed the flathead into the keyhole and twisted. He knew this trick wouldn't work on a lot of locks back on Earth, but out here there wasn't much reason to lock anything. Most locks on the belt were built to say, "Hey, I don't want anyone in here right now, but check back later." Everyone was part of the colony. Everyone drank the Kool-Aid. Everyone but Sam, that is.

The handle turned with a cracking noise and Sam tucked the screwdriver in his back pocket. He went in, giving one last look around before pulling the door behind him. It was still a desert out there, just how he liked it. The back of the government building was nothing more than a hallway leading to the front. There was a series of doors lining the hall and Sam tried them all. Each of the first three opened to an empty office until he found the last one to stick in his hand. He grabbed the screwdriver again but couldn't get this one to give. Sam took a step back, breathing hard, wondering how much more undetected time he had. He tucked the screwdriver away and put his ear to the door. He could hear sound, muffled and far away, but something was making noise behind that door. "In for a penny, in for a pound," he muttered and threw his weight into the door. A jolt went up his shoulder and down to his hip. The door was solid wood, not budging at his feeble attempt. He rubbed his arm, trying to get the needles out while he searched the unlocked offices for something useful. It was a shovel in the second office that piqued his interest and soon he was ramming the butt end into the handle. It finally gave way, the handle busting off and falling to the floor. After a little more twisting of the screwdriver, he was in.

There was a stairway before him, leading down to a turn and a second flight. Sam took them, deciding that if there was someone down here who wanted to stop him, they'd be well aware he was coming. The screwdriver wouldn't do much to protect him. He wondered for a second if he should go back for the shovel, then dropped the thought.

After the second flight he landed into a room full of jail cells. There were only dim lights but he saw them immediately, *the kids*. There were eight in all, after a quick head count, ranging from around three years old, to fifteen or so. A few approached the bars to their cells, watching him but not speaking.

"Oh god," said Sam. "What happened to you? Why are you down here?" His hands were on his head, looking wildly back and forth until he froze on a little girl he'd seen when he first scoped it out. She was no more than four, possibly less and his heart ached. "What did they do to you kids?"

No one was replying and Sam was afraid there was something majorly wrong with them. It wasn't just children in jail cells, that would be bad enough. These kids had a look in their eyes, a different look that he couldn't quite place. The little girl was standing at the cell watching, holding a cross-bar with her soft, pink hands. Sam went to her, trying to hold himself together long enough to do something about their situation. He knelt down, speaking in a gentle voice.

"Hey there, Honey. Did some bad people put you down here?"

She didn't reply, only tilted her head, her wild eyes fixed on him like he was something to study.

Sam tried again. "I want to help you. I want to get you out of here. Do you want to come out?" When he still got no response, he patted her hand softly, fighting back tears at the look of her sweet face. She bit down across his pinky and ring finger and tried to tear them off his hand.

Chapter Ten

The Rock-Hoppers were on an invisible, electronic grid throughout the belt. It prevented them from crashing into one another and kept travel times consistent. They were self-piloted and most of the time, that was a luxury. Currently, Robin Visser, Kaia Gammen and Oscar Ramirez were cursing their transportation, trying to find a way to override the auto-pilot and get the damn thing moving. It had been so long since they'd had to perform an emergency override, none of them knew how to do it. When they arrived at the belt forest, it was already too late. Tiffany was hysterical, crying into one of Arjen's shoulders as his mother was on the other. He had tears of his own running down his cheeks. He looked to the trees with a clenched jaw. Zane and Marlow stood nearby, also holding each other.

Robin joined them first, popping the door open as soon as the 'Hopper would let him and stumble-running to them.

"Where is he?" His hand was on his youngest son's shoulder, heaving breaths between his words.

Arjen pointed but shook his head. The rest of the workers and responders were scattered in a circle about twenty feet away. Some of them paced. One sat, rocking, while he held his knees. Another had his hard hat over his heart. Robin did another stumbling-run to them, viewing his oldest son's mangled body for the last time. He couldn't keep looking at Wesley, but Robin found his cold hand and held it, weeping bitter tears as he kissed it. After a few minutes, he rested Wesley's hand on his chest and looked up to the man still holding his hard hat, now at his side.

"Tell me what happened," Robin said in a soft, frail voice.

The man flinched hearing Robin speak. He wouldn't look at the mourning father but he recounted the son's death the best he could.

"We calculated the landing spot. I was ready to haul it. I had plenty of clearance but we didn't see the branch it got snagged on. These damn trees are so strong and so tall. It spun off there like it was thrown. I was too slow. I shoulda dropped my tools, I shoulda ran, but I couldn't think. Wes…he *did* think. He tackled me and…" The man stopped, using his hat-holding arm to wipe his face. Robin noticed for the first time that his other arm was in bad shape. He turned to Robin with an agonized face. "It shoulda been me, that damn fool should've left me to die."

Robin fully agreed with the man's words but didn't voice his opinion. Kaia and Oscar stood behind him and helped him to his feet. Arjen, Tiffany, Zane, and Marlow were with them. All of them were looking past the destroyed body of their former brother, son, husband, and friend.

Kaia was listening intently, holding a hand to her ear and nodding. Finally, she said, "Okay, keep him there until we arrive."

Oscar looked at her. "What is it?"

"Someone broke into the government building. The children are out."

~ * ~

When the group arrived in the courtroom within the government building, Sam was cuffed to the witness stand with a security guard standing by. The judges, Robin, Kaia, and Oscar sat together, the tears barely dry in their eyes as Arjen and Isolde watched from the gallery.

"My son has just been killed and you took the opportunity to break in here and release a bunch of sick children?" Robin was already standing from his bench seat.

"If they're sick, why are they in cages?" Sam yelled. "Something is seriously wrong with them. What have you done?" He pointed a wrapped hand, blood showing through the bandage.

"I will not be accused. *You* are the one on trial for endangering their lives." Robin was jabbing a finger, trying to get closer when Kaia held him back and Oscar made him sit.

Kaia took over. "Listen, both of you. This is a very bad time for all of us and no time for an interrogation. I move we postpone any further actions until tomorrow."

"Second," said Oscar. They led Robin out of the room.

Sam didn't fight the guard moving him to a cell of his own. He just gave a look to Arjen and Ice and said, "You know what's going on but you hide it. The blood is on your hands as much as theirs."

Ice looked to Arjen and his steel-set jaw. Neither of them replied.

~ * ~

"There has to be a manual," said Zane, climbing over the seats of the 'Hopper. "Do you think it's only in their data-pads?"

"Maybe," said Marlow. "But what if those are broke? What if it goes off course for whatever reason? There has to be another way."

They'd been put in a Rock-Hopper and set on a trajectory by Tiffany as she went with Wesley's body to the medical facility. The two of them had no way of controlling the 'Hopper, currently headed for the Visser's homestead. They'd exchanged glances when Kaia had said, "The children are out." Marlow reminded Zane of Sam's message weeks ago. "The kids are down there," he'd said. Now they were out, and Marlow quickly put two and two together on who'd let them out.

"I found a panel," said Zane, now at the very back of the ship, tucked behind the last row of seats. Marlow joined him, peering over the seats as he popped the panel open.

"That's it," she said.

"It has an emergency stop switch." Zane's hand hesitated over it. "But what if we can't get it going again?"

Marlow strained, hanging over the seat, crammed next to him. "I'm sure we can get it going again, and look, we've got almost two hours of oxygen left."

"Oh yes, that's very reassuring. Two hours to sit out here, thousands of miles from the nearest island."

"Well, we're only getting further away. Once it lands, we can't get it going again without a data-pad." She added, "I'll hit it if you won't."

"Fine, no, I'll hit it. You're practically hanging upside down. I don't want you to accidentally hit the self-destruct."

"Hah, hah."

Zane hit the emergency stop button and had to confirm on the screen that he truly wanted to do it. He confirmed and they felt the engines cut, then reverse thrust until they came to a complete stop. Their 'Hopper was now stranded between islands. They could see Ceres far in the distance, glowing with life as well as other specs of islands hanging in the endless void.

"Um, Mar, there is no reprogram option."

"What?" she said, feeling a chill ripple across her skin.

"The only options are the emergency door release, which is grayed out, thank goodness, and 'Home.' Where do you think home is?"

Her eyes brightened. "Ceres. It has to be, right? That's where all the ships are docked and repaired when not in use. It would only make sense in an emergency that it would return to the repair shop if it could."

"Makes sense. Okay, here we go." Zane hit the home button, confirmed it, then was given a thirty second countdown to return to his seat.

They strapped in and watched the ship turn and head in the direction of Ceres.

"Thanks for scaring the shit out of me," Marlow said.

"Sorry." Zane looked at the stars in the distance.

Within a half hour they approached Ceres and entered the 'Bubble-atmosphere. Their ship found a spot near a hanger, across from the *Iris*, resting like a sleeping giant. They noticed a red light flashing on their 'Hopper when they got out.

"Must be requesting an inspection or something," said Marlow. "Since we did the emergency landing, you know? Let's get out of here before someone notices." She looked around. "Where is the government building from here?"

"It's down the road," said Zane. "Maybe a mile. Follow me."

They headed down a rocky, dirt path, away from the hanger. There was a row of trees they focused on. Getting out of sight was their first goal, then they'd see if they could get any details on what would cause a father to leave his son's dead body.

The trees were clusters of banyans, halfway between the shipyard and the government building. They were the perfect place to get a better vantage point while staying out of sight. Marlow grabbed Zane and they had to duck off the road to avoid being seen by a patrol of second shift workers roused from sleep to go search for the missing children.

They sprinted for the trees, working their way to the front row, then they went up. Zane went first, with speed and skill from all the practice he'd been getting. Marlow had been calling him "Monkey" lately when they'd get outside. It didn't take him long to zip to the top as she took time to catch up. Soon, they both looked through a break in the upper leaves. The patrol they'd seen had passed through the opening for the road, then went back when they saw the clear path. Marlow and Zane were perched like a pair of birds for ten minutes, watching the various patrols around the government building and down towards the apartments before Zane said,

"How are we going to get home? When this is over, are we going to be in trouble?"

"Probably," said Marlow, then she leaned in. "Look."

There were two grown men, one on either side of a girl no more than ten. She was struggling as if possessed, whipping her head back and forth and snapping at them. They dragged her by the arms, flinching back each time she lunged.

"What in the world," Zane whispered.

"These are the ones they experimented on," said Marlow. "This is what Sam was talking about."

"Oh Mar." But Zane had little defense for what they were witnessing. "Maybe she's sick and just doesn't want treatment."

"I thought the 'Panel prevented illness," Marlow reminded him.

The girl snapped her teeth just inches from one of the men's faces. He let go of her arm to defend himself and fell back, tripping over his own feet. She turned on the other man and swung her free hand, clawing across his forehead and into his eyes. He yelled and shoved her with both arms. She stumbled back, keeping her balance before she caught the legs of the man on the ground. She went down, and he took the opportunity to pin her, straddling her smaller body while his partner came over, loosening a length of rope, starting with her legs, then her arms. They carried her off like a pig on the way to the spit.

Zane turned to Marlow. She was about to give him a solid, "I told you so" when they heard growling in the dark of the trees.

"Whuah…" said Zane, turning around, nearly losing his balance. He was leaning against Marlow and her arms strained to hold the branch. Their eyes were fighting to adjust to the dark. The growling continued, low, just behind where Zane had been sitting. The back door to the government building slammed shut, the sound barely audible, but they saw movement in the tree when it did. A figure sat atop a branch, much like themselves.

"Hello?" said Marlow.

A head poked out. A human boy, just a few years younger than Marlow by their best guesses. He tilted his head, watching them. He had general belt clothing on, a blue shirt and modal-blend pants but no shoes or socks. His eyes were wild.

"Are you…?" started Zane.

"You're one of the missing kids," Marlow finished. "Don't worry, we won't turn you in. What's happened to you?"

"Take," he said in a grunt. "Take from family."

"They did?" said Marlow leaning forward and making Zane hold his own weight so she could point at the building below.

The boy nodded.

"What did they do to you?"

He gave her a puzzled look. She tried another route.

"Did they…" She motioned a needle going into her arm, and his eyes widened as he nodded. "Are you hurt?" He shook his head. "We've got to get you somewhere safe." She looked around. "Shit. We can't get a Rock-Hopper to fly. Where can we hide him?"

Zane shrugged. "This whole place is on alert. He's in a pretty good spot."

"We can't leave him up here," said Marlow, louder than she meant to. "Sorry." She watched the ground. "Earlier, those guys came past here but didn't go all the way to the shipyard. They may not be searching there."

"The *Iris*," said Zane. "The ramp was open. We could find a good spot in there to hide him for now. We know the ship pretty well."

"Yes. We just need to be careful. They may be cleaning or doing repairs."

"Or they left it when they heard the alerts."

"Let's hope you're right." Marlow looked to the scared but stone-faced boy. "We're going to find a better place for you to hide. Will you come with?" She waved for him to follow, not sure if he understood, but they started down the tree anyway. About halfway down, they noticed he'd left his perch.

When they reached the ground, the boy was right behind them. Zane checked the road and waved them on. They all sprinted toward the shipyard. The boy was fast, probably faster than them if he really tried. It didn't take long, and they were on the front side of the *Iris*. The shipyard was still clear of people. Zane's theory didn't seem farfetched. It was likely all the workers cleared out to help search. They swooped around the far side of the ship, heading for the open ramp. Zane and Marlow were halfway up it when they saw the boy had stopped.

"What is it?" said Zane. "Come on."

"We want to help you," said Marlow. "Please."

The boy didn't drop his inquisitive look but slowly approached the ramp, testing it with one bare foot, then the other. When he felt it to be acceptable, he joined them inside. Marlow led them down the hall, trying not to reminisce about her first time on the ship and the doubt that she felt. The doubt that had finally been gone until it was reopened again that day.

She reached their old bedroom and the door slid open. Her thought had been right. Outside of the regular doors to the bath house and workout studio, most others had been locked to them during the trip and only opened to someone else's data-pad. Their room had been public entry until they locked it from the inside, which she did as soon as they were in. The ship's functions ran on a version of the enhanced solar power the TechBubbles used which would be more than enough for some dim lighting. All their guesses had been right so far. The problem was where they could go from here.

A few hours passed. The boy sat in the corner where Honey's nest had been. Zane sat cross-legged on the bed and Marlow paced. They were unable to get much out of him. His vocabulary was minimal as far as they could tell. Something had been done to him but they couldn't get out what it was.

They heard movement down the hall, clunking steps of boots. Marlow put her ear to the door as Zane led the boy to the bathroom to hide. The boots stopped, right outside and a rapping began.

"Marlow? Zane?" It was Arjen. It sounded like he was alone, according to the footfalls.

She knew he could open the door if he wanted. Once the boy was hidden and Zane came back out with a thumbs up, she opened it.

Arjen gave them a confused look as they couldn't hide the guilt on their faces.

"What are you two doing in here? How did you get here? I've been searching the belt..."

"Our ship was acting funny when we left the forest," said Marlow. "We found a panel and told it to return home. It came here and..."

Arjen narrowed his eyes. "You overrode the 'Hopper to bring you here?"

"Home," she said. "We didn't know what that meant but figured it would be better than it breaking down." Zane nodded behind her.

"Then you chose to hide out in your old bunk on the *Iris*? Why didn't you come find me?" His arms were crossed.

"We heard the message," said Zane. "The children were loose or something and people were running around. We don't have data-pads, how were we supposed to call you?"

Arjen considered their words. "Are you two okay? Did you run into anyone on your way here?"

"No," said Zane, too quickly.

"We saw a girl," said Marlow. "She was being dragged against her will. Something was wrong with her. What's going on?"

Arjen sighed. "Remember our friend Sam?" They both nodded. "He got it in his head that girls like the one you saw are being experimented on."

"They're not?" said Marlow. "Then what was wrong with her? With *them?*"

"Of course, they're not. We're not mad scientists out here. It's a condition of the belt," Arjen said, like it was no big deal children were being tackled and hogtied. "Be happy you weren't born here."

"A condition?" said Zane. "What kind? Can we get it?"

Arjen shook his head. "Not as far as I know."

"I thought the *wonderful* NutrientPanel prevented *all* sickness," Marlow said, with no lack of sarcasm.

Arjen sighed. "It does. This is…something else. Smarter minds than mine are working on it."

"What will happen to those kids?" said Marlow. "They had the girl tied up like an animal."

"Believe me, it's a last resort, but the condition is something similar to that. They've become feral. Like they've gone back to a primitive state. We're doing what we can to help them and I'm hoping we'll have a solution soon, but right now, they're a threat when they're free. They don't understand that we're trying to help."

"But they can understand," said Zane.

Arjen leaned a hand on the doorway. "You two don't understand what we've gone through to try to help these kids. They're belt kids, so that makes them all of our kids. If we could—"

"You haven't tried hard enough," said Marlow. "They will listen."

Arjen narrowed his eyes at her. "You're pretty adamant about this. Did something else happen you're not telling me?"

Marlow exchanged glances with Zane and nodded.

"Yes," she said. "But you can't freak out and you have to let us do it our way."

"What does that mean?"

She whispered, "We have a boy in the bathroom. He's scared. He trusts us though. He didn't try to hurt us. If you let us talk him through it, we can get him somewhere safe without having to tie him up and cage him."

"In the…" Arjen quieted his voice, "bathroom? What were you trying to do? Why didn't you tell me that right away?" He reached for his data-pad but Marlow grabbed his arm.

"No. Don't call anyone. We saw what was happening to the others. We were afraid…"

"I get it," said Arjen. "It's not a good look, but you have to understand the belt. We're it. The people here will do what they can to survive."

"I still don't see how that involves locking up children."

"They were causing harm to their parents and caregivers. We had to do something. Now listen to me, the best thing for that boy is to be away from people so he can't harm them. Until we can figure out a treatment, it's the best we've got. Do you understand?"

"Tiffany…" said Zane.

"What?" said Arjen.

"Uh, nothing. Just thinking about the scratches on her. Are they from the kids?"

Arjen nodded. "She's a devoted teacher, but there's just not a need for her right now. There's nothing she can teach these kids until we find a cure."

"She still thinks she can help them," said Zane. "That's why she's so frustrated."

Marlow felt her heart sink. All the terrible things she'd thought and said about this woman were now kicking her in the gut.

"That's it," said Arjen. "I wanted you guys to have a chance to live a semi-normal life here, with the property, the classes and all. I didn't want you involved in all our mess just yet, but it looks like the mess has found a way. Now please, can we take James back to his cell? They aren't just left down there. I swear. We feed them and take care of them but they aren't ready for society."

"He'll follow us if—" Marlow stopped as Arjen was already shaking his head.

"He might follow you out of the *Iris* but there's no way he'll walk back into that cell."

"So, let's find him another place."

"Marlow…" said Arjen.

She turned to Zane and saw only remorse.

"I wish we could do something," said Zane. "But Arjen's right."

"Fuck," said Marlow, grabbing her hair like she meant to pull it out.

All of a sudden, Arjen's eyes lit up. "You really want to help him?"

"Yes," she said.

"Help me get him back in custody today and tomorrow I'll bring you to our scientists. There may be a way you can help."

"Really? How?"

"You'll have to talk to them. Just trust me for now." Arjen pulled a pouch from his pocket and held it out to Marlow. "Would you mind? It's got a sedative but he won't take it from me."

She looked at him incredulously. "Are you serious?"

"It beats wrestling him and tying him up."

Marlow just stared at him until Zane reached out and took the pouch.

"I'll do it."

"Zane." she said.

"We can't leave him here all night." They locked eyes and she broke away first. Zane popped the top of the pouch and went to the bathroom.

The sedative worked fast on the hungry teen. They helped Arjen carry him out of the ship and loaded him into a Rock-Hopper for the remaining transit. Arjen met the guys who'd carried the girl in earlier. They took the sleeping boy and headed into the government building. As the door closed, Arjen let out a long breath.

"Hell of a day." He looked at the Earthlings with bloodshot eyes. "I told Tiffany and Mom I'd meet up with them at the medical facility."

"Oh god," said Zane. "Wes. I'd completely forgotten."

Arjen nodded, close to tears, as if he finally let himself think about it again now that the kids were taken care of.

"If I put you on a ship will you make it back to the homestead this time?"

They both nodded. The unspoken understanding that the first ship didn't just "break down" as they'd said, went silently between them.

"Okay then, hop in." He was leaning over the 'Hopper they'd taken with the boy when he felt them both hugging him from behind. Arjen turned, blurry eyed with sporadic breaths and they all shared an embrace.

"He was a great guy," said Marlow.

"Yes, he was."

Chapter Eleven

The next morning, Marlow and Zane sat at the table between the houses. Honey waddled around their feet, quacking happily while picking at a handful of grain they'd scattered for her. Robin Visser joined them, looking more resolved than the day before. A night's rest, no matter how little they all got, had seemed to do some good for him and Arjen. Tiffany was yet to make an appearance.

Life in the belt would go on. It would have to or life as they knew it would cease. They couldn't count on the Earth to repopulate. It was a wasteland now. It was truly up to their little colony to continue on, and the pressure on Robin and the leadership must have been immense.

He had a remarkable way of not showing it as he spoke to them. The political family roots were strong.

"You two are going with Arjen to meet with our development team today, right?"

"Yes," said Marlow. "I'm not sure what we can do but we want to help. Those kids responded to us, better than anyone else. Maybe…"

"I'm sure they can find use for you. Just remember, the belt is only as good as its next generation. We can't pull brilliant minds from other countries. We're it."

The Earthlings nodded. Arjen came out, well dressed in a black uniform that made him look like he was ready for a wedding or more likely…a funeral. He was matching his father as Robin stood, ready as he could be.

They left as a group on a Rock-Hopper heading for Ceres. Halfway, as they sailed past the belt forest, Robin put a hand to his ear.

"Right, good, send it through."

Robin sat in silence, his eyes growing wider by the second. He looked back at Arjen, shaking his head. After a minute he touched his data-pad.

"What is it?" said Arjen.

Robin shifted his eyes to the kids behind him, then grunted. "Oh, they may as well hear it."

Marlow and Zane were at attention as Robin relayed the message.

"Our other ship, the *Knox*, reached the international space station. Since Sam made all his discoveries viewing Earth from orbit, we wanted them to apply recording devices that would transmit video back to us. Lisa's team boarded the ISS to try to piggyback on some of the tech already available. When they entered, they found the rest of the crew." Robin put a fist to his mouth. "Their flesh was gone. Some of it clearly eaten or torn off. Their bodies were propped up, like you would on Halloween to scare children. Some appeared to be waving. Closed off, in the last lab, they found the rest of the decayed flesh and organs. There was a message carved into the wall, 'He's going to kill all of us so he can live.' It was dated July, twenty-eighty-eight."

"Sam killed them?" said Zane.

Robin nodded. "And pretty early on it sounds like."

Arjen was holding his head. "He was on my ship. He..."

Robin patted his shoulder. "You couldn't have known."

"But he could've done the same to us." He turned. "To *them*."

"We're okay," said Marlow. "I just can't believe Sam would do that."

"Think about it," said Arjen. "He got up there knowing no help was coming. He told us that. He knew he was the last ship full of provisions, but provisions only last so long with a crew. If he could keep them all to himself..."

The whole cabin was groaning at the thought of it all. Finally, Marlow spoke.

"What's going to happen to him now?"

Robin spoke in a hard voice. "He goes to trial."

They landed on Ceres at the government building. Zane and Marlow were, once again, instructed to wait in the 'Hopper while Arjen and Robin went in to meet with Kaia and Oscar. After a half hour, Arjen came walking out with Isolde at his side. They met the Earthlings at the 'Hopper, explaining the trial was taking place, but they were no longer needed in the room.

"It's just crazy," said Marlow.

"It's been a crazy couple of days," said Ice. "We're due for a few normal ones again." She turned back. "How's Honey?"

"She's okay," said Marlow. "Still can't figure out why she can't get her eggs to hatch. She walks the island now in between nesting."

"Oh, you let her free?"

"Yeah. She seems okay with it."

They were all in the ship, and Arjen picked the route. They lifted off the ground, gaining altitude but not leaving the atmosphere. Soon they were crossing a range of mountains. Zane was glued to the window.

"Is that a volcano?" His hands were splayed on the window like a kid in a fudge shop.

"Yes," said Isolde. "But it's not active."

Zane followed the volcano, its split ridges carved over millions of years. He wondered how different Ceres looked before they introduced the TechBubble. He'd wait for a better time to ask this question. On the other side of the range was another group of buildings. These were strangely shaped compared to the others they'd seen. One had a giant dome in the middle, another with a long flat roof. There was the usual cluster of banyan trees around the perimeter but a large maple stood in the middle of the scene, its branches too tall for Zane to ever reach.

They landed and felt the looming volcano behind them. The sun lay in the distance as it always did and Marlow looked up, puzzled.

"Why is the sun always up here? I get that you moved the islands to face how you wanted but isn't Ceres a planet?"

"We redirected its rotation," said Arjen. "Its angle. You know how some places on Earth could have sun for an entire day? We've worked that out, but used the TechBubble to absorb it as energy and spread the heat so it's not roasting over here. The other sides still have light and heat, thanks to the 'bubble, but a lot of that is ocean now."

"My dad would have loved this," said Zane, as they walked to the entrance of the lab building—flat roof, not dome—and entered.

They were met by Mateo Ramirez and Ice's sister, Admani Gammen, descendants of the founding families, and head developers of new technology.

Mateo looked similar to Oscar, light brown skin, dark eyes and a goatee. Admani looked like she was from another family all together. If Ice was midnight black, Admani was closer to dusk. She kept her straight, brown hair at shoulder length and must have given up six inches to her sister. Her thin nose and lips betrayed her as well. They hugged and Zane couldn't look away.

"That's your sister?"

"Zane," said Marlow.

"It's okay," said Ice. "Different fathers. As I told you, not everyone out here is into the whole 'marriage' thing."

Admani broke her hug and reached out a hand. "I'm Admani. Illegitimate sister of Isolde."

Zane laughed and took it. "Sorry."

"No problem." She turned to Marlow. "You're the one, huh?"

"The *one*?" said Marlow. "I'm just Marlow. I don't know about that."

Admani smiled big at her, then turned. "This is my boss, Mateo."

"Boss." He scoffed. "I'd say partner, really."

They exchanged greetings and were led back to a laboratory. There were a couple techs in white coats with goggles and gloves on, working at their stations. Mateo walked them through to a back room with the letters "CSO" on it. There were two seats at the back of the room in front of a long counter with various microscopes and a machine like the one the doctors on the *Iris* used for blood samples. Mateo and Admani sat at the back while Zane, Marlow, Arjen, and Isolde took up a row of wooden chairs across from them.

Mateo rubbed his hands together. "So, let's get right to it. Arjen told me you ran into one of the children yesterday." Marlow and Zane nodded. "Let me explain their condition, the best we understand it at least. We're a few generations into life on the belt. Using myself as an example, my grandfather was Juan Carlos Ramirez, born on Earth and had a son, Oscar. I think you've met my father by now. He was also born on Earth. He was part of the initial colonization. I was born here, on Ceres in twenty-fifty-eight. My wife, Layla was born here as well. She gave birth to our son, Antonio. He's second generation belt. His parents were not born on Earth. He is like the children you saw yesterday."

"What?" said Zane. "Was he…?"

"No," said Mateo. "He was not loose, but he does have the same condition as the other children. Some call it 'the belt disease,' some just call it 'feral.' Whatever the case, feral is a good term for you to best understand it."

"So, they're like animals?" said Marlow. "The boy we met?"

"You could say that," said Mateo. "They respond like animals. They live in their brain stem at all times. Fight or flight, food, survival, it's all they care about."

"Why?" said Marlow. "Just because they weren't born on Earth?"

"That's the part we're trying to understand."

"What about you guys?" said Marlow, pointing to Arjen and Ice.

"Dad was born on Earth," said Arjen.

"Mom," said Ice. "She was a toddler when she was brought out here."

"So, if you have kids…?" said Marlow.

They both nodded.

Mateo took back over, "They would likely end up feral, like my son."

Marlow felt her guts turning as she remembered Wesley's conversation about Tiffany, how she was afraid he'd get her pregnant. She went as far as to give him the cold shoulder so she wouldn't end up with a feral child. From seeing the kids, Marlow understood her concern and felt like an even bigger piece of shit for hating her.

"That's the bad news," said Admani. "Let's talk about the good."

"The bad is pretty bad," said Zane. "You can't have children out here without them turning into animals."

"Yes," said Admani.

Marlow read between the lines. "Oh, Jesus," she said, putting her head in her hands. "When I said I wanted to help…" She looked up at the two scientists. "Even if I have a child here, they'll only become feral on the next generation."

Mateo nodded but had a sly smile as he did. "True but here's a thought. Our parents had a gene, a *human* gene, if you want to call it that. They obviously passed it on to us or we'd all be feral too, somewhere though, that gene is lost. It doesn't move on to the next generation. If we could find that gene, isolate it and reproduce it, we could save the next generation of children out here. *All* generations of children." He put his hands out to signify the entire belt. Before Marlow could reply, Admani joined in.

"We have a chance for a major discovery of what makes us human. What will keep us being human. Otherwise we could all be dead within a hundred years or less."

"That's a nice was to put it," said Marlow.

"It's true," said Mateo. "Every child born to belters has ended up feral. The boy you met was one of the first. With each delivery, we were hoping for the chain to be broken, but it's held true." He lost his smile now. "We're out of options. We've tried everything we can think of."

Marlow's eyes went wide. "So, you *have* been experimenting on them."

"Marlow," said Arjen. "This is not some evil scientist stuff. We're trying to save their lives. They can't just go into a program out here for special needs children. Everyone serves a purpose in the belt. If our entire next generation can't operate the machines…"

There was a long pause in the room. The air was stale with grief and doubt.

"What about them?" said Marlow, finally. "Can we save the kids already alive?"

Admani looked hopeful. "We want to say 'yes,' but we won't know until we can isolate that gene. We'd plan to take stem cells and cord blood. It's where all the building blocks are. Maybe we could find what we're missing."

"I believe it will save them," said Mateo, leaning forward. "It may take time, but just like we've learned to use the hagfish DNA for ourselves, we could use this gene for our children."

Marlow was taking heavy, purposeful breaths. "What do you need from me?"

The faces of the belters lit up.

"You'll do it?" said Mateo.

"If it means we can save those kids and future generations, how can I say no?"

Zane, who'd been silent up to this point, spoke up, "Just how are you getting her pregnant?" He looked suspicious.

Admani laughed. "You'll play a part but not *that* way if that's what you're thinking."

"No, no," he said. "Right, but..."

"Yes," said Mateo. "You'll be the father."

Admani put a hand on each of their shoulders. "The mother and father of the future."

~ * ~

They all agreed there was no time to waste. Once Marlow decided, she wanted to get the first part over with. Dr. Vell was called to assist with the fertilization. Once Zane's sample was ready, Marlow was given a sedative. She awoke on an exam table, alone. Her groggy feeling was minimal and soon, Admani stepped through the door.

"Awake? How do you feel?"

Marlow rotated her neck. "Fine, I think. Can you free me?"

Admani undid her straps and took her hand, helping her to her feet. Marlow walked under her own power, with Admani holding an arm just in case. They met the rest of the group outside the building.

Zane was leaned against the maple tree, talking with one of the lab techs. Mateo and Ice were in their own conversation that stopped when Marlow walked out.

"There she is," said Mateo. "The savior of the belt."

"Please don't call me that," said Marlow. "That's a lot of pressure."

He put a hand on her shoulder. "We're just happy you're here."

"How soon will I…?"

"We'll check back in a week for a blood test."

"Okay."

"Should we go?" said Ice. "It's almost time for the funeral." She waved on Zane and they climbed in the Rock-Hopper. Mateo and Admani met them at their seats.

"It was good to meet you," said Admani. "I'm sure we'll be talking more in the future." She raised a crossed pair of fingers.

Mateo was somber. "Thank you, Marlow."

She nodded as the door closed. The 'Hopper took off toward a white mountain peak in the distance.

Chapter Twelve

Ahuna Mons, the tallest mountain on Ceres, was the chosen funeral home for the belters. A group of Wesley's closest companions, co-workers, and family gathered at the peak. A row of 'Hoppers parked on the east side while a lone one sat on the west. Arjen, his mother, father, and Tiffany each stood at a corner of the casket. They said their final words and watched the belt forest workers seal Wesley's final resting place. The family carried the casket to the lone Rock-Hopper and loaded it on the back. They rode together in silence as the ship lifted off, Wesley and his family taking one last journey together. When the 'Hopper exited Ceres' atmosphere, it turned until the casket faced the direction of Earth and launched it with a small thrust. They turned to watch him go, drifting toward their former home, in reality for some, in spirit for the others. It was a beautiful and terrible way to go, Marlow thought. Better than being buried to decay in the ground but launching him off to space meant…he was really gone.

Hours later, Sam was brought to the same mountain. There was less procession. Only a guard leading him, as he was shackled to his casket. The judges were there, Oscar, Kaia, and Robin. Arjen and Isolde arrived with Marlow, upon Sam's last request.

Sam stood, a foot from his grave, his weak arms held tight by the guard, as Robin read him his final rights.

"Samuel Bozeman of Earth. You are hereby convicted of murder, cannibalism, and endangering life on the belt. A unanimous conviction of death has been decided by the judges. You have chosen to forgo lethal injection and—"

Sam's yelling cut him off, "Because I didn't do that. Any of it!

Listen to the files from the station. It was Captain Young."

Robin raised his hand for silence. "Our team has reviewed the files and there was no record of what you mentioned."

"I can show you when they get back. Just give me a few more weeks."

"Our team is perfectly capable of following your instructions. They did not find any record of wrongdoing. Only your own."

Sam shook in the guard's arms. "Fuck me. You're the murderers! My blood will be on your hands."

"No." Robin stepped forward, raising his voice to match Sam's. He pointed a bony finger. "Your decisions have forced our hands. This is your doing. Now, one more word and your final wish will go unmet as well."

Sam raised his hands in exasperated defeat. He shook his head as the tears began.

Robin put a hand up to Arjen to wait, then, as Sam's weeping slowed, Robin nodded. Arjen took Marlow over, stopping five feet and gripping her arm to stop with him.

Robin began again, calmer, "Your last request was a conference with Marlow. You have one minute."

Sam looked up at her, trying to control his emotions as the guard tightened his grip on his bicep to the point of pain. Sam gritted his teeth.

"Guess I've only got a minute." He sounded like he was about to hyperventilate. "I chose you because you're the only one that even pretended to trust me since I was saved. Looks like it wasn't enough. First thing, I did not kill and cannibalize my crew. Captain Young was the one. When the signs became clear that Earth would never be sending another ship, he devised a plan. At first, he wanted Janet to join him, live out their last days fucking and eating what was left of us."

Marlow made a face.

"Sorry," said Sam. "It's true. Only, Janet didn't agree and told the rest of us. It was too late though. Young managed to kill the other crew members. Janet and I were the last two. She thought she could save me because Young wanted her alive. She'd closed me into one of the labs, trying to talk him down, only, he was in a blind rage at that point. I could hear things weren't going well and I came out, just in time to see him finish the job. I sprayed him in the eyes with biocide, this cleaning spray we used and it gave me the upper hand.

"When I was done, I was truly alone. I—"

"Time," yelled Robin.

Arjen began pulling Marlow away. The guard did the same, leading Sam to the casket. Sam stepped in willingly, then yelled out,

"You were not an accident, Marlow."

The guard was struggling to get him to lay down. Sam's skinny frame fought to get free and continued to yell.

"They didn't 'happen upon' you. Remember that. They use everyone for their purpose."

Robin growled, "Get the needle. His decision goes out the window if he's going to do this."

A silent man Marlow hadn't noticed before, walked over to the scene. He held a needle up, and she realized he was the man who she'd woken up to after her reaction to the medication on the *Iris*. Dr. Crouch? He jabbed the needle directly into Sam's neck and within a half-minute, he dropped to the ground.

Arjen saw the look on Marlow's face as they watched the events from afar.

"Just a sedative," he whispered, as if that made it all right to sedate a man before you send him to the vacuum of space to die.

They loaded Sam into the casket and the judges helped carry him to a 'Hopper. The ride was the same as Wesley's, only no one went with Sam. He took his final journey alone.

Part III

Chapter One

The ensuing months passed on the belt with less disturbances. They confirmed Marlow's pregnancy, and she began weekly checkups right off the bat. Zane began his apprenticeship at the belt forest with Wesley's right-hand-man. His first big project was to build a house for himself and Marlow. They'd sanctioned a special plot of land on the medical complex island. More and more, the gravity of carrying the future of the belt inside her began to weigh on Marlow. They wanted her close by for good reason. If her child didn't "work," then what would? She knew they counted on her. Everyone did.

Of the few trips they let her take to other rocks, she saw it in everyone's eyes. She'd become a savior and it made her sick. Other belt mothers gave her advice, and part of her weekly checkup was meeting with the lone midwife. The part that worried her was the advice she got was all labor-related, as if there was no plan for her to ever touch the child once it left her body. Though it hadn't been discussed, she found this to be a likely outcome. It was a question she should ask, would *have* to ask before the time came but she didn't dare. Inside her grew a human, possibly the last human to have any humanity left in them. It was equally invigorating and heartbreaking. Her child could be the savior for these people or end up as a science experiment gone wrong. Either way, it wouldn't really be hers.

She still held out hope for a third option. In the perfect world inside her head, they would get what they needed during the delivery, between the cord or whatever, and they let her raise the child from there.

No testing, no experiments, just her and the child. It was something she never imagined for herself. Even before Jason died, she didn't think of children, or future generations. She had accepted that they might be it, and they would just have to enjoy their days together. Even if help came, it would be so they could live comfortably in a shelter during their last days.

Three months in and Marlow went from feeling like she had a temporary parasite living off her that would soon be handed over to the development team, to feeling love for something the size of a plum. While she envied Zane—his job of procreation over with—moving on to a "real" job, she'd finally come to accept her role of staying alive and growing a human.

It was dull work, outside of the emotions, but came with no shortage of guilt. Everyone had to work to support the belt, contribute in some way. She was pampered, in a way, and it didn't feel right. She was beginning to think of the development and medical staff as her family. Zane would be at work for twelve hours at a time. Sometimes he'd even go out after work. It was the most they'd been apart since they'd met. She gave it to him once when he got home later than ever, complaining that he'd be out all day, doing who-knows-what while she sat at home watching the skies, hoping he was all right. He'd even been late to respond to her data-pad message. Zane hadn't taken the critique well, but in the end, told her he'd be home as soon as his shift was over the next day so they could do something fun together. She spent the rest of the night feeling like a piece of shit, shaming the poor gay-boy whose only real commitment to her had been survival on Earth, not to father her child or be in a sexless marriage. They'd survived: he didn't owe her anything anymore.

She apologized the next morning, telling him to stay out as long as he wanted and that she'd find something else to do. To her surprise, he actually took her up on her offer.

It was another night when she'd stopped watching the skies and decided taking a walk around the trees would do her some good. It would be her third of the day, but she needed something to do. She marked her place in Wesley's old e-reader and set it down on her dresser. Honey had a grade-A nest in their new place. It was one of Marlow's few jobs she'd tasked herself with, fixing a good place to lay eggs that would never hatch.

"Come on," she said, standing up, and Honey knew the command. They walked together most days and Marlow joked to the doctors that soon they'd be waddling together, though she wasn't showing yet.

Their house was off to the side of the medical complex, partially hidden by the limbs of a banyan tree. The path was a simple loop across the front of the complex, then sweeping around the rear under the trees and back to the house. Honey slowed her, but she was desperate for the companionship, even if they spoke a different language. She carried the duck for the first part across the yard, then she'd set her down to scavenge for good leaves to bring back to the nest. Marlow was the only one ever scavenging. There were times she felt like the duck just humored her so she'd have something to do. There were also times they had full conversations while they walked. Ducks were good listeners after all. She heard the buzz of a Rock-Hopper landing as they turned the corner behind the buildings.

Under the banyans was a world of its own. It reminded her of Earth when she was a child, though it was never this clean, it had the smell of life. Her mother used to take her to the only park in the small town she grew up in. It was lined with trees and had a swing set that was still in order. With each push, she'd get a little closer to the sky. She remembered her mother's smile over her shoulder. Each time she'd look back and say, "Higher." until her mother said she'd gone as high as she could, laughing and shaking her head at her daughter's fearless spirit. With each memory it clicked into place further how much of her mother's existence was to give Marlow a good life. From finally leaving her dad, to begging for a vacancy at a shelter, then finally taking to the road during the war until they could find a safer place. Was that how she'd be as a mother? Giving up her life just to see her child try to touch the sky from a swing set? Would she get a chance?

She was stirred from her thoughts when they rounded the last medical building, holding some choice nesting leaves, when she saw a figure circling around the back of her house. She dropped the leaves and picked up Honey, walking quietly to see if she could sneak up on the nosey neighbor. She followed the path she'd seen the figure take, around the back, heading towards the front door. When she got to the edge, she peered to see a man knocking at the door.

"Marlin?" she said, stepping out from the shadow. He turned, his face lighting up.

"Little Earthling. I'd heard the news, you're gonna be a mother."

She stopped. "I am, if you want to call it that."

"I'd call it that. Are you excited? Feeling funny?"

"All of that I guess." She was petitioning the dirt for something to say, but all her pregnancy-related thoughts were too jumbled to say aloud.

Marlin smiled, digging in his pocket for something. "Oh, I'm sure you get enough pregnancy questions already. What I want to know is, do you still know how to play cards?"

Marlow invited him in. She did, in fact, remember how to play cards. They traded victories as they talked.

"So, you're with the 'Panel team here?" she asked.

"When I'm not flying."

"Right. Were you on the ship that went back?"

He nodded. "That was a dull one. Probably because we'd just landed and Robin scrambled a team together and my dumbass volunteered to go back."

"Why?"

He shrugged. "'Cause I like to fly. I don't know. I don't have anyone waiting for me back here. I figured why not? After the camera placement, we hit Mars on the way back and did some gathering. I know it's another planet and all but once you've seen it, you've seen it. It's been good to be back for a bit."

"What about the space station, did you see all that?"

"No. It was Lisa's team that boarded it. I heard it all firsthand but that was the highlight. Otherwise they just installed the tracking cameras."

"Do you think...?" She lowered her cards.

Marlin waved a hand. "I don't know what to think. It was some awful stuff they found. If he did all that, well, he deserved what he got."

"But they never proved it."

"Him being the only one alive was some proof, and our people confirmed he'd been eating the corpses."

Marlow shuddered. "Ugh."

"How about another topic?"

"Okay, but one last thing. Before he died, he said that I wasn't an accident, that I wasn't happened upon and they'd *use me for their purpose.*"

Marlin waved a dismissive hand. "He said a lot of crazy things, now some of that is true if you think about it. It's no accident that you're here. You fought to survive the Earth in the condition it was in. That's no small feat and you *are* here for a purpose." He motioned at her belly. "But that part just worked out."

She eyed him for a few seconds.

"Ever the inquisitor," said Marlin. "Now tell me how you're finding life on the belt."

They talked and played cards for the better part of two hours. It was the best time she'd had in the past few months. She made Marlin promise to come back and visit her again.

He left with a goofy wave and headed for the 'Hopper as she stood in the doorway watching the stars as he flew off.

Chapter Two

Three months later, Robin sat as his desk in the government building. A call came through from the communications team. He answered it with a tired voice,

"Visser."

"Sir, we've got a message from the cameras."

"It spotted the ship?" Robin sat up, his dreary state out the window.

"Yes sir, sending it through now."

"Thank you."

Robin pulled up the video on his data-pad. The ship was small as it broke Earth's atmosphere but it was clear what he was seeing.

"The *Mack*," Robin said, shaking his head in disbelief. "Lana…"

~ * ~

Arjen and Isolde arrived to meet with the counsel within the hour. They'd reviewed the short video on the way over. Arjen replayed it a second and third time before Ice made him stop.

They stood in front of Robin, Kaia, and Oscar. Arjen was doing the talking.

"We've got to move now." He paced the room as he spoke. "Sam said the last trip was six months ago. They may not be back for another year. If ever."

Oscar held up a hand. "Now just think about this for a minute. Where have they been the past three years?"

"We don't know until we ask them."

"Even if you leave this very minute you probably still won't catch them. We must rely on the camera to tell us where they're going."

Arjen slammed a hand on the table in front of them. "Then it will be too late."

Robin stood, raising his arms to calm the room. "Please, everyone. We all want to know who is on that ship, but we need to make the wisest decision here. If it's really Lana's team out there, why haven't they come back to us?"

"Who else would it be?" said Ice.

"We don't know," said Robin. "That's why it's a risk sending a team to chase this old ship."

"We have to try," said Arjen, looking to the door as if he meant to steal a ship and go on his own.

"Just wait a minute," said Oscar.

"I agree," said Kaia to gasps from the room. "It's worth a shot and we still have Lisa's team if Arjen misses them."

"Hold on," said Oscar. "We can't authorize another trip just to chase ghosts."

"They're not ghosts," said Arjen. "You saw the video. Now take all the time you need *authorizing*. I'll be getting the ship ready for travel." He turned on a heel and Ice followed him out, smiling.

Oscar gave an angry look to Kaia while Robin stared at the door, confused as to what his next steps were.

~ * ~

It took a few torturous days for the *Iris* to be prepped with enough materials for the NutrientPanel to make it the minimum six-week journey. Marlin slaved at it, itching for another trip after months of belt life. It was on the third day since the video came across their feed that Arjen and Isolde boarded the ship on Ceres. He looked out the display window, squinting, as if he would see the *Mack* go flying across the sky and they'd throw their flashers on and take off after it like an old cop show.

Ice strapped into her seat and waved him to sit as the engines rumbled to life. He finally did, clicking his harness into place with shaking hands.

"Have you slept at all?" she asked, putting a hand on his.

Arjen twitched his shoulders. "I've got time once we're in the wormhole."

"Okay." She took her hand back, leaning into her seat, ready for the kick of takeoff when the engines cut. Ice put her hands to her face, not knowing what was happening but not wanting to see Arjen's reaction, whatever it was. They heard the lowering of the ramp. One of the counsel had changed their mind, probably not her mother. Arjen was out of his seat within seconds, cursing his guts out when he saw a lone figure coming towards them.

"Dad?" said Arjen. "What is it? You can't cancel the trip now. Not after being the deciding vote." Arjen felt like a teenager pleading for a later bedtime.

Robin was puffing by the time he reached Arjen. "I didn't change my vote. You need to see this first." He pulled up a video and cast it to a nearby display. They watched Earth, full of gray clouds with a blip in the middle they knew as their old ship the *Mack*. It exited the atmosphere and passed the ISS with a clear flyby. The camera rotated to follow the moving object. It wasn't leaving the way it had come. It was heading past the moon.

"Is it...?" Arjen asked. "Did it...?"

Robin nodded, patting his son on the shoulder. "We think it entered the wormhole. It's heading our way."

Chapter Three

The belt was a different place for the following weeks. Marlow noticed the development team's interest in her waned even the slightest. All the talk about the "ghost ship" coming back had people split on what would be aboard the *Mack* when it arrived. *If* it arrived.

For mostly non-superstitious people, Marlow heard more mystical discussions than ever before on the belt. She hoped to get a front row seat but highly doubted they'd let her anywhere near a ship full of unknown threats. Zane, however, would find a way and be her eyes and play-by-play. He'd promised her that. She, on the other hand, was tasked, as always, with growing the child like nothing was going on. They focused on her keeping her stress levels down, but her boredom levels were at an all-time high as a result of it.

When they'd first heard about the ship, her weekly card game with Marlin got cancelled, as he was needed to prepare for the trip. She knew he'd wanted to go. He enjoyed their card games, but she could tell he was just as antsy to get out of the belt as she was sitting around it each day.

The good thing was, they'd entrusted her with a data-pad shortly after pregnancy. As if now she finally needed the ability to open doors and program Rock-Hoppers to take her places. No one owned the 'Hoppers. There were a finite amount of them flying around the belt by request. If she took one, most people wouldn't make much of it; they'd just call another. That's what she counted on during her outings. As long as she showed up to her doctor appointments, which were built into the data-pad, they didn't bother her. It was probably the reason she was given one in the first place.

She'd been out a few times in the weeks before Marlin stopped showing up but nothing major. They'd turned her away at the belt forest. She'd barely gotten a smell before they loaded her back up and sent her away. After the incident with Wesley, none of the workers would dare be responsible for the future of the belt riding around in her stomach standing under any of those tall trees. So, she'd found her way to the library. There were tons of Earth history to bury her nose in, and a kind, old librarian named Linda who was happy to help her find whatever she was looking for.

It wasn't until the week before her card games ended that she met Rami. He was a second-shifter with a love for small American towns. She found him pouring over pictures of Winter Garden, Florida in its heyday, around twenty-twenty.

"Doesn't look like that anymore," she said. When he looked up, she added, "Much colder too."

Rami smiled at her, and she knew her comments were a mistake. He had the awestruck look a lot of people got when they found out who she was, like meeting a celebrity they always had a thing for.

"Will you tell me about it?" he asked, patting the seat next to him and she found herself sitting.

Winter Garden was pulled up on a display in front of him as he swiped from slide to slide of the cute downtown area.

Marlow pointed at the pretty trellises lining the walkways. "Those would've been firewood long ago. Not that anyone would be living down there."

Rami's mouth was open and he caught himself. "Did you live there?"

She shook her head. "No, just passed through. I was in Inland by the end."

"That's awesome." He cupped a hand over his mouth. "I mean...not the way it ended. I just..."

Marlow held up a hand. "I get it. You like looking at it when it was good. Who doesn't?"

"You too?" he said, clicking a 'home' icon. "Want me to bring up Inland? I'm sure they have—"

She was shaking her head and squinting. "No, it's not cool to me. I lived it for too long. I hope to never see it again."

Rami let out a breath, his hand frozen at the screen, not sure what to bring up now. Marlow pushed herself up from the seat.

"Sorry to be a buzzkill. I'll let you get back to it."

"Oh, okay. I mean…you don't have to…we can look at other stuff."

"I'd really better be going." She'd turned and headed for the 'Hopper she'd procured outside, expecting him to follow, but he just sat stunned from his encounter with the Earthling. Marlow was a person who'd been to some of the places Rami dreamed about and lived to tell him they were all uninhabitable. She truly was a buzzkill but she was good at it.

She saw him again a few days later when Linda found her a file on duck care. She was amazed they'd even kept one from the archive as she pulled it up for Marlow on a screen at a personal table. Marlow was leaning in, trying to read a part on eye discharge when she heard Rami's soft, but excited, voice.

"That's right, you have a duck."

She turned around, half frightened, half annoyed. "Oh, hey, yes I do. I'm guessing you don't know much about caring for one, do you?"

"Can't say that I do. They look like amazing creatures though."

"Yeah, until she gets this junk coming out of her eye and I can't figure out if it's serious or if it just needs to run its course. We don't really have medication for ducks out here."

"That sucks," said Rami, leaning on the table.

She feared he wasn't going to leave, then he sat down at the adjacent table. "Best of luck." And went to clicking away on his own screen.

"Thanks," she said and went back to her file.

After reading for a bit, she glanced over and saw Rami was looking at pictures of Inland. She held her gaze for a while, and he didn't seem to notice, then it was her turn to comment.

"Go back," she said and he jumped.

"Hey. Didn't see you." He was holding his heart.

"Sorry. That last picture of the house. Can you go back to it?"

Rami swiped the screen, and she saw the house she'd visited on her last day on Earth. It was the place where she'd slid across a cold, dirty floor, hoping to be able to do anything with a container of flour and a Paula Deen cookbook. Her lips tightened, thinking back to how bad it was. The wannabe-rapist, the cough, the starvation. Rami saw the glistening in her eyes.

"Should I...?" He held his hand to the home button.

Marlow rubbed at her eyes. "No, sorry. Just brought back some memories."

"You want to sit? They have some others too."

"No. I need to go take care of Honey. She's got this eye thing."

Rami looked at her for a bit. "Oh, the duck, right?"

"Yeah."

"Do you need any help?"

Marlow stopped as she was clearing her screen to leave. "Help?"

"With the duck. You being pregnant and all."

"It's just a duck. I can handle—"

"No, sorry. I wasn't implying...I just see you here a lot and you're always alone..."

"*You're* always alone," said Marlow, crossing her arms.

"I am," he admitted. "It would be nice to not be alone once in a while, but I'm not really one to go meet people at Club Earth."

Marlow laughed. "Yeah, me either. Zane took me there once. Feels like a meat market."

"That's kinda the idea."

There was a lull and Marlow felt her body pulling for the door. "I've gotta get back to Honey. I should be okay to take care of her but what about tomorrow?"

He looked confused. "Tomorrow?"

"You going to be here again, looking at pictures of Florida?"

He smiled. "Oh, yeah, probably."

"Want to play cards or something instead?"

Rami didn't hesitate. "Yeah. Definitely."

They picked a time and she headed off, excited to have a card partner again so soon after Marlin left.

~ * ~

For the next few days, they met and played cards, all kinds of games Marlow had never heard of. Their data-pads would display their own hand while they pulled up the games on the main monitor at the table. Marlow realized how old-school Marlin was for carrying around a deck.

It was a week before the *Mack's* arrival that she finally invited Rami to her house. It was a night that he wouldn't have to work and late enough that Zane would be home.

The second phone number Zane received at Club Earth was the one he'd ended up dating. He was a tall, red-headed guy who liked rubbing Marlow's belly as it grew. She wasn't fond of being touched sporadically but liked him enough even so.

"I've got a great game the four of us can play," said Zane. "Peter and I played it with Dave and Dan the other night. You'll love it." He was laying across the couch, his head in Peter's lap as Marlow lounged in the chair. She was getting to the point of having one comfortable position that quickly wore itself out.

"Just don't be weird, okay?" said Marlow.

"Weird?" said Zane. "How do you mean?"

"You know how I mean. He is just a friend of mine. Don't try to sell this as some double-date, couples thing."

"I wouldn't dream of it, Mar." Peter poked him in the side and he giggled. "Okay, maybe I've already been calling it that."

"Yup," said Peter. "I'll try to keep him in line tonight."

"I'm glad somebody's taken that job from me," said Marlow.

"Hey," said Zane, but Marlow held up her hand for silence.

"I think I hear him." She got up and brushed down across her stretched blue shirt as the boys giggled. "Shut it."

She went to the door and realized it would be weird to swing it open before he knocked. She stood waiting until two quick knocks sounded in the house. She looked back at the boys, giggling once again and waving their hands for her to open it. When she did, Rami looked surprised, standing with one hand behind his back and the other brushing an eyebrow.

"Hey," Marlow said, after three, awkward seconds.

"Hey." Rami swung out his other hand, revealing a bouquet of magenta flowers tucked nicely into a thin vase. "For you."

Marlow took the vase, admiring the blooms, recognizing them from the cherry trees she'd seen in the belt forest. "Thank you. These are lovely."

She ushered him in as Zane and Peter sat up straight, looking far from innocent. Marlow gave them an evil eye.

After moments of stale conversation, Zane brought up a game on his data-pad and sent it to the projector. They all joined in and the competition was on. Peter and Rami had the advantage of having data-pads their whole lives. Marlow and Zane caught up as the night went on. They broke into teams, and after Marlow and Rami beat Zane and Peter's team in a word game four times straight, Peter threw up his hands and walked off to the bathroom.

"You forfeit?" said Marlow, taunting Zane. "Giving in to a feeble pregnant lady and her nerd friend from the library?"

"Hey," said Rami.

Peter came back into the living room holding a bottle. "I was gonna save this until you went to bed," he pointed the top of the bottle at Marlow, "but you beat us so bad, I had to bring it out early."

Marlow waved it off. "Have at it. I don't mind. Where'd you get that anyway?"

"Some guys homebrew it on the security team."

"Oh, I bet it's gross. Thank God I can use pregnancy as an excuse."

Peter gave her the finger. "You try working twelve hours with a dude who never stops talking about his ex. You'd take what you can get."

Zane laughed. "He's talking about himself." Peter gave him a playful punch in the arm.

"I don't bring up Brian that much, do I? Now I'm self-conscious." He made a face at Zane.

"No, Honey," said Zane, pulling him into a hug. "I was just messing." Their duck came walking out of the room at the sound of her name. Zane looked over the couch. "Sorry, other Honey. My bad."

"That's her," said Rami, excitement all over his face. "Can I see?"

"See," said Marlow. "There she is. You want to pet her or something?"

"I think so. I'm not sure."

Marlow called Honey over and pulled her into her lap. "Go ahead. She doesn't bite. She might just nibble a little."

Rami stroked her back and she gave him a mumbling quack for his efforts.

"She's so cool," he said, looking her over. "Her eye's okay now?"

"Yeah. I tried a few things from the book, but I think it took care of itself in the end."

"Good girl," said Rami.

Marlow lifted her and set her in his lap. "I've gotta pee. You take her for a minute."

Rami looked scared, like a person being handed a newborn for the first time.

"I'll be right back," she said, seeing his expression. "Hand her to Zane if you need to."

It turned out he didn't need to and spent another ten minutes petting and examining the duck. Peter and Zane were getting loose-tongued the further they got into the bottle. Rami stayed dry in support of Marlow and soon the redhead and his Indian boyfriend were at the door.

"I'm going to make sure he gets home safe," said Zane with a sly smile.

"Right," said Marlow. "Make sure his bed is still soft while you're at it."

Zane saluted her and she smiled as they walked out. Rami raised a hand, then turned back to her.

"I guess...should I let you get to sleep then?"

Marlow glanced at her data-pad. "Unless you wanna watch a movie or something."

"Yeah, that would be cool."

He stayed and she put on the romantic classic, *Terminator 2: Judgement Day*. They settled into the couch, a gap between them that Marlow closed quickly. As the movie picked up, she put a hand on his, claiming that that part always scared her. Rami locked his fingers into hers. As the T-800 was lowered into the molten steel, Marlow had a head on Rami's shoulder, listening to his breathing. It was a comfort she hadn't felt in a while, like she was in the right place at that moment.

When the credits rolled, Rami stroked a hand across her hair.

"You still with me?"

Marlow looked up with sleepy eyes. "Sorry, I think I am getting tired now."

"That's okay," said Rami. "I had a nice time. Maybe you can come to my place sometime soon."

"I'd like that." She stood, waiting for him, licking her lips quickly before he looked up at her.

Rami faced her, and for a second, she thought he might kiss her, then he leaned in for a hug, said goodnight and headed to the door. She watched him climb into the 'Hopper and fly off, shaking her head as he went out of sight.

Chapter Four

Marlow didn't see or hear from Rami after that night. The way it ended, she realized almost seven months into pregnancy was not the time to start a relationship. Rami obviously knew that. She was like a monkey in the zoo to him. He must see her and Honey in the same light, interesting to look at, observe, even pet a little but it stopped there.

She'd never felt so dumb. It hadn't been since the kiss with Wesley that she'd been so embarrassed.

Zane and Peter were discussing plans to move in together which meant Marlow would be alone for good after that. Who would want to be with the girl carrying the belt's future? That would be a lot of pressure even after the pregnancy. Again, she thought back to Tiffany and her schooling. Her animosity toward the woman faded long ago, but her fear for her own future never left. Fear that she'd be a fucking queen-bee, only used to populate the hive until they figured out how to fix what was lost from Earth. Zane would make his contribution, but she'd carry it for nine, damn months while they treated her like a china doll.

It was three days before the *Mack's* expected arrival when she woke from a nightmare. They'd delivered her baby, but had to perform a c-section and did so with a rusty machete, much like the one she'd been attacked with her last day on Earth. The baby came screaming out of her, clawing the sides of her already mutilated stomach. It killed the doctors, then they were alone with corpses and no one to sew her up. The baby turned, crawling on all fours like a hunched animal, ready to pounce. Then it jumped at her.

She'd flinched awake hard, smacking Zane with a loose hand. She'd decided that day she would talk to Tiffany, not to bury the hatchet but to find out what her real assignment was back when she and Zane were handed off. She never seemed happy about it and maybe Marlow could get out of her why.

Marlow felt lucky to see the Visser homestead was empty of Rock-Hoppers when she landed. Sure, it meant Tiffany could be gone as well but it was a starting point. Finding her way to the school or *basement* with the feral kids would be a harder mission, one she hoped to avoid.

The walk felt strange, recalling all her first memories of being in the belt. When they'd first landed and their world was upside down. The stars and sun in view at all times. Jupiter as well. The canopy of trees she'd practice kickboxing under. The table where they always started their pointless schooling and Wesley, the memories of him hurt the most. His jokes always pulled her out of her moods, usually moods she'd got into because of his wife. Their kiss. She hadn't forgotten it and as wrong as it had been, it was still a sweet memory to her. Mainly because it never went further and it told her he cared for her as much as she had for him. If only Rami was as funny as Wesley...

She approached the door to Tiffany's house and wasted no time. She rapped on it three times, then turned away to check her back as if anyone would be following her. The door opened to the confused but model-like face of Tiffany.

"Marlow? Hey." She stretched her arms out and they bumped bellies in a hug. Marlow looked down, they had matching humps, blocking the views of their feet. She didn't know what to say and thankfully Tiffany said it for her.

"It's his," she said. "It must have been on our last night together because the next day was the accident."

Marlow's eyes were wide. "Wow. I...that's amazing."

"Yes." She took Marlow's hand. "I should've told you by now. I've just...it's been a hard time and a good time over the past six months or so. I waited for a long time to even tell the family."

"I understand. I know you were a bit afraid of raising a child the way things are."

Tiffany's eyes narrowed. Marlow was afraid she'd already said too much. Wesley told her that when they'd been alone, never in front of his wife. Did she know? Did he tell her about the *day* or even days in the forest? Tiffany seemed to let it roll off her shoulders and led her to the outdoor table.

"We pregnant ladies need our rest," Tiffany said as they sat. "So, what brings you out here? I'm the only one around if you were looking for Arjen or Robin."

"No, actually I wanted to catch up with you," said Marlow. "I didn't know about *this* but I'm happy for you."

Tiffany nodded and Marlow felt like she should continue.

"Are you happy?"

"Oh, yes, I…" Tiffany waved a hand and tears began forming. "He would've been a great dad. I think you know that. It was his dream to have children. Never mine. When the kids here continued to be born with their disabilities, I dedicated my life to trying to help them, to teach them, regardless of their condition. I just wanted to leave that at work. At the end of the day, I could come home to my husband and do whatever we wanted without the worry that our child would soon be locked up with the rest of them."

Marlow nodded, not sure how to follow that or get back to her real questions.

Tiffany continued, "It's just me now. I'm it. I am excited though. When I lost Wes, I dreaded every day, waking up and him not being there. But now our child will live on as a daily reminder of him."

There were no safe questions, so Marlow asked anyway. "If the child is…?"

Tiffany reached over and patted Marlow's belly. "That's what you're for."

Marlow felt that old anger creeping up. The condescending tone in her voice, like Marlow was just a servant that was carrying a child so Queen Tiffany's could live a fuller life.

"Is that why I'm here?" Marlow asked bluntly.

"Excuse me?" She was teetering already, like a boxer about to go down and Marlow knew she had to strike.

"I was picked up for that reason. I was going to be the *mother* whether I wanted to or not. Wasn't I?"

"Marlow, now, I don't know what you're talking about."

"Really? So, you're just that bad of a teacher that you found a career for Zane within the first week but couldn't find anything for me?"

"Now wait a minute. I am a great teacher, no matter what you—"

Marlow stood up, barley towering over the woman. "I'm sure you are if you're actually teaching and not just biding your time. Just admit that you knew. That your brother-in-law went out there to find somebody to give them babies to experiment on." Her fists were clenched at her sides, fighting to hold them down and not point fingers. Tiffany stood in defense.

"You silly little girl. You think you're that important, don't you? That our whole way of life out here depends on you?"

Marlow heard her words but could see the fear in her eyes betraying each syllable. "Fine then. If I'm just some Earth scum Arjen picked up on his shoe, I'm sure you won't miss me if I take a jump off of Ahuna Mons in the morning." She turned on a heel and headed to the 'Hopper.

"Marlow…" Tiffany raised a hand but didn't dare to follow her.

Good luck without me, Marlow thought. *I hope your baby turns out normal.*

Chapter Five

It was not subtle when Arjen turned up at her door in the morning. Zane had just left for work when the knock came. Marlow waddled over and opened it, sighing when she saw him.

"I'm not really gonna do it," she said, turning from the door and walking back to drop a handful of grain for Honey. "Come in, though, if you want."

Arjen was speechless but did step in, resting a hand on the couch.

Marlow grunted as she stood up from her squat to feed Honey and leaned on the other end of the couch.

"Did she say she thought I was actually going to jump?"

"Well…" Arjen started, "you make threats, I felt like I needed to come by and see you."

Marlow ran her hands down her body. "Here I am, all two hundred pounds of me."

Arjen laughed. "There's no way you're topping one-forty, even with the baby."

"Feels like more."

"Probably because you've been underweight for years and now, you're healthy and with child."

"Yeah. About that…"

"Let's sit," said Arjen, then pointed back at the door. "Unless you've got a mountain to climb."

"Shut up." Marlow sat down across from him on the couch.

Arjen rubbed a hand through his blonde locks and looked her in the face. "Ice wanted to be here but I told her no."

"Okay…"

"This is not on her. Let me start back a bit. You remember the story of my dad, right?"

"Being dropped off by his parents to come out here?"

"Yes, at thirteen. Really, he was pledged to the belt, if you will, at four. His whole life has been planned out for him to be out here as a representative of our family. To continue on the political tradition and join the government when he was old enough. So, that's what he did. Then he had me and tried to pass that on…it's hard being fit into a box when you're so young. I think you know that. So, you know the story, I rejected that and went to become a gatherer. I swear that might have had something to do with my parents' separation. They'll never admit it, but Dad worked so hard to prime me to be the next to join him in our small political party out here. When I rejected it, it hurt him. It took him some time but now we mostly get along."

Marlow had been taking in the story with a confused look. "Why are you telling me this?"

"Because the belt had to do something. When Dr. Ramirez was dying, he tasked Oscar and my father with finding a solution to the feral children. After he died, my father was adamant about fulfilling that wish, maybe more so than Oscar since he was still mourning his father. So, he took it and ran with it. The clear, scientific data we had was, if you were born from parents also born on the belt, you'd become feral. We'd tried with different combinations over the years but eventually all the Earth-born people were outside of reproductive age."

Marlow felt heat wash over her. He was finally admitting it but she had to let him say it aloud.

"We set up the trip to Earth, the only other place people might still be alive. It was a small chance, but we had to take it." He pursed his lips at her and continued, "You can thank Zane for sitting on the roof every night. That helped us find you. We did come across others but they weren't in the condition for space travel."

"Or breeding?"

He gave her a pathetic face. "Yes."

"How did you know I was?"

"Blood. When I wrapped your foot, I took the best sample I could.

I got a positive result on the portable tester I brought with while you guys were inside the church. I highly doubted the accuracy but it was good enough for us and Dr. Vell said we were a go. We'd been searching for weeks. Our hope was all but gone when we found you."

Marlow was facing him, legs crossed on the couch with her jaw tightening over and over. "You sure didn't act like it."

Arjen shrugged. "That's why they sent me. The political background I did have was good for 'relations' as Dad put it. You were our last hope but you were a human in a desperate situation. We didn't want to spook you. I learned early on that you wouldn't do anything just because we asked but only if you'd truly decided it was what you wanted to do."

"So, what then, the kids getting out, Sam…what was all that?"

"Unplanned. Completely."

"Bullshit. What were you going to do if that hadn't happened? Just wait to see if I got knocked up by my *gay* friend?"

Arjen's silence lasted long enough for her to answer her own question.

"I was already pregnant?"

He nodded, solemn. "Dr. Vell didn't want to wait. Dad didn't either. As soon as I turned over the sample a pregnancy plan was set into place."

"But the first time I saw her…"

"Your first visit was truly to create a special 'Panel to get you healthy again. She did confirm your fertility then but your next visit was the one."

"When I had the reaction…?" Marlow dragged her last words, knowing how wrong they were.

There was no reaction to the medication. She was out so they could fertilize the egg. Her breathing picked up. Arjen was waiting, as if he expected her to punch him straight in the face but she wouldn't give him the satisfaction. Somehow it would mean they were even. He stole her from Earth, lied to her over and over, had people impregnate her against her knowledge and let her believe she was doing it out of her own free will. They would never be fucking even.

She stood up, walked into the bedroom, screamed, then came back out. Arjen looked like he was on the verge of tears.

Marlow's arms were crossed as she spit her next sentence at him, "So, did Daddy tell you to come over today and calm the fucking water? You great diplomat. You lying piece of shit."

Arjen stood up. "No. And you can't tell him." He lowered his voice. "I might have a better offer for you."

Marlow's eyes went wide. "A better offer? From *you*? Why would I trust you ever again?"

"Because I received a message. It was from the ship heading toward us. It was from Lana. If you haven't heard, I have a *history* with her. We were both gathering leaders. She had her ship, the *Mack*, and I had the *Iris*. We were always on separate trips, working opposite of each other. But we messaged, and when we were home at the same time, we'd spend time together. I wouldn't call it a relationship. We were apart too much but we always talked, by time delayed messages depending where we were, about one day, finding a place we could just be together. They were just fleeting thoughts, when you miss someone and you want to say something nice, share a dream with them. But our place couldn't be the belt. The baths, the tech, everything here is great but something is missing and our children are proving that to be true. We were never meant to live out here. We're aliens and we always will be. Maybe we can genetically engineer a gene to replace what we're missing from Earth but for how long? Eventually it'll be something else and we'll run out of time."

Marlow tilted her head. "What are you saying? You want to move back to Earth? To Mars?"

"Further. Lana's message says she found another wormhole and found a place, *our* place."

"Where?"

"Far away. I don't really know. The wormhole trip takes months, she says, but there's a planet. Three actually. But one in particular that she says is what we've been searching for all along."

Marlow was pacing the room. Her anger at Arjen was fading and that was making her angry all over again.

"So, you drop this on me that I've just been used all along and now you're saying what? You want me to come with? On another trip to some new world? Is that the offer?"

Arjen nodded. "You, Zane, I'm still figuring out who I can trust with this."

"What about your dad? You said you weren't telling him."

"Yes. Like I said, all his cards are here. He's not leaving and I think he'll oppose us leaving."

"I can see why. It sounds like you don't mean to come back from this trip."

"If it's what she says it is…"

Marlow nodded slowly. "What happens here? If we leave that is?"

"Well, first, you have the baby. Let them do what they need to do, then we go."

"Without the baby?"

"It probably depends how all that turns out."

"Fuck, Arjen, do you hear yourself? I don't know if I could just leave my child up in a lab and take off."

"So, we take the baby. Give them the cord, the stem cells they can get from it and we go."

"This is insane."

"Staying here where we don't belong is insane. You being an All-mother that keeps popping them out for science is insane."

Marlow threw up her hands. "You're the one who stole me from Earth."

"It was the mission. I had to do it for our species. I thought Lana was lost forever. I didn't know what she'd found. All that's changed now. When we found you, there was no other option for us or for you. Now there may be."

"And we just trust her, after years missing out there?"

"I do."

"Why hasn't she come back until now?"

"She was probably scouting it out, making sure it was safe for the rest of us."

Marlow sighed. "I've gotta talk to Zane."

Arjen stepped forward and grabbed her arms. "You have to understand what I've just told you. If any of this gets back to my father, or Oscar…"

"Does Ice know?"

"Yes."

"And…?"

"She's still deciding. But she won't talk. In the end, she'd want us to do what was best for us."

"So, who can I talk to?"

"Me, Ice, Marlin, Zane…just don't let him get to talking with his boyfriend about it. And no data-pads. This cannot leak."

"But they all know she's coming back. Do they think she just plans to stay?"

"She'll take care of that. She'll have a story."

"More lying. Can't wait."

"When necessary."

Marlow rolled her eyes at him. "So, I just have the baby and we slip away quietly in those huge ships."

"We'll figure that part out when we get there."

Marlow was pacing again until she stopped at the bedroom doorway. "This was the strangest conversation I've ever had. I should've punched you when I had the chance."

Arjen turned a cheek to her. "You still can if you want."

She waved him off. "My heart's not in it."

~ * ~

Later in the afternoon, Marlin stopped by with a deck of cards.

"You hadn't been answering my messages," he said, standing in the doorway, looking around. "I was afraid you'd found a new card buddy."

Marlow winced. "I kinda did, but come in."

"What? Are they here? I can…"

"No, no. Just come in." She led him to the couch where they

usually set up their games. "I thought you were leaving, I had to find another person to play with."

"Yeah, it was a scramble until we realized we weren't going, then I had to fix the mess we'd made. Took me a week all together." He set down the deck. "Look, I'm not here to play cards. I think you know that."

"Yeah."

"Arjen told me he discussed the plan with you."

"I just can't believe you all want to leave here."

Marlin gave her an intense look she'd never seen before. "You ever meet somebody that made you realize all the somebodies you'd met before were just not the same?"

Her mind immediately flipped to images of Jason. She nodded but didn't reply.

"That's how we feel. Me, Arjen, Ice. We go on the gathering trips because being here doesn't feel like home. You notice how cool and calm Arjen is when he's out there and how antsy he is on the belt? It's no trick. We all feel it, even though we were born here. Tell me you don't."

"I feel a lot of things." She patted her belly for emphasis. "But I think I know what you mean."

"I'm not here to tell you what to do. I just wanted to talk to you before it all goes down."

"I understand. It's just a lot to think about, especially coming from Arjen after everything he's told me."

Marlin put his head in his hands. "Don't be too hard on him. He was trying to save the belt. Really just taking orders from above."

"I'm done talking about all that, Marlin. You knew about it too. Don't tell me you didn't."

He put out his arms, palms up.

Marlow stared him down. "That's what I thought."

Marlin grabbed his cards and stood up. "Any apology I'd offer would be weak. Just know, despite everything, we want to make this right. Don't let your pride keep you here."

Marlow stood up and had to balance herself on the couch. "My *pride*? What the fuck, Marlin."

Marlin raised his hands, backing toward the door like he was at gunpoint.

"Think about it," he said and ducked out.

Marlow was out shortly after him.

Chapter Six

The TechBubble surrounding the clothing factories waned. Carol, who'd clothed most of belt with her team, stood in the cotton field, watching with horror. Her feet were frozen in the dirt. Her top assistant, John, came running up and grabbed her arm, dragging her from her spot.

"Carol. We've got to go."

Her feet found her way, stumbling behind John like a drunk being dragged from a fight. A Rock-Hopper loaded with four others sat open. There was already a fight going to keep the door open or seal it up. John ran, pulling Carol and waving his other arm.

"Wait! We're coming."

The 'Bubble wavered like the air above an open flame. It was shrinking in as it failed. The temperature was dropping rapidly and the 'Bubble was barely able to keep the atmosphere in place. John and Carol were still thirty yards back as the other people in the Rock-Hopper were starting to see their breath.

"We can't wait anymore," said Michelle, one of the sewers. She clicked on her data-pad and the others watched with shame as the glass door sealed shut. The process took a few seconds to establish the seal and it had never dragged on so long.

From the edge of the field, Carol raised a hand before she collapsed. John looked back to help as the TechBubble failed. He turned toward the 'Hopper with pleading eyes as he felt the oxygen rush from his lungs. He fell forward into the shriveling grass, feeling his body swell as he lost consciousness. The cabin was full of screams and sobs as the Rock-Hopper took off.

~ * ~

Oscar paced as Robin and Kaia looked on. His son Mateo stood next to a sobbing man, Gilbert, from the TechBubble team. Oscar finally stopped directly in front of him, ignoring his condition.

"What are you going to tell their families?"

"I don't…" Gilbert couldn't get his words to form.

"You were too busy to care about their lives?"

"No sir, I just…" Gilbert had no real excuse. Going from rock to rock, day after day, checking the working parts that supported the TechBubble was tedious work. Especially when they rarely had any major issues. It had been almost a year since he'd even had to evacuate an island for repairs. Even then, the 'Bubble hadn't failed like it had today. He could admit to himself he'd gotten lazy. He'd marked off the clothing manufacturing island as "all systems check out" when he'd not even gotten out of the 'Hopper. It was just bad timing all around.

"How many others should I worry about?" said Oscar.

Mateo jumped in. "I've got Nick hitting them one by one, thoroughly."

His father didn't even look at him. "Let's hope he actually checks them out." He went back to pacing the room. "You've endangered the belt, maybe all of the belt. We won't know until other 'Bubbles start failing. Your sentence will be decided—"

Mateo interrupted. "Then let him out there to help."

Oscar gave him the look only a father can. "You think I'm going to let him back out there?"

"He's a good tech. He got lazy. We can all agree but holding him here isn't going to do any good."

Robin caught Oscar. "He's right. If we're concerned about TechBubble safety, we need to get everyone out there to check them out. Just as a precaution."

Oscar turned to Gilbert, now with his head up and eyes still red. "Are you fit to check systems?"

Gilbert nodded.

"I need an audible answer."

"Yes, sir."

"Then get your ass out there."

It took the better part of a day to do a full system check on each island. In the end, they found the clothing manufacturing island to be the only one to have the freak system failure that it did. They didn't know if this was concerning or good that only two people died from neglect. Mateo convinced his father to lighten Gilbert's sentence on the argument they needed 'Bubble techs more than ever and so far, there wasn't a next generation of them coming.

It was less than twenty-four hours before the *Mack* made its triumphant return. Part of the belt thought it to be a reunion with their former neighbors and friends, others felt it to be the dawning of a mass exodus. Arjen was cautious with who he let into the secret group of "explorers" as he called it. "Deserters" would likely be the name they would be called if it all went as planned. The belt was quietly splitting into pieces with very few knowing about it.

Marlow and Isolde were still on the fence as Zane was content with staying. They lounged around the living room as Zane made his points.

"We just got here, Mar. Not even a year ago. Life is good. I don't want to spend any more time crammed into a spaceship sailing toward an unknown land. We've done that. Can't we just enjoy it?"

Marlow wanted to bring up Peter as his reason for staying but felt it unfair to blame him for being happy and content.

"It's different for you," she said. "I'm happy for that but I don't get to go work in the forest and come home to my cute red-headed boyfriend. I'm just here to deliver them their future."

"That's a pretty commendable job. You should be proud."

"*Proud*, Zane? I'd be proud if I chose it. They impregnated me a few weeks into our trip out here without telling me. That's pretty fucked up."

"Yeah, but it's worked out so far. Hopefully the baby gives them what they need."

"And if not? What then? They'll probably want another. Do you think I'll have a choice on that one either?"

"That's pretty selfish, Mar. These are their kids. You have something no one else does and you want to keep it for yourself because you weren't asked politely."

"Oh, shut the fuck up, Zane. You try carrying a baby knowing that when it's born, it's just going to be an experiment. It's not just about the pregnancy."

Zane looked at her, tilting his head. "You want to *keep* it now?"

Marlow sunk her head to her hands. "I don't know but I feel it moving. You've felt it. It's crazy, having this little human inside me, *our* little human. That's probably the weirdest part. At the beginning it was easier but now...I don't know. I guess I'm just connected and I'm afraid they'll take it from me and I'll never even get to look at it or hold it."

"Oh, come on," said Zane. "I'm sure they'll let you hold it. They may even let you keep it after they figure out the gene thing."

Ice had been listening quietly, now she was rocking back and forth, shaking her head.

"Ice?" said Marlow.

She stood up. "I've gotta talk to Admani." And walked out the door.

Chapter Seven

The next morning when Zane was at work, Marlow returned from a walk with Honey to see a 'Hopper landing near her house. She was happy to see a bouquet of white flowers clutched in Rami's fist as he looked around for her. He smiled as he approached.

"Hey." He held out the flowers. "Still got that vase?"

She took them. "Yeah. What are you doing here?"

"I uh…I'm gonna be honest. I was advised to stop seeing you."

"What?"

"After that night we watched *Terminator* and all. I kinda bragged to the guys at work and word travelled. The next thing I knew, by the end of my shift, Robin Visser stopped by to 'have a word with me' about you."

Marlow's brow furrowed. "What did he say to you?"

"N-nothing bad. Just that you were a very important piece of the belt and you couldn't be distracted right now. He was afraid a relationship may change your mind about things."

Marlow stomped her foot like a four-year-old having a tantrum. "That…oh, he thinks he can control every part of my life." She looked up at Rami and noticed he'd backed away a few steps. "So, why are you here going against his advice now?"

"Because Arjen told me to come."

Her face split into an unbelieving smile. "What does Arjen know about any of it?"

Rami scratched his dark hair. "I don't know. He said he heard it from the librarian or something. It's a small colony. Everyone knows everything."

She raised her eyebrows. "Do they?" And waited to see if he'd say anything about their potential trip.

"I mean, word gets around about these kinds of things. I think I knew Zane was dating that Peter guy before you even did."

"Hah, that's possible. I don't get out much. So, Arjen just sent you by? That's all?"

Rami shrugged. "I mean, I wanted to come but I was afraid. He'd talked to me about it and said to make it soon and not to wait. I guess he's talking about the baby?"

Marlow sighed. Rami was not in on the secret. It was probably for the best but it meant she could only tell him so much.

"Probably," she said finally, looking at the flowers in her hand. "I should get these to the vase. You want to come in?"

He looked around. "Yeah, just don't…"

"I won't tell anyone."

They went in the house and she gave one last look around before locking the door behind them. Rami gave her a look and she reassured him with a smile.

"Just making sure nobody surprises us. Have a seat, I'm gonna grab that vase." She tucked into the bedroom and grabbed the dying, magenta flowers out of the vase, rinsed it out in the bathroom and replaced them with the white ones. She brought them out and sat next to him with the flowers displayed on the table in front of them.

"So, what have you been up to?" she asked. "Besides avoiding me, that is."

Rami laughed. "Working, fearing Robin Visser coming to my house while I'm sleeping."

"Tell me that's a joke."

"I mean, it is, but I did have a nightmare about it."

She patted his leg. "Really?"

"Yes. I don't know what it is about that guy. Just freaks me out."

She took his hand and stroked it. "So brave to come see me anyway."

"Yeah, I just *missed* you I guess."

"I actually missed you too."

"Actually?"

"Well, a few weeks ago, I would've never thought…I'm sorry,

I'll stop while I'm ahead."

"I get it. I'm a bit of a weirdo. My Florida obsession and all."

"Yeah. And other things."

He turned to fully face her on the couch. "Like what?"

"Like, why you haven't kissed me yet. Is it the belly?"

"No, no. I was just afraid of what you'd think and you know, women of the belt can be pretty straightforward. It's not always on the men out here."

"Fine," said Marlow and leaned in and kissed him. His shyness went out the window as he kissed back. His lips were firm and decisive, unlike any of his personality she'd witnessed so far. They went back and forth for a minute. Marlow teased him with her tongue, then tucked it back in. Rami grabbed the back of her head, running a hand through her hair while his other locked fingers with her. When they pulled away, they were breathing hard. She was smiling at him, her hair hanging down to her breasts as he watched her reaction.

"I should've done that a week ago," said Rami. "I'm sorry I didn't."

"There's still time," she said and went in for another kiss.

This time she raised up on her knees, leaning down to kiss him as his hands found their way to her back. Soon he was on her neck, brushing her hair gently to the side while making her skin shiver with his lips.

Marlow let out a moan then scooted back, pushing him off of her. Rami looked quizzically at her as she re-centered herself on the couch, then she pushed him onto his back, his head resting on the arm. She straddled him the best she could with the space she had, looking down at her belly as her cotton dress hung over it.

"Is this weird?" she asked.

He put a hand on each side of her. "No. This is…great."

Marlow smiled and leaned down, kissing him and running her hands down his body. He was taking it in as she worked her hips. She pulled her head up, using a hand on his chest to prop herself, while her other hand went between his legs.

"Oh…okay," he said, meeting her hand, gripping her wrist. "Are we going a little fast?"

"I don't…" Marlow said.

"I just don't want you to regret this afterward. We've only known each other a few weeks."

"We don't know what happens tomorrow, Rami. Right now, we have each other. I'm okay with that if you are."

His hand loosened on hers. "Okay, I just—oh."

Her hand was back in place, gripping him through his pants. He let her work for a minute, then reached under her dress and found the edge of her panties, sliding his fingers over them until he found his way inside. She released him and sat up straight, letting out jagged breaths as he warmed her up. After a minute she was tugging at his pants, standing just long enough to drop her panties as he stripped himself. Marlow climbed back on, her dress hanging down over them as he entered her.

"Ah," he said as she picked up the pace. Her hips and belly surrounded him in a way he'd never felt before. It was such a good feeling being encompassed by her, but he couldn't relax. He could feel the end not far away. Marlow saw the expression on his face change and she slowed.

"Is this okay?"

He nodded. "Yes, just…I'm not going to make it long."

She leaned down and kissed him on the forehead. "Just promise me you'll keep going until I say."

He shuddered as he agreed and she continued. It wasn't long before Rami felt himself release. He let out a cry and gripped her thighs. She kept pumping, tightening her hips and focusing on harder, forward thrusts. Then she was crying out, squeezing his shoulders as her hair hung in his face.

They were both sweating and out of breath. Marlow kissed him and stared off. She found it hard to look at him now. She couldn't help but see Jason on their last encounter, when he still had the lungs to do anything strenuous. He'd looked up at her and smiled, saying that they would find a way to beat the Earth, together. She'd held him long after the sex was over, subconsciously knowing to take in that moment. Now she was reliving it with someone else and it made her heart hurt.

"Marlow?"

She looked back down at Rami and smiled. "Thanks for visiting me."

He smiled back. "Yeah, hey, any time."

Chapter Eight

Arjen was up early with a message on his data-pad. *I'm back, but not for long. I hope you've made your decision.* He stumbled out of bed and onto the lawn, watching the skies from every angle. He went back in, threw on some clothes and was on a 'Hopper headed for Ceres within minutes.

The shipyard was teeming with energy. The workers stood ready while Robin, Carlos and Kaia huddled together. Marlin stood under the *Iris* with Captain Davis. Isolde stood alone until Arjen landed. He climbed out and joined her.

"Surprised you didn't sleep here," said Ice.

He held up his data-pad with that morning's message.

Ice nodded. "Don't you have the inside track."

He cleared the screen and stretched his back. "You decided?"

Ice cracked her neck. "You the recruiter?"

"I just want us to have a chance at something else."

"You don't think being here is a chance? We could've been born on Earth."

"You know what I mean."

"This your head or your heart talking, Arjen?"

He paused for a few seconds, looking up at the sky as the *Mack's* broad frame came into view. "Both."

They touched down, the big bay door lowering to the dirt and the crew of the *Mack*, lost for the last three years, stepped out. There was a smattering of applause as old friends met up for hugs, handshakes and pats on the back. There were only four of them, three men and one woman. Lana was not with them. One man, Williams, shook Robin

Visser's hand, looking around as he did.

"Carol?" said Williams. "She didn't come?"

Robin shook his head and put an arm around the man, leading him away from the group to tell him about the TechBubble failing on Carol's island.

Williams took in the story with a stern face. "I understand," was all he said.

Arjen greeted a few of the crew, looking past them, hoping to catch a glimpse in the blackness of the ship bay. Isolde was next to him, her eyes went wide when they saw it, two figures walking out of the darkness onto the ramp. One was unmistakably Lana. The other was unlike any being they'd seen before. It was tall, rising over six feet with a long neck stretching down to its back. It had two human-like arms coming from the upper body and four legs spaced out like a dog or horse, only the feet were like monkey's, four fingers and a thumb. Its neck and head were smooth and gray. Its eyes bigger and wider-set than Lana's.

The figure was talking to Lana as Arjen stopped at the bottom of the ramp. He couldn't understand what it was saying, the garbled, guttural words coming out in short bursts but Lana seemed to. Its mouth was wide, almost ape-like with rows of flat teeth.

Finally, she came down the ramp, the creature trailing behind.

"Arjen." Lana wrapped him into a hug and for a second, he forgot all about the monstrosity behind her.

"You're here," he managed as a crowd gathered behind him, staring, some holding up their arms in defense. Lana broke away.

"Everyone," she said to the group. "This is Bruuth. He is from the planet Wyan. We met along our travels. He and his people are the reason we're still alive. They took us in when we were lost."

The crowd was speechless. Lana's smile teetered but held on her face. Bruuth stood behind her, like an attack dog she'd told to hang back. Robin finally broke the silence.

"Well then, welcome Bruuth."

He stuck out a hand and Bruuth looked to Lana for confirmation. She nodded and he reached out one of his arms. His thick, three-fingered hand engulfed Robin's.

Arjen stared at Lana, dumbfounded. She hadn't mentioned this part in her messages.

Robin and Bruuth broke their handshake and Robin pulled in Lana for a hug.

"We thought you were gone for good," he said.

"I did too," she replied.

Robin looked at Bruuth who was taking in all the attention with furrowed brows.

"Will he understand me? If I…?"

Lana shook her head. "A few words here and there. Mostly curse words though. I can translate. What do you want to say?"

"Well, obviously you and I have a lot to discuss but start by welcoming him here and explaining that Oscar, Kaia, and I would like to talk with him."

"Okay," she said to Robin, then turned to Bruuth and began making guttural noises.

Bruuth lowered his head, listening, then grunted back to her.

Lana said, "He said he would love to talk but first he wants to take a meal with his companions on this new land." She looked around. "Do you mind cutting down a limb off that banyan? They're vegetarians and well…let's just say they won't let a piece of it go to waste."

Robin tilted his head at the trees in the distance. "They eat trees? Wait, there're more of them?"

"Yep, two more aboard the ship. We didn't want to overwhelm everyone, so Bruuth volunteered to be their ambassador. Just keep everyone off the *Mack* for now, okay?"

"O-okay." Robin looked back to Oscar and Kaia and they were more shocked than he was.

He motioned for two of the crew men who'd planned to check out the ship and explained the situation, sending them on a mission to cut down a tree branch.

After Bruuth thanked them for the meal, he dragged it up to the ship and disappeared. No one dared board the *Mack* with three aliens aboard. Arjen finally got a moment with Lana while they had their meal and Robin was distracted with other crew members.

They were walking slowly away from the shipyard as they talked.

"I feel like you left out a detail," he said.

She smiled. "You kind of had to see the Wyans to believe me. Didn't you?"

"I would've believed you. Is that…" He stopped to look around, then whispered, "Is that where we're going? Wyan? *His* planet?"

"Yes. It's a beautiful planet. It makes anything we've done here look like a poop."

"A *poop*?" Arjen laughed.

"Sorry, Wyan speak. Obviously, a different word." She made a sound that almost sounded like "glub." "Means poop though and it's commonly used to describe things of waste."

Arjen shook his head in disbelief. Not only had Lana disappeared for the last three years, found another world, and lived to tell the tale but she'd met an alien race and learned their language. He realized his former attraction to her as an equal, a partner, was turning into admiration and awe as she spoke.

"I received your reply," she said. "What's this about the pregnant girl?"

"Marlow. She's a long story but she is the proposed solution to the feral children. She's from Earth. Her sperm donor is also from Earth. Mateo and Admani think they can use the DNA, cord, blood, stem cells, all that, to replicate the genes that are missing and…"

Lana held up her hand. "Then what? What other genetic disorder will they get from being born out here?"

He shrugged. "They don't know. They hope this will solve it."

She stopped short of the line of banyan trees where Zane and Marlow had hidden out the day the children broke out.

"You know it won't, Arjen. Not long term."

"I know."

"People need real air, water, wind, rain, and food. My god, do we need real food. We've given up all of that for convenience and we didn't see the outcome."

"We've done well for a long time out here."

"Two generations, and that's it. Then it's all but over."

"Maybe not if Marlow's—"

"They're going to use her until she's sucked dry of every useful gene in her body, then they'll dispose of her. Am I wrong?"

"My father…" He stopped himself.

His father would lead the charge on just what Lana said.

Lana put her arms on his shoulders, her wavy, chestnut hair stopped just below her chin as she looked straight into his blue eyes.

"I want you out of this lie they're living out here."

He looked back almost hypnotized by the green orbs piercing into him.

"I do too."

Lana's lips curled up as she leaned closer. "Then let's get everyone we can on that ship and get the hell out of here."

He pulled back. "But the pregnancy…"

Lana sighed and let go of him, starting the walk back toward the shipyard. "How soon is she due?"

"They plan for a c-section if she doesn't deliver in a week."

"Okay, but we've gotta try for it to be sooner than that. I'm not sure how long the crew can hold out and not get into the fact that we're not staying."

"I'll do what I can but how are we going to load and transport enough 'Panel for everyone when we don't even know how many are coming?"

"We have a cryo-room on the *Mack*, remember?"

"Huh," said Arjen. "I didn't think you ever tried it."

"Desperate times." She looked down as she spoke. "Getting out there the first time was…challenging, to use one of your dad's diplomatic terms. We were afraid we were going to lose the whole crew. The wormhole was never ending. We were running low on 'Panel. Finally, I put them all in cryo-sleep. I had enough supplies to last me a month on my own. It was a lonely time but someone had to be awake if we ever came out of it." She looked away for a second. "I thought of you every day. I wrote you a bunch of notes I hoped you'd find one day." She shook her head, pursing her lips to keep the tears at bay. "Don't worry, I destroyed those sappy things.

"I found myself going to the cryo-room and talking to the crew even when they were under. I'd just stand at the door, day after day, telling them stories, I mean, God knows I had nothing to report. I made up stories about this new place we were going to find and how we'd all live happily ever after. I was borderlining on insanity by the end of that month I spent alone. I remember one of the last stories I told them was of the wormhole coming to its end and dropping us directly into Alpha Centauri. It would be so bright and warm, I said. The next day I did see a star but we weren't in it. It was much smaller than the sun but there were planets orbiting it. I focused in on the one that gave me the best readings. That was Wyan. The rest...well, I'll tell you on the way out there, before we all go to the cryo-room."

Arjen was shaking his head slowly. "I...wrote you some notes too. Though, I think I still have them."

"Will you read them to me?"

"On the way," he said. "First, we have work to do."

Chapter Nine

Marlow waited on Zane's report of the landing. He should've been back by then and she circled the medical buildings, watching the sky for signs of a 'Hopper. Finally, she saw one when she was making her turn around the back of the buildings. She waddled back as fast as she could across the yard in time to see Arjen climbing out.

"Arjen? What happened up there? Did you see Zane?"

"No. I'm not sure he was there but don't worry, I'll give you the details."

She waved him inside and she sprawled across the couch, forcing him to use the chair. She felt weird having anyone else sit on the couch after the way her and Rami used it the day before.

Arjen held up his data-pad, showing a picture of Bruuth standing next to Lana.

"God, what is that?" said Marlow.

"That is a native to the place we're going."

"What? Is it a monster? It looks like it would eat us."

"Actually, they're vegetarians."

"Are you fucking kidding?"

Arjen smiled. "No, I actually witnessed them demolishing a tree branch."

"That's crazy."

"Yeah, but Lana is in with them. She knows their language and is even working on a translator for the rest of us."

"Cool, I guess."

"Yes, but the thing is, we need to leave soon. The crew was one thing, having Bruuth here is going to throw off the whole plan."

"Then why did she bring him?"

"I don't...I didn't ask."

Marlow sat up. She hadn't seen Arjen so off his game since he last talked to her about losing the ship and having nightmares about the crew. He was drunk then, and though he said "crew," she now knew he meant Lana.

"She's special to you, huh?"

He looked out the window as if he'd see her. "Yeah, but listen, I want what's best for us. You, Ice, Zane, Marlin. Whoever we can trust. We know that's not here, don't we?"

"Yeah but—"

"So, we have to be prepared to do what we must."

"What are you saying, Arjen?"

"If things go south, we have to be prepared, baby or not."

"What about the belt? I thought we'd agreed to give them the cord at least."

Arjen rubbed his nails through his hair. "If this choice is to give it to them and have to stay or leave while we still can..."

Marlow nodded slowly. "Okay, but it won't get that bad with your dad, will it?"

On cue, Arjen's data-pad notified him of a message. He looked down.

"Shit."

"What?" said Marlow.

"They've already got Lana with the judges. He told me he'd wait until tomorrow. Fuck."

"What does that mean? They're questioning her?"

Arjen was up, heading for the door. "Yes, and if you remember how Sam's questioning went, they didn't waste a lot of time."

She caught him before he was out. "What are you going to do?"

"Intervene. Try some diplomacy. If that doesn't work...just get ready. Do you understand?" She nodded and Arjen finished with, "If I come or I call, just be ready."

He ran to the 'Hopper and took off. Marlow started clicking on her data-pad.

~ * ~

Zane arrived at his house to see Rami getting out of a 'Hopper, smiling and waving.

"Hey Zane, you ready for the movie?"

Zane gave him a confused look as he brushed past him and went into the house.

"Mar, Mar!"

She popped out of the bedroom holding Honey and Zane wrapped her into a hug.

"I got the message. What's happening?"

She looked over his shoulder at Rami, standing in the doorway looking concerned.

"Is everything...?" he started.

"Just come in," she said.

He did, closing the door behind him and Marlow began,

"Thanks for coming. I had to get you both here without saying too much. So, Zane, I had to use the code words. Sorry if I freaked you out."

"Code words?" said Rami.

Zane said, "Monkey feet. It's our code from back on Earth. In case we came across a bad situation when we were out scavenging or people we didn't know showed up at the bunker. It's a warning call to hear those words." He looked at Marlow. "I'm glad you're safe."

"Yes, sorry."

Rami looked at her, still confused. "You just told me you were starting a movie and I had to get here as quick as I could or you would start it without me. I was confused but I figured I'd humor you. Why didn't you just tell me?"

She looked around as if she was checking the room. "I didn't want it out there on a data-pad."

"What is happening?" said Zane.

"The ship. Arjen just came by. Things may change with the trip. They're interrogating Lana. Arjen is afraid they're not going to let her...let *us* go."

"Really?" said Zane. "They wouldn't force you to stay, would they?"

"Wait," said Rami. "Where are you trying to go? On another gathering trip?"

Marlow sighed. "Further. I'm sorry I didn't bring it up yet but I've only just decided I'm going. The ship that came back found another planet, a lot like Earth. A place where kids won't grow up to be feral. There's rain, wind, and everything."

"Like Earth?" said Rami. "Why wouldn't you tell me? That sounds amazing."

"Because it's likely causing civil war right now. Do you think Robin and Oscar are just going to leave here? They and their families have spent years colonizing the belt. They don't plan on ever leaving, only building it bigger."

Rami's eyes changed like a light bulb went off. "And they need you to build it. So to speak."

Marlow nodded. "You can see why some would be opposed to it."

"After you have the baby..."

"They may want another."

"No, but...would they?"

"If it doesn't work. If my genes don't do it. I could just keep having children while they figure it out."

"God," said Rami. "I really hadn't thought of it like that. Visser would do that?"

"If he knew he was losing me. That's why I called you two. I'm not asking anything of you. I just want you both to know why I've decided to go."

Zane was nodding slowly, looking at her with tears in his eyes. He hugged her again.

"Can I go?" said Rami. "Would they take me?"

"Yeah," said Marlow. "But don't do it just for..." She couldn't finish.

He smiled at her. "I'll do it for me, if that's okay. Being around you will make it even better. Hey, they may even have a city like the ones in Florida."

She smiled back through tears. Zane let her go, holding his forehead to hers for a minute then pulled away.

"I've gotta go see Peter." He kissed her on the head and was out the door.

Rami watched him go then turned back to Marlow.

"This is crazy. I…should I pack? I don't know what to bring. I've never left the belt."

She hugged him. "You'll figure it out, you nerd."

"So, how soon are we talking?"

"I don't know. I'm waiting to hear from Arjen. It probably wouldn't be a bad idea to be packed but it could still be a week if he can smooth everything over."

"Well, goodness, I'd better go make sure I'm ready then. Should I come by later and we actually watch a movie?"

"That sounds good. I'll let you know if I hear anything from Arjen."

Rami grabbed her hand and kissed it. "I'll see you later then."

"See you."

Rami went out the door.

Within a minute, Honey was quacking and waddling at her feet. When Marlow was nervous the duck always picked up on it. Marlow went to the bedroom, only to be followed, then back to the living room, almost stepping on a webbed foot.

"Jesus, Honey. You just want out for a bit?" The duck headed to the door. Marlow followed. "Just stay close to the house."

She opened it and heard a horrible scream. She peeked out to see Rami get thrown against a Rock-Hopper, his head bouncing off of it in a dizzying wobble. He staggered away and focused long enough to see Marlow at the door. His face was a bloody mess.

"Monkey!" he screamed, ducking a punch thrown by one of the men assaulting him. Then he finished as he was grabbed from behind, "Monkey fee—" His words cut off when his face smashed against the solid glass of the 'Hopper. It didn't crack but something did as the man had him by the hair now, giving him two more solid collisions with the 'Hopper before letting his limp body hit the ground.

Marlow let out a whimpering moan. "No…" Reaching out a hand before she saw the men turn toward her. She slammed the door behind her, turning the barely used lock. As she was dragging the chair to block the door, she remembered Honey. Marlow paused, looking around the room wildly, hoping she'd followed her back in when the door was kicked in. It swung open with a bang against the chair she'd been pushing. She stumbled against the couch as the men came in.

"We're not here to hurt you," said the first one. Though she could see Rami's blood on his shirt.

There was nowhere to hide in the house. Marlow didn't wait, lunging forward with a kick she'd practiced many times with Ice's guidance and without. It had been many months though and it landed softer than she'd hoped. Still, the man was caught off guard trying to field a kick from a woman a week away from delivering a baby. She swung a fist at the other man, grazing his face as he ducked back. Her second blow landed, a knee to the midsection and he groaned, doubling over as she raised an elbow to strike the back of his head. She was focused until then, going through her fighting routine to disable an opponent until she saw Honey laying a few feet outside the door, her neck unnaturally bent backwards. She wasn't moving. The sight gave Marlow just enough pause for the first man to catch her elbow just before it struck his partner. He spun behind her, getting her in a rear chokehold. Then the second man was on her. She felt cold steel in her neck shortly before her eyes closed.

Chapter Ten

Marlow awoke, groggy and shivering, though she could feel blankets on her. Her head felt sweaty and feverish. Her vision wouldn't clear for the longest time and she feared she'd damaged it in the fight. She remembered Honey with a sickening pain. Had she tried to defend her? A little duck with no real claws and smooth bill? It didn't matter, what mattered was she was dead and Rami? She didn't know. She could only hope they'd left him alone after the initial attack. Even then, his injuries would be terrible.

She realized she couldn't feel much of her body. Her chest and up was at least tingling. The rest was hard to tell. She tried to rub her eyes but her hands wouldn't move.

She blinked, trying to clear the film. She could make out the room, familiar but she wasn't sure why without more clarity. She wanted to scream but didn't want to alert the men if they were still nearby. Finally, Marlow could tilt her head enough to rub her face on her shoulder. The first thing she saw was the sheet pulled up just below her breasts. The real fear struck her immediately and then she did scream.

They had gotten their baby after all.

Marlow screamed but her voice was weak. She had to force herself to calm down, realizing if they took the baby, what kind of scar she must have, if they even stitched her up. Surely, they would though, they'd want her alive to make more, assuming they didn't already have what they needed. Maybe they did and she'd been dumped like trash. Her usefulness gone and now she'd been discarded and forgotten. Her heart ached for her child. She didn't even get to see it. She didn't know its gender, its features, if it had hair or was bald still. It was still odd to think it might look like Zane. It might even *favor* him.

The real thought hit her that she may never see it. If she died or not, they may never let her, "for the good of everyone," they'd say. Would they even give it a name? Or would it just be Test Fetus #1? The thoughts enraged her but her body was powerless to act. All she could do was cry as she sank into another bout of shivers.

~ * ~

Marlow passed out for a bit. She didn't know how long, only that time passed and she hadn't been conscious. She realized the distant banging sounds were what woke her. She craned her neck. There was a door on the left side of her that she watched with eager attention as the noises got closer. Soon she heard thumping footsteps and the handle jiggled. There was heavy breathing just outside but no voices. One of the men from earlier tucked in, then the second. They looked frazzled, only checking to make sure she was still in the bed but otherwise ignoring her.

"Do you think he...?" started one but the other shushed him, holding his ear to the door.

He whispered low, only for the other man to hear. Marlow watched them, unsure what they were afraid of and not knowing if she should yell for help.

Her answer came quickly with the plodding sound of running. There must have been three or four people coming. She decided whatever the outcome, her situation was about to change drastically. The plodding stopped and one of the men motioned the other to help him lean on the door. "There," could be heard from the hall. One of the men looked at the other with a deep-rooted fear in his eyes. He let up just enough as something slammed the door. The man went flying off the door, tripping backward and taking out a rolling, instrument tray. The other man doubled down, planting his feet when a second slam came. He was raised up off the ground for a second before landing back, shaking it off and repositioning himself. The wood of the door was cracking and splintering with each hit. He had to know, the next one would be it, but still he held. The plodding could be heard, then a grunt as Bruuth came crashing through the door, shoulder lowered and four feet pushing hard. The man flew back into his partner and they continued into the wall, hitting it with a cracking sound as they fell into a heap.

Bruuth was focused on them while Lana came over to Marlow.

"My girl," Lana said. "What have they done? Oh, god." She looked her over like she didn't know where to begin.

Marlow recognized her from the picture Arjen showed her.

"My arms," said Marlow.

"Okay." Lana went to work to free her arms. "Just be careful. I think…"

"They took the baby," Marlow admitted.

Lana looked past the sheet. "Yes. Let's just focus on you right now." She looked over. "Bruuth?"

He joined them and made a grunt even Marlow could translate as sympathy for her situation.

Lana spoke to him in the Wyan language. It was odd to see a human pulling it off but he seemed to grasp every word, nodding before reaching two strong arms under Marlow. Lana stood next to him, supervising.

"Does it hurt?" She looked down at Marlow's blanket-covered waist.

"No," said Marlow. "I think I'm numb."

"Right, well, now's the time to move you then. Come on."

She waved for Bruuth to follow her and they went back out the splintered door. Marlow realized during the events that she wasn't far from home. The medical facility hallways were empty. She wondered if Mateo and Admani were around, hiding in offices, or gone. *Who'd performed the c-section?* she wondered. *Them? Dr. Vell? Dr. Crouch?*

The entrance came into view and Lana held up a hand. They turned back, heading toward the rear exit under the banyan trees where Marlow had worn a path during her pregnancy, though, her pregnancy was over now. Lana pushed open the door and Bruuth ducked through. They turned the corner and saw Marlow's house. The 'Hopper still sat there with blood dried down the side of it. *Rami's blood*, she thought. Though Rami was nowhere to be found. Honey either, she noticed. Lana ran over to the 'Hopper, activating the door.

"Wait," said Marlow. "I have a bag packed, just inside the bedroom there. Can you grab it?"

Lana turned as if she meant to tell her no, there wasn't time, but instead she grunted something at Bruuth and ran to the house.

Bruuth loaded her across the middle row of seats, managing to lay her down the best he could. He looked at her and said something she imagined was, "Is that okay? Do you need anything?" Something like that, but really, she had no clue. Her head was starting to pound and the feeling in the rest of her body was coming back. It was not a good feeling. The ride to Ceres would be painful, no matter how smooth the 'Hoppers were.

Bruuth was in the back row, leaning over to keep an eye on her as Lana shot out of the doorway, holding Marlow's bag. Two figures came out of the medical center simultaneously. Lana tossed the bag before she jumped in, clicking at her data-pad as she did.

The glass door closed maddeningly slow as the figures approached. They reached it just as the seal began. One of them went to jamming some kind of bar to try to break the seal when Bruuth slammed his hand on the glass. It scared them enough to drop the tool and the Rock-Hopper began its launch sequence. They turned to their data-pads in frustration. Lana gave them double middle-fingers as they lifted off. They were headed to Ceres. Out of the frying pan and into the fire.

Chapter Eleven

The *Mack* was surrounded by every able-bodied man and woman the belt had to offer. They were being commanded by Robin Visser. The belt had a major shortage of useful weapons, so they carried anything they could swing or disable someone with, from brooms to wrenches, all the way down to a stick broken off a nearby tree.

Marlow, Lana, and Bruuth landed at the side of the government building.

"The ship," said Marlow, and groaned at the pain she felt on each word.

"I know," said Lana. "It's going to be a bit of a walk, but if we landed too close, we'd get overrun."

Bruuth climbed out first, reaching back in for Marlow and she cried out in pain as he lifted this time. He looked to Lana who explained her anesthesia and pain meds were wearing off. They started toward the row of trees separating the government building and the shipyard. Bruuth stopped when a group of people came out from either side.

Marlow gave a weak smile as Arjen and Ice rushed over.

"Arjen," said Marlow. "They…they took…"

"I know," he said, petting her head. "I know."

"Be strong," said Ice. "We know you are."

Marlin, Captain Davis, and Admani joined them.

"You're with us?" said Marlow to Admani.

Admani smiled. "I wouldn't let my sister go off to space without me."

"So that means you're coming?" said Marlow to Ice.

She just nodded, facing the shipyard.

Lana looked around. "Where are Doth and Gow'on?"

"The other Wyans? I haven't seen them since we split up," said Arjen. "They were supposed to meet me back here."

"Shit," said Lana, looking ahead. "Are we going to rush them?"

"No," said Arjen. "We have to resupply the ship. Even with the cryo-sleep, we'd never make it there."

"It won't take much though," said Marlin. "The *Iris* is still loaded. It'll just be a haul across the yard."

"The yard's pretty crowded right now," said Isolde.

"We need a distraction," said Arjen. "I have an idea but it's a bit of a reach."

~ * ~

Robin Visser stood with the mob surrounding the *Mack*. Normally even-keeled people brandished sticks, hammers, and brooms half-heartedly. If you presented them with a foe, they were just as likely to strike up a debate as to actually swing the weapons. Still, the threat was there. Acting as a human shield was all that was really required of them to "prevent the loss of our future" as Robin put it.

A Rock-Hopper came swooping in and landed on the side of the *Iris*. The mob was on it in a hurry, but before the door opened, a second one landed closer to the *Mack*. They were split now, making semi-circles around the ships when a third came. Before it landed, the first 'Hopper's passengers were jumping out and running wild, then the second's joined. The children from the basement of the government building were set off by the daylight and the faces of those who put them away. Still, they were the children of the belt. Most of the people went defensive and tried to calm them. Some of the kids took off for the trees, others tried to bite the nearest adults. The third 'Hopper landed to less attention. Ice and Lana helped to get Marlow into Arjen's arms as Bruuth led the way to the ship. The few left in their path thought twice about swinging a weapon at the alien.

Lisa, the other gatherer leader, stood in their path screaming.

"Hey. Everyone over here. The kids are just a distraction."

A few stragglers joined her along with Robin and Oscar. They blocked the ramp to the *Mack* and Bruuth stopped short. More of the mob joined, sealing the way they'd come with bodies.

"Son," said Robin. "What are you doing? What's going on here. Put down this poor girl."

Arjen took a breath and raised his voice for everyone in the shipyard to hear.

"She wouldn't be like this if not for us. We took her from Earth. Coercing her with lies that just got deeper as we went. Then we impregnated her against her will and made her think it was her idea."

Robin stepped forward and cut him off. "It was you who did all these things. Tell them."

The mob was muttering out questions and some were calling insults.

Arjen lowered his head for a second, then turned to the ones behind them.

"I did lie to her. I'll admit to it all. But I want to set her free now. She isn't bound to us. She isn't our slave. She's a human, one of the last ones from Earth."

Oscar joined in. "What are you saying? She accepted her situation with free will. What other choice did she have before we rescued her?"

Arjen stepped over to Bruuth, raising Marlow to the alien's arms. "She deserves the choice to have a natural birth without being assaulted and having her baby cut from her body." Her pulled up Marlow's shirt, revealing the scar across her abdomen. The bandage was soaked with blood. Some in the crowd gasped, others looked to Robin for answers.

Robin raised his hands. "Calm everyone. These are more of his lies. This poor girl was having complications. We did what was best to save the child *and* the mother. She could have died."

"I was attacked," said Marlow.

Her voice was weak but the closest people heard and the wave of shock began passing through the crowd. Then came another voice.

"Move aside," said Kaia. She was walking with the other two Wyans at her sides and Zane and Peter behind her. They each had big backpacks, packed tight for a long journey.

"Kaia?" said Robin, meeting her at the ramp with Oscar next to him. "What is...?"

She pushed him aside. "Let them through. They just want to go back to their planet."

The Wyans followed her signals and went up the ramp, keeping Zane and Peter between them as they went.

"What is this?" said Oscar. "They're taking them as prisoners?"

Kaia shook her head. "They've chosen to go, the same as these folks." She motioned to Arjen's group as Admani, Captain Davis and Marlin joined them. They took their cue and walked onto the ramp. Bruuth leered at the two government officials still trying to block the way and they moved aside. Robin looked at Marlow with pain in his eyes. Was it for her pain, for her situation, or for the belt's? Marlow mustered up a weak frown at Robin. The group was headed up the ramp as Robin caught Arjen's shoulder.

"Son, now listen. You can't just leave your people, your *father* here. You don't know what you're getting into."

Arjen looked him in the eye, regretting that it had come to this as some of the crowd was still out chasing the children.

"I've got to try, try something you haven't. Maybe I'll get a different result than this."

"This was *your* doing," said Robin. "Your hard-headedness for that girl will be your downfall."

Arjen nodded at him, done arguing, afraid it was just a stalling tactic. "Goodbye, Dad." He patted his shoulder and brushed by him.

Kaia joined the other judges at the bottom of the ramp, watching it raise as her two daughters from different lovers stood at the top. Admani blew a kiss. Ice put her hand on her heart and Kaia smiled as tears filled her eyes.

Chapter Twelve

The *Mack* was loaded to little resistance. What was left of the crowd watched in indifference. No one dared enter the ship with the aliens in it. They didn't know there were only three on board. Kaia kept Robin busy, reminding him, and the crowd, that violence was how Earth came to its end.

The *Mack* took off in a hurry, as soon as Marlin and the Wyans finished transporting the cargo from the *Iris*. Arjen and its crew couldn't relax until they were out of the belt. There was no threat of heavy artillery or missiles. Defense had never been a focus of the belt since they thought they were alone, but Arjen didn't trust his father's desire to control everything.

They cleared Ceres while Captain Davis joined Captain Williams on the bridge. Arjen and Lana poured over every monitor the ship had. It wasn't long before they saw her, Lisa tailing them in the *Knox*. They knew it had to be her. Within the hour they approached the wormhole. On their last look, the *Knox* had stopped, perched above one of the islands, watching as they entered. They wouldn't know if she decided to follow after all. The distorted reality of the wormhole made it hard to see much in any direction but they hoped she was just giving them a final send-off. One final, "Go on, get out of here."

Marlow was back in an exam room much like the one on the *Iris*, only this one had a real hospital bed rather than just a cold table. Admani was with her as well as Julie, one of Lana's crew who doubled as a medic and crewman.

They changed her bandages, disinfecting her to be certain it was done right and gave her a strong dose of painkillers. She was able to sleep for a few hours as everyone was still settling in. When she woke, Arjen was sitting in a chair, reading something on his data-pad.

"Hey," he said, looking up. "How you feeling?"

"Insanely better than before."

"Glad to hear. Are you up for a few visitors?"

She tried to sit up and thought better of it. Arjen saw her attempt and showed her the controls to raise her back.

"Okay," she said. Arjen turned and opened the door. The first thing she saw was red hair. "Peter?"

"Hey," he said, waving and smiling at her, then he stepped out of the way and Marlow felt her whole body go numb.

Zane stood in the door, cradling a baby, *her* baby. His face was huge with excitement.

"It's a girl," he said, walking over to her. "She looks a lot like you."

Marlow couldn't speak as Zane set the newborn on her chest. She held her gently like she was in a dream. Her little brown eyes opened and shut a few times before she was staring at Marlow, swinging a loose hand wherever it would go. She had a dark head of hair and clearly, Marlow's nose. The rest they'd figure out in time.

Marlow ran a hand through the baby's hair, spiking it up then flattening it back down.

"She's beautiful," she said through tears. "I didn't think...how did you...?"

"It was Kaia's idea," said Zane. "We wrapped her up and put her in one of the backpacks. Thankfully she seemed to sleep through most of it."

"But how did you get her away from them?"

"The Wyans helped. Everyone is afraid of them, though they're pretty docile. They led us through, and nobody really paid attention to Peter and me."

Arjen and Ice gathered with them.

"You're gonna have to start thinking of names," said Arjen.

"I will," said Marlow. "Maybe when I'm not hopped up on painkillers."

They all stood around, watching the new mother and the daughter she was never supposed to have.

Chapter Thirteen

They were three days into the trip when an all-ship meeting was called. Lana stood at the head of a big conference table. Around it were three Wyans at the end, the sisters, Admani and Isolde, who didn't resemble each other, Arjen, Captain Davis, Marlin, Peter, and the Earthlings with their baby named Avani for its meaning, Earth, and Lana's four-member crew.

Lana began, "As I've told you, this journey will be just under two months. We do not have the supplies for everyone to stay awake using resources. The cryo-room will be utilized for most of you. Marlow will stay awake to feed and care for Avani." Lana gave a smile to the baby. "And I will stay awake to maintain course and be her support if she needs it. Our friends the Wyans fear and do not understand the cryo-sleep so they will stay awake as well. They also do not understand English so I'm working on in-ear translators to fix that. Thankfully, I'll have plenty of time." She got a laugh out of the English speakers of the group. "We'll have a final round of cards tonight, per Marlin's request, then I'll set you all up for the rest of the trip."

She took questions from the group and gave the Wyans the translation. The *Mack* supported a large garden that had been tweaked by their needs to feed the three of them the best it could for the remainder of the trip.

There was a rousing game of cards that night, much like on the *Iris* but with more nervous excitement hanging in the air. None of the newcomers truly knew what they were going to wake to find in two months' time, but they were optimistic for the opportunity at a new life. When the games were over, a last 'Panel was taken in by the recent belters, while Lana's crew ate packaged food. She explained how on Wyan there would be no more NutrientPanel and Marlin expressed his aversion to learning to eat actual food to laughs from the group.

Everyone gave Avani a kiss on the head for good luck before they went into the cryo-room. They each found a place along the walls and Lana locked the door and set the timer to wake them up a few days before arrival.

Marlow gave a last wave with her hand, then Avani's as she stood at the small window within the door, feeling the emptiness of watching her closest friends being locked away for the next two months.

"Just you and me," she whispered to Avani, who cooed in her arms.

Chapter Fourteen

A few days later, Marlow knocked on the door to Lana's quarters. She called, "It's open," and Marlow stepped in.

"Hey. I was just bored. Avani doesn't want to sleep so I was walking the halls trying to keep her from crying."

Lana nodded, setting down a tiny tool next to a small, tan object.

"Want me to carry her for a bit? I could use a break."

"Sure." Marlow handed the baby over. "What are you working on?"

"Translator," said Lana, looking back at it. "Still quite a few kinks to work out."

"Cool. Well, if you need someone to try it out sometime…"

Lana smiled as they exited her room. "I'll keep that in mind."

~ * ~

Another week passed as Marlow grew closer to Avani, understanding her desires and quirks better each day while she grew further from the only other English-speaking person still awake. Lana was always locked in her quarters with the door closed. Marlow would bother her from time to time. She'd always oblige her, come out and take a turn holding or playing with Avani, but then she'd be right back at it.

Marlow was headed for Lana's room when she passed the two other Wyans, Doth and Gow'on. She couldn't remember which was which, only that they were shorter than Bruuth. She smiled and waved. Lana seemed annoyed to see her at the door, but she took Avani out of her arms and went down the hall. Marlow was left stretching, trying to rub her own shoulders that ached from hours of baby holding. She saw the device Lana had been spending so much time on, sitting on the table. There were no tiny screwdrivers or anything nearby. Maybe it was done. She didn't know. She figured Lana would tell her when it was ready so she could try it. She just hadn't heard and was bored and lonely. She stepped into Lana's room. She knew she had about twenty minutes as Lana would do her normal lap around the ship, singing songs and pointing out objects to Avani. She really seemed to have a gift with children.

Marlow felt her fingers gripping the little device, turning it over as she heard the thumping of Wyan feet down the hall. She pushed in a miniscule button and it gave one, green flash at her. Without thinking, she stuck the piece in her ear and brushed some hair to conceal it.

The Wyans were almost to the door, mumbling something in their guttural, grunting language. Then she heard it, a small voice in her right ear.

...*jump in the lake bare,* it said. There was another grunt from the other Wyan then the voice again, *freeze your reproducer, it was rain season.*

Marlow's eyes went wide. She'd just heard a rough translation of their conversation. She contemplated alerting them that she could finally understand and to please tell her something, anything to break the monotony of space travel. She realized they didn't have translators. Besides a bunch of motions toward the tiny device in her ear, she couldn't say jack to them that they'd understand. She decided to test it a bit further in a different way. Just as they were passing, she stepped out of the door. One of the Wyans jumped back, surprised by her, holding up his hands, then dropped them when he saw who it was. The other laughed at him, grunting and Marlow heard, *like a spooked child,* as he pointed. The one she scared looked at her, grunting as well before he turned to his friend and they continued down the hall. What she heard in her earpiece sent chills down her body. *Watch it, you're nothing but food for the Night Chasers. All of you.*

Marlow put back the device with a shaking hand and went to find Lana. She knew the route she usually took as they went together from time to time. Marlow was always relieved to have someone else to hold Avani but still desired conversation with another adult. She shivered as she walked, trying to get her breath under control. Surely, *food for the Night Chasers* was just a threat in their language. Like, useless piece of shit, or something. Lana would clear it up, she'd been there.

Lana was coming off the bridge, holding Avani on her shoulder as she gurgled out happy noises, watching the door frame passing just over her head when Marlow found her.

Marlow tried to sound casual. "Hey."

"Hey. We were on our way back."

"Cool." She reached out her arms. "I don't mind taking her if you want."

Lana frowned. "Okay. Thought you needed a break."

"Yeah. I got one. I do have a question though." She took Avani into her arms and hugged her tightly.

"What's that?"

"Who or what are the Night Chasers?"

The look in Lana's face betrayed her. There was a fear that passed over her eyes before she could help it. She gave Marlow a quizzical look.

"Why do you ask that?"

"Don't be mad. I went into your room and tried out that translator you've been working on. I just wanted to see if you got it working yet. You've been spending a lot of time on it."

Lana's eyes narrowed. "Did you? And...?"

"Well, I must've scared one of the Wyans because he said, 'you're nothing but food for the Night Chasers, all of you.' Who are they? Is that just a saying or something?"

Lana sighed, stopping in the hall, staring down before she looked up to meet Marlow's eyes.

"I'm not going to lie to you. Arjen said to not waste my time with that."

"Okay." Marlow was feeling the fear running up and down.

She was hugging Avani, trying not to squeeze too tight.

"The Wyan's planet is beautiful, covered in glorious mountains, beaches, farmland. A lot like the best parts of Earth, but it has a strange rotation pattern around its star. For years they'll have nothing but sunlight. Seriously, just midday sun as you'd know it on Earth. This is the area they live in. As you can imagine, the other parts of the planet are very dark and cold during these years. Now, the time is coming again where their years of sun will be ending and they'll have a month of darkness."

Marlow was bouncing Avani too strongly and Lana put a hand on her to slow down.

Lana said, "Come to my room so you can let her lay on the bed for a bit."

Marlow did and soon Avani was cooing at the ceiling of Lana's room as she lay on her back.

Marlow was eager to continue the story. "So, it's just going to be dark while we're there for a month?"

Lana tilted her head. "Yes, but…on the other side of the planet, the side normally in the dark, there are creatures. The Wyans call them Night Chasers because they stay in the dark. During the years of sun, they stay on their side, in the dark, feeding on other things that grow in the dark and even each other but during the darkness that's coming…"

Marlow's lips barely moved. "They feed on the Wyans."

Lana nodded. "And that's why we need your help."

Acknowledgements

I have to start with Erin and Dustin. You guys suffered through most of my early stories, corrected my grammar and gave me the honest feedback I needed. Bossman Studios Writers Group for life. Sarah H. for reading early stuff. Brittany for reading later stuff and Jennifer for saying, "I liked this one the best." I guess you weren't lying. Maybe you were. It doesn't matter anymore. Soon you'll find out what happens to Marlow. Stefanie with an F for being generally awesome. Aunt Sharon for being willing to handle the casting and doughnuts. Haunted MTL for being my first. It was good for me. I hope it was for you. Thanks to Rogue Phoenix Press for saying, "We want more," rather than, "That's enough." Azuza for the title. The park across the street for offering cold, pensive walks for idea building. Anyone who sees a little of themselves in these characters, remember, this is fiction. Also, did I get your nose right? Anders...check your messages, man.

About the Author

Scott Boss is an author, musician, and computer EMR teacher. He likes to take his Dad-bod up the beautiful, hiking trails in Western North Carolina, along with his family. He started writing when he was seven with *The Hammer Head Worm* comic series that the public has been spared from ever seeing. Scott loves to cook and listen to heavy metal at the same time.

www.ingramcontent.com/pod-product-compliance
Lightning Source LLC
Chambersburg PA
CBHW071502170626
46811CB00007B/2683